I've travelled the world twice over,
Met the famous: saints and sinners,
Poets and artists, kings and queens,
Old stars and hopeful beginners,
I've been where no-one's been before,
Learned secrets from writers and cooks
All with one library ticket
To the wonderful world of books.

© JANICE JAMES.

THE CRYING CHILD

Summoned by her brother-in-law to a tiny fishing village in Maine to comfort her sister, Joanne faces shock after shock. What was the mystery of King's Island? And was Mary, her sister, becoming dangerously unbalanced? Why did she risk her life by solitary night-time searches? Joanne found herself a reluctant ally of the unsympathetic Dr. Graham until she too heard that terrible crying and saw the figure in black. Even then Joanne refused to believe the evidence of her ears and eyes.

*Books by Barbara Michaels in the
Ulverscroft Large Print Series:*

PATRIOT'S DREAM
WITCH
THE CRYING CHILD

BARBARA MICHAELS, 1927–

THE
CRYING CHILD

Complete and Unabridged

ULVERSCROFT
Leicester

A-4

First published in Great Britain 1972 by
Souvenir Press Ltd.
London

First Large Print Edition
published January 1981
by arrangement with
Souvenir Press Ltd.
London
and
Dodd, Mead & Company, Inc.
New York

British Library CIP Data

Michaels, Barbara
  The crying child.—Large print ed.
(Ulverscroft large print series:
  romantic suspense).
I. Title
823'.9'1F   PS3563.E747C/

ISBN 0-7089-0568-4

Published by
F. A. Thorpe (Publishing) Ltd.
Anstey, Leicestershire

Printed in Great Britain by T. J. Press (Padstow) Ltd.
Padstow, Cornwall

FOR KAY
with apologies for my comments
on San Francisco weather

1

FROM the air, the island doesn't look big enough to land a plane on. It's a pretty sight, from above, calling to mind all sorts of poetic images—an agate, shining brown and green, flung down in folds of sea-blue satin; a blob of variegated Play-Dough, left in a basin of water by a forgetful child; an oval braided rug on a green glass floor.

Or a hand, in a brown-and-green mitten. The hand is clenched into a fist, with a thumb-like promontory jutting out on one side. Across the broad end there is a range of hills that might be knuckles; at the other end, the land narrows down into a wrist-shaped peninsula. There are beaches there, like fur trim on the cuff of the mitten; the rest of the island is thick with foliage, sombre green pines and fir trees for the most part. The house is surprisingly distinct from above. The lighter green of the lawns and the grey outline of roofs and chimneys stand out amid the darkness of the pines. The only other distinctive landmark is the cluster of buildings that make up the village, along the thumb promontory, and its harbour, which is formed by the junction of thumb and hand.

And that's where the figure of speech fails. You could compare the house to an oddly shaped ring, up on the knuckles of the hand, but the village doesn't suggest any analogy. A diseased imagination might think of sores or warts; but there never was anything festering about St. Ives. It was just a charming Maine town, and not even the events of that spring could make it anything else. There was no lurking horror in the village. It was in the house.

I certainly wasn't aware of horrors that morning in May. I had worries, plenty of them, but they were comparatively simple ones. I didn't know, then, how simple.

Fortunately, fear of flying was not one of those worries. If I had had any such weakness, the plane I was in would have reduced me to a quivering jelly. It was the smallest winged thing I had ever been in. After the big jetliner that brought me from San Francisco to Boston, this object looked like a squat beetle with stubby wings. The pilot flew it like a hot rod; with his long hair curling around the base of his neck and his grin almost buried in blond beard, he wouldn't have inspired much confidence in a timid flyer.

Although I was in a hurry to reach the island, this charter flight from Boston wasn't my idea; it was Ran's. A brother-in-law who is also a millionaire has certain advantages. As Ran pointed out, the alternative arrangement would have taken a lot of time: another plane from Boston to Portland, then a bus or train or taxi from Portland to the coastal town of Richmond, which is the closest city on the mainland to the island; then a privately chartered boat. The ferry only runs once a day—in the summer. In the winter, I assumed, the inhabitants would have to swim.

It was a long swim. King's Island—they insist on the possessive form—is the farthest out of all the islands of Casco Bay; so far out that it isn't on the regular ferry route, which chugs like a commuter bus between Portland and the other islands that cluster thickly between the arms of Cape Elizabeth and Cape Small. The inhabitants of the island say that's fine with them. They see enough tourists during the three summer months. The Inn, with twenty rooms, is the only hotel. A few private homes take in boarders, but there

3

isn't a motel or a resort hotel on the island. The Fraser family owns most of it, and they have always refused to sell to developers, so there are no cabins or summer cottages.

Ran's last name is Fraser.

I suppose owning things gives rich people the feeling that they can manipulate human beings as easily as they do inanimate objects. Ran has certain tendencies in this direction, but he gave up trying to boss me after I ran away from home. I was twenty at the time, and a college graduate; but I'd been living with Ran and Mary for ten years, and he carried on like a Victorian father whose daughter is planning a career in a bawdy house. His original idea was for me to hang around the family homestead on Long Island after I graduated until I hooked one of the wealthy young males he kept dragging home. When I insisted that I wanted a job instead, he offered me fourteen (fourteen—I counted them) different positions in Manhattan, from an assistant editorship in the publishing house he controls to running my own interior decorating business—which he would buy for me. I literally had to elope, down the stairs at 2 a.m., with my suitcase under my arm—but not with a man. My companion on that flight

4

wasn't a human being, it was a bizarre quality called pride.

I took a job in San Francisco because it was about as far away from Ran and Mary as I could get, and I needed that distance to keep myself from crawling back. I was so homesick and so broke those first three months that I almost did weaken. It took Ran another three months to forgive me. He called on New Year's Eve. After that he and Mary called almost every week, just for company and gossip. But the last two calls had been something else. It was because of those calls that I was in the air over the coast of Maine in a plane that looked like a sick lightning bug.

The first of the significant calls came in April. It was Ran telling me with curt brevity that Mary had lost her baby. That wasn't how he phrased it. In fact, he corrected me when I used the word.

"Baby? It wouldn't have been that for another six months. Foetus or embryo; I never can remember which comes first . . ."

The words sounded callous, and so did his voice. I wasn't shocked; I thought I knew why he was so determined to avoid the emotional overtones that particular word carries. So I didn't sympathize; I didn't offer to

5

come back east, though I knew how desperately unhappy Mary must be. I also knew that Ran would resent any suggestion that he wasn't the only thing or person Mary needed.

I'm ten years younger than Mary. She brought me up by hand, like Pip's sister, after our parents died in an automobile accident when I was nine. There's no one left, now, except a distant cousin in Milwaukee, so there are a lot of reasons why Mary and I have always been even closer than sisters usually are. But I knew Ran was a little jealous of that relationship. Oh, he loved me like a brother. He had taken me into his heart and home without hesitation when he married my sister. But the combination of money and masculinity made him very sure of himself; he resented the hint that any woman he cherished could possibly need anything, or anybody, else.

Yet not even Ran could realize how much losing this baby could mean to Mary. She had been pregnant twice before, and had miscarried both times. Then there was nothing, for six long years, despite all her efforts—and, to do him justice, all Ran's efforts. The doctors said there was no physical reason why they couldn't have children. It wasn't until recently that I had realized how much Ran must have hated it all—especially the fact that his gangling adolescent sister in law knew all the gruesome details. Mary wasn't reticent; the problem was so important to her that she had to talk about it. The schools didn't go in for sex education in those days, but I got all I needed from Mary.

I wrote to her, of course, after Ran called. I got a brief scrawl in reply, and a promise that she'd write at length later. That letter never came. Instead there was Ran's second call.

It was typical spring weather in San Francisco—cold. I was huddled over my imitation fireplace trying to work out a sketch for an ad for face cream. It wasn't my job. Beauty Aid is one of our big accounts, but junior artists don't originate layouts. Still, I thought, maybe if I came up with something spectacular . . .

When the phone rang I jumped, I was concentrating so hard. As soon as I heard Ran's voice I knew something was wrong. He has a deep baritone voice that gets softer and deeper when he's upset. That night it was almost a bass rumble.

"When are you taking your vacation?" he asked.

"First two weeks in June," I said; and the funny feeling at the pit of my stomach began to spread out. "You know that, Ran; we discussed my coming to visit you—"

"Could you come now instead? And stay longer?"

"I've been at the agency less than a year. They don't—"

"What about an emergency leave?"

There was a long silence. Then I said, "Start from the beginning. What's wrong with Mary?"

"Nothing physical. She's fully recovered from the miscarriage."

"Don't make me drag it out of you, Ran. Do you think I'm that dumb, that I'll flip when you mention mental illness?"

There was a little chuckle from the other end of the line.

"That's what I like about you, Jo—that hard core of brutal honesty. Yes, her illness is mental. Melancholia, depression, whatever you want to call it. A nervous breakdown—"

"Never mind what I call it; or what you call it. What does the doctor say? I assume she's seen a doctor?"

8

"A dozen doctors. Gynaecologist, neurologist—"

"Psychiatrist?"

"Well . . ."

"For God's sake, Ran—"

"Wait a minute; don't jump on me with both feet." He was laughing again, I could hear him, and the anger that I use to veil my fears, even from myself, spread and grew stronger. Before I could say anything, he went on, soberly,

"Of course I took her to a psychiatrist, after the other doctors found nothing wrong. The man she saw was first-rate, and Mary seemed to like him. Trouble was, he couldn't take her on full time. And that's what she needs, apparently—five days a week, fifty-two weeks a year."

"There are other psychiatrists."

"He gave me the names of three others. Mary has seen all three. The third man was a disaster. She took a violent dislike to him. Now she absolutely refuses to see another psychiatrist."

"But Ran, surely—"

"Jo, you are a bright, intelligent girl, but you don't know the answer to every damned

9

problem in the world. Don't tell me what to do until you hear what I've done."

There was a brief silence; I could hear him breathing. It was uncanny, hearing those puffs of restrained anger from three thousand miles away. Then he said briefly,

"Sorry."

"I don't mind."

I didn't. I was glad that he was just as concerned as I was, under his seemingly careless laughter.

"Psychiatry is helpless, Jo, without co-operation from the patient. What am I supposed to do, drag her in there kicking and screaming? I tell you she won't go!"

"I see your point. I suppose it was the miscarriage that brought this on?"

"Brought it on, but fails to explain it. Look, Jo, let's not tear the thing apart now. In lieu of analysis, which she isn't ready to accept, the doctors think peace and quiet and a complete change of scene might help. I've got a house, on an island off the coast of Maine, and we're going up there for the summer. Can you join us? As soon as possible, and for as long as you can stay?"

"An island? Why an island?"

"Because that's where the house *is*," Ran

said. "Of all the stupid questions . . . Will you come or not?"

"There is the little matter of my job."

"Quit."

"I love fresh air, but it's low in calories."

"For God's sake, Jo, you know I can get you a job any time you say. So far as that goes—"

"We went through this before, Ran."

"Yes, and I came around, didn't I? I admire your independence—even if I do call it pigheadedness when you aren't around. But there are more important things than pride, Jo."

He fell silent, then, and all at once I could almost see him—his tall, lean body slouched in the big leather chair, his thick dark hair standing up on end because he had been running his fingers through it the way he did when he was annoyed. And he was always annoyed when some lesser human specimen intimated that his plans were less than perfect. I got to be pretty familiar with his moods in the years when I lived with him and Mary; so I knew, now, what the silence meant. He was trying another approach. In my mind I saw his heavy dark brows lift and an ingratiating smile lighten a mouth that was, in repose, rather too thin and too long for geniality. The voice that finally spoke was just the voice I expected.

"Honey, I'm sorry. I'm in a lousy mood, or I wouldn't be so overbearing. I'm not ordering you; I'm begging you. Mary wants you. And you are just about the only thing she does want."

It might have been calculated—it almost certainly was—but that statement broke through my defences. Not because he admitted that Mary wanted me, but because of his admission that she didn't want him. He was not a humble man.

"Okay," I said. "Okay, I'll come. It'll take a while, there are so many things . . . But I'll be there."

I was still sitting by the phone, trying to sort things out, when the doorbell rang. It was the special-delivery mail man, with a letter from Ran. It contained a plane ticket and detailed instructions for reaching the island. All I had to do was call Ran's office when I had made my reservations, and everything would be taken care of.

Fifteen minutes between New York and San Francisco is good time, even for air-mail special. I didn't have to look at the postmark to know that Ran had sent the letter that morning, before he even bothered to ask me to come.

II

The next two weeks were filled with furious activity and with an increasing anxiety that made all activity more difficult. I took the time, though, because this way there was a slight chance that I might be able to get a job when I came back to the West Coast. I didn't expect the agency to offer to hold my job for me, and they didn't. But at least, by offering to stay long enough to train my successor in my peculiar ways, I avoided serious hard feelings. Of course, by the time they heard my excuses they couldn't have blackballed me without making like Scrooge. I have an unfortunate habit—not of embroidering a story, exactly—but of bringing out its more dramatic features. And in the process I tell more than I should. I don't do it for effect, I don't even approve of it; I just can't seem to help it. Mary used to say that I could bump into a lady at the grocery store and by the time I was through apologizing I would have told her I was breaking up with my boyfriend and described the dream I had the night before.

Anyhow, I managed it somehow—left the job on good terms with all concerned, sublet my apartment, and packed three suitcases. It sounds simple, but I've left out all the little things, the details that sound so insignificant and take so much time. By the time I got on the plane I was so tired I slept most of the way across the country. And when I reached Boston, the plane Ran had hired was waiting for me.

We landed on the island. I'm sure I don't know how we did. Of course I knew that the island really was large enough to allow a small plane to land; I knew it in my brain, anyhow, even if I didn't know it in my insides. But as we came down, my interested eyes failed to find a flat space bigger than a front yard anywhere among the acres of fir trees and the miles of rough cliff-line. I did see the field finally—if you could call it that—it looked like somebody's corn field. So I chickened out and closed my eyes. The landing was what I can only call exuberant; we bounced a couple of times more than necessary.

Ran had said I would be met. I guess I expected him, or Mary, or both; I was conscious of a pang of disappointment when I scanned the faces of the people near the small building that served as a terminal, and failed to see a familiar one. I started walking towards the building, and as I did so a lounger removed himself from the wall against which he had been leaning and came towards me.

It's hard for me to remember my first impressions of William Graham. I must have been struck by his height; he's really tall, six feet four or five. He has one of those long, weatherbeaten New England faces that change very little between the ages of twenty-five and sixty. The features seem to be all sharp angles and the skin is tanned—not just sun-browned, tanned like old leather. Will has sandy hair and light-brown eyes. They look like amber in the sunlight. And in direct sunlight, and only then, you notice his freckles, just a scattering of them, across the bridge of his nose.

Then he smiled. I didn't exactly stagger, but I felt like doing so. It was the most amazing transformation I've seen outside of an old Lon Chaney movie. His face got rounder and years younger; his pale amber eyes glowed as if a light had been switched on behind them.

15

"Will Graham," he said, and put out his hand.

"Joanne McMullen," I said. I let him have my hand with some trepidation; it was the first time my not-so-dainty digits had been swallowed up by a man's hand. But I needn't have worried. His handclasp was firm, but gentle and businesslike. His eyes were fixed on my face, and I fancied I could hear the facts clicking into place in his brain. Female, early twenties, five-nine, one hundred and twenty-five pounds (approximate), brown hair, blue eyes, no visible scars or deformities . . .

"You must be a friend of Ran's," I said inanely. The clinical stare was making me nervous.

He didn't bother answering, but turned away to greet the pilot, who was coming up with my bags. They were apparently old buddies.

"Hi, Vic" said Will Graham.

"Haw'rya, Doc," said Vic.

He hadn't mentioned that he was a doctor. I was beginning to feel like a subnormal child; nobody was telling me anything. Ran had sent a perfect stranger to meet me, without warning me, and the stranger seemed

16

to feel that the mere mention of his name was sufficient identification. Finally Graham took my suitcases and started walking off with them. The pilot gave me a grin and a flip of the hand and went off in another direction. I stood there, looking from one retreating back to the other. There was nothing else to do but follow the doctor. I didn't exactly have to run, but I had to walk faster than I normally do. I caught up with him at the door of the terminal and I remarked moderately,

"You could at least say, 'Heel.' "

He glanced down at me.

"Huh? Oh. Sorry."

He didn't sound sorry.

We got into his car. It was a blue station wagon, the saddest, most battered specimen of automobile I had ever seen. It started with a scream and settled into a series of agonized grunts. Clearly the doctor was one of those rare men who regard a car as a means of transportation rather than a love object. That should have raised him in my estimation, but I was feeling sulky.

"I don't even know who you are," I said.

He gave me an amused glance.

"You shouldn't get into cars with strange men."

"Just what I was thinking."

"Ran asked me to apologize. He meant to meet you himself. When he had to go away, he asked me to take over."

"But who are you? Do you live here? How long have you known Ran? How is he? How is Mary?"

"Wait a minute, wait a minute. Yes, I live here. I've known Ran since . . . Must be about fourth grade."

"Fourth grade!" I don't know why that fact, and its obvious corollaries, surprised me so, but they did. "You're a native? Lived here all your life?"

"Yes."

"Then—Ran used to live here too."

He glanced at me in surprise.

"It's his grandfather's house. His grandfather's island, you could say."

"I didn't know that. I wonder why he didn't tell me."

"Maybe you never asked."

"Maybe I didn't get around to asking," I admitted. "I have had other things on my mind. Oh, why beat around the bush? You're a doctor and an old friend of Ran's. You must know why I'm concerned about Mary."

By then we were driving down the main

18

street of the village, and the doctor, concentrating on a traffic jam which consisted of two motorcycles and a jeep, was ostentatiously silent. It was a pretty little town, with old houses and a few blocks of new but discreetly designed modern shops. Down the side streets I caught glimpses of the harbour, with white-sailed boats and a few larger motor craft. A charming town . . . But I was in no mood for charm. The good doctor could communicate more with silence than another man could in a long speech.

"How is Mary?" I asked.

Instead of answering, he asked me a question.

"How old are you?"

"Twenty-one," I said, without thinking; and then, annoyed, I snapped back, "How old are you?"

It worked.

"Twenty-nine," he said; and turned red—with anger, not embarrassment.

"Then perhaps I have as much right to doubt your qualifications as you do to question mine."

"On the defensive, aren't you?"

"Am I?"

We had left the town—what there was of

it—and were on a road that skirted the shore. Inland, the island was wooded and green, but this terrain was sandy, with sparse vegetation. To the left the sea shone amethyst and aquamarine in the sunlight. I took several deep breaths.

"This is silly," I said. "Why don't we stop picking at each other? I gather I am going to see something of you in the next few months. It will certainly be better for Mary, not to mention the general social situation, if we try to get along."

"Fine with me."

"Then can't we talk about Mary without one of us getting mad?"

"I'm not mad," he said calmly.

"But you're not talking."

He made a funny noise which, I learned later, was a laugh. He turned the car, so abruptly that I fell up against his arm. He fended me off, without prejudice, and completed the turn, on to a narrow gravel road which led up towards the centre of the island. There was a gate, which stood open, and a "Private Property—No Trespassing" sign.

The change in terrain was extraordinarily abrupt. Within a minute we were driving in a green gloom, under trees whose massive branches interlaced above. Graham brought the car to a stop. He turned to face me, one arm resting on the steering wheel, and produced a pack of cigarettes, which he offered me.

"And you an MD," I said, taking one.

"I am one of the twenty per cent that hasn't quit."

He lit my cigarette; and I turned too, sitting sideways on the seat so that I could see his face.

"Conference?" I said.

"We're not far from the house. I think it will be easier to talk candidly without Ran or Mary around."

"Where shall we start?"

And that was the last question I asked. I still don't know how he did it, but from then on, he had complete control of the conversation. He would have made a first-class district attorney. And of course he was talking to me—old blabbermouth. I described our childhood days, Mary's and mine, and told him about our private jokes and our battles; Mary's tantrums and the way she had walked the floor, night after night, when our parents were killed. There is something very seductive about being allowed to talk about yourself, by someone who really listens. That's why it took me so long to see what he was doing.

When he referred for the third time to those temper fits of Mary's, I began to wonder. I stopped talking, the flood of my eloquence damned by suspicion, and the slow, thoughtful nod of his head told me those suspicions were justified.

"What do you think you're doing?" I demanded.

"Confirming a hunch," he said calmly. "I couldn't get this from Ran, naturally."

"Naturally. Only from a stupid, loose-lipped—"

"Only figuratively." His eyes focused on my mouth and I felt the colour rise in my cheeks.

"You didn't want information. You only wanted confirmation. I know what you're thinking, and you're wrong! Mary is—"

"A spoiled, pampered neurotic who can't endure the slightest frustration."

A cold, final appraisal.

And it was false. I tried to remember what I had said, how I had failed in showing him the Mary I knew—the girl who had comforted a bereaved, hysterical child, confining her own desperate sense of loss and inadequacy to the four walls of her room; the woman who had handled my confused adolescent failings with wisdom and humour. But I knew the failure wasn't all mine. He had made up his mind about Mary before he even met me.

"You are wrong," I said.

"I wish I were."

"Just tell me one thing. Are *you* Mary's medical adviser?"

It sounded even nastier than I had meant it to, and he flushed angrily, up to and including his ears. They were big ears.

"I'm the only medical man on the island," he snapped. "Mary has no adviser, medical or otherwise. She won't talk to me. That's why I have to sneak behind her back like this."

"I didn't know you had a degree in psychiatry."

He took a deep breath. His eyes were as hard and as dull as pebbles.

"I know enough about the usual psychoses to know that Mary is not that sick. Believe me, I've made it my business to find out. The symptoms just aren't consistent. They don't make sense. The obvious conclusion is that she's deliberately provoking her own—"

"I won't listen to this!"

I shouted; but my voice was drowned, subdued to an insect's croak by the twilight greenness that crowded in on the car. The forest was old, untended. I could smell the damp, fecund scent of rich black mould and growing plants. Usually I like the woods, but this forest was different. It was pressing in on me. The trees were too close together and the sunlight couldn't get through.

"We can't talk," I said. "Let's go on, please. I'm anxious to see Mary."

It was a relief to come out of the trees on to an open windswept clearing with gusty clouds hurrying across the great unhindered expanse of blue sky. In the middle of a wide stretch of green lawn the house was waiting.

I never believed in haunted houses, but I won't deny that every house has its own atmosphere. Some make you feel welcome the moment you walk in the door. Others repel. It's a purely physical thing, of course—a question of proportions and light and the repetition of forms that soothe some personality types while they create in others a subtle distress. I know that must be the explanation, because I've been in brand-new houses, still smelling of paint and plaster, that made me so uncomfortable I wanted to turn and run out. So it can't be ghosts. Unless the troubled spirits are already there, bound to the land on which the house was built . . .

Ran's house had no such atmosphere. It was a big, sprawling place, altered and added on to over the years; and, as the unstudied grace of flowers growing wild in a field surpasses any artificial flower arrangement, this house was more beautiful than many architect-designed structures. The original central portion must have been two hundred years old; its elegant severe lines still showed through the Gothic embellishments added by a later owner. There was a tower. There was a cupola at the very top of the house, with a domed roof. There were gables galore, and wooded fretwork along every roof and window edge. The wide veranda that swung across the front and side of the main section was curved, and the supporting pillars were turned, and the porch eaves carried a row of wooden "icicles". Oddly enough, the effect was attractive. For one thing, the house was big enough to carry the ornamentation without becoming over-burdened. It was freshly painted—a glistening sugary white—with very dark grey shutters. The chimneys were of lighter grey stone. In winter, under a lowering sky, the place may have had its eerie qualities, but now, framed by a freshly mown lawn, with flowers and shrubs in blossom, it was as sunny and inviting as a house could be.

The doctor swung the car around the curved drive and stopped in front of the porch steps. Mary must have been watching for us. The engine had scarcely died before the door opened and she came running out.

My first sight of her, in her bright linen dress, her face flushed and smiling with welcome, was such a relief that I shed a few tears as I flung my arms around her. Mary is so tiny, compared to my stalwart five-nine, that she always felt fragile when I hugged her. So it took me several seconds to realize that her ribs were almost standing out under her skin and that the arms that circled my waist had no more strength than a child's.

I held her off at arm's length. I kept the smile on my face; but it wasn't easy.

Thin—good heavens, she was thin! There were grey hairs in her short dark curls. The flush wasn't healthy red blood, it was make-up, skilfully applied, but discernible. But it was her eyes that shocked me most. Mary always had circles under her eyes, even when she was in the pink of health; the dark circles and the petite body gave her that air of fragility which so many men found so appealing—and which was completely deceptive, because she was as strong as a horse. But the marks weren't circles now, they were purple stains. Her eyes burned with a feverish glitter.

"You look great," I said, with such palpable untruth that Mary's face took on a faint mocking smile.

"I look like hell." She linked arms with me and turned me towards the steps. "But you should have seen me a month ago."

"Where's Ran?"

"Boston. He had to go down this morning on business. That's why he couldn't meet you."

I glanced over my shoulder. The doctor—whose existence Mary had not acknowledged by so much as a nod—was taking my bags out of the car.

"Sorry I can't say that the substitute was an improvement."

"Sssh." Mary's hand tightened convulsively on my arm. "He'll hear you."

Her voice was so strained I glanced at her

27

in surprise. Before I could reply she turned away from me and addressed the doctor.

"Just leave them, Will. Jed will bring them up later. Unless you can stop for a minute—"

"And spoil your reunion? Thanks, Mary, but I've got things to do. Ask Ran to call me, will you?"

When the car drove off, Mary seemed to sag.

"Well," she said brightly. "What are we doing standing out here? Come in."

The inside of the house was as charming as the outside. The hall was shaped like welcoming arms, circular, with white-painted panels around the lower half and a bright, flowered wallpaper above. The staircase rose up at the back.

"Did you have any lunch?"

"Stop acting like a hostess," I said. "I had lunch at least twice; I lost count over Des Moines or thereabouts."

"Coffee, then. I know you can always drink coffee."

"Later. What I'd like now is a shower and a nice long talk."

"Of course. You must be tired after that long trip. I'll get Jed to bring up your bags."

As I followed her slight form up the stairs, I

wondered why Ran had talked of apathy and withdrawal. Mary was changed, very much changed; but I found her high-strung and nervous rather than apathetic. Was this a recent development, or was she different with me? I could hardly wait to talk to her, in one of those confidential sessions we used to enjoy. And I didn't intend to pull any punches. Something was bothering her, and I meant to force it out into the open, even if I had to be brutal.

My room was lovely—a great high-ceilinged chamber on the corner of a wing, so that it had windows on two sides. There was a fireplace on one wall, and the furniture consisted solely of early American antiques, or expensive reproductions thereof. A rocking chair sat in front of the fireplace, and the bed had a blue-and-white quilt.

But after the first glance of approval and pleasure I forgot the room. Mary was standing by the fireplace. Her hands were twisted together. Her head was tilted and her eyes had the blank look of someone who is listening to a sound beyond the range of normal hearing.

"Mary," I said sharply.

She gave a little start, and smiled.

"I'll call Mrs. Willard about some coffee—"

I went to her and took her by the shoulders. She was so small, looking up at me with an odd, birdlike tilt of the head. It was an unfamiliar gesture to me. It reminded me of a child ducking its head in anticipation of a blow. How the devil had she learned that look? Ran wouldn't strike her, not physically . . . Perhaps it was not a physical blow that she feared.

"What are they doing to you?" I asked.

The words surprised me as much as they did her; I hadn't even realized I was thinking along those lines. But, as is often true of unpremeditated comments, this was the right thing to say. Her look of surprise turned into one of pitiful relief.

"I knew you'd help me," she whispered. "You won't let them take me away, Jo? They want to."

"Not Ran?"

"Ran and that Graham. He's a doctor. He watches me all the time. They think I don't know it, but I do. It takes two doctors. But if one says so, they can always find another one. They help each other."

"Nobody is going to take you away," I said.

30

Her hands clutched at mine.

"You promise?"

"Not while I'm on my feet and capable of speech."

I got her to sit down in the rocking chair and I squatted beside her. There were tears on her cheeks, but she was smiling.

"It's such a joy to have you, Jo."

"I've missed you too," I said, and took her hands. "I'm so sorry, my dear—about the baby."

She looked down at me.

"You don't understand, Jo."

"I want to understand. That's why I came. Mary, what's the matter? It can't be the baby, not only that . . . What is it, Mary? Something to do with Ran?"

"What is it?" she repeated dreamily.

"Is it Ran?" I repeated. "Some trouble between you?"

She shook her head.

"You don't understand," she said again. "He's closer all the time. But I keep hearing him crying."

Ran?

He was the only one she could be talking about, and yet . . . Closer all the time? Yes, that was fine, the way marriage ought to be,

31

especially after a shared loss. But it didn't fit with the other things she had said, about Ran's conspiring to have her committed. And—Ran crying?

"Ran?" I said.

"Ran?" She laughed, a sudden, bright laugh. "Ran doesn't cry," she said. "No. But *he* cries. It is a boy, you know. His name is Kevin."

2

RAN didn't get back till late that night. I was the only one waiting up for him. Mary had gone to bed right after dinner. When I offered to come up with her she refused. Mrs. Willard always helped her. Mrs. Willard knew about her medicine. Mrs. Willard would take care of everything.

Mrs. Willard was the housekeeper. A big, square woman, she must have been at least fifty, but she moved with the vigour of a girl, and she cooked like an angel—if angels cook.

Except for the Willards' niece Flora, who came in to help out occasionally, Mrs. Willard and her husband Jed made up the household staff. The terms of address were characteristic of the pair; I couldn't imagine calling Mrs. Willard by her first name any more than I could have called Jed anything else.

My first impression of Jed was that somebody was kidding me. This wasn't a real man, it was a caricature of a Down East type that might have appeared in a bad novel, forty

33

years ago. Tall, lanky, with stooped shoulders and a face like that of an elderly bloodhound, he spoke in a slow drawl. He wore overalls, the kind with the metal buckles on the straps.

It was Jed who interrupted us just after Mary's astonishing speech. Later I realized that I should have been grateful to him; God knows what I might have said, or done, in my first shock. As it was, I could let out my feelings on him, spinning around with a start and a stifled shriek that echoed the creak of the floorboards.

"Oh," I said. "You startled me."

Jed put the suitcases down and straightened up to his full height, which was considerable. He smiled at me. It was an effective smile, considering its extent, which barely cracked the surface of his cheeks. Despite its melancholy, his was an affable face. It was also amazingly expressive. Each feature seemed to be capable of independent movement, and he could convey as much emotion in the twitch of his nose or the lift of a sandy eyebrow as other people could in a long speech. I assumed that he had developed this talent because he didn't get a chance to talk much. I was wrong; but certainly in the first meeting Mrs. Willard talked enough for both of them.

34

She was right behind him, and she practically filled the doorway. I never thought of her as fat, though. She was massive, all over, from her shoulders, broad as a man's, to her big, solid feet. Even her hair was abundant; the bun at the back of her head would have bent the neck of a lesser woman. She wore gold-rimmed glasses, which enlarged her eyes. They were beautiful eyes, as blue as cornflowers, but they were lost in the vast pink expanse of her face.

"I'm Miz Willard," she announced. The tone of her voice turned the words from a statement into an inalterable law. "This is my husband, Jed. You must be Mary's sister. It's good you've come. She needs company. The Good Lord knows I don't have time. This is a big house. Not that I can't handle it. I've never seen the house yet I couldn't handle. But it don't leave much time for sitting and talking. I like a house to be nice. If you got a job to do, do it right, that's what I say."

Wordlessly I put my hand out, and she took it. She moved well for a woman of her bulk, not gracefully, but with neat efficiency. The blue eyes were as shrewd as they were beautiful. I saw them darken a little, as if with concern, as she glanced from my face to Mary's.

"I come up to see if you were ready for some coffee. I just made it fresh. Some hot doughnuts, too. Mary needs fattening up. I suppose you're on a diet, like all the girls, but you just forget about that for a while. You could stand some flesh yourself. Ran said if he wasn't back by seven we should go ahead and eat, but that's a long while from now. Never mind about them clothes, I'll put 'em away for you later. Come and drink your coffee while it's hot."

She swept Mary off, and I followed them down the stairs, half hearing Mrs. Willard's voice as she talked about the doughnuts, the menu for dinner, the prospect of Ran's arriving in time to eat it, the weather—heaven only knows what other subjects she covered. I was preoccupied with my own thoughts. Among them was relief. God knows what I might have blurted out but for the fortuitous appearance of the Willards. This was worse than I had imagined. This was bad, so bad that it had to be handled with infinite care. A surge of anger rose up as I thought of William Graham. Why hadn't he warned me of this? And how could he possibly mistake an obsession of this sort for spoiled petulance? Even I could see how dangerous this was.

And I didn't have the faintest idea of how to respond to it. I had to know more. I had to talk to Ran.

But as the day wore on, I began to have second thoughts. Was it possible that Dr. Graham didn't know of Mary's delusion—that it was a new development? For the rest of the afternoon her behaviour was absolutely normal. She was edgy and easily tired; it would have been obvious even to a stranger that she had been ill. But there was not the slightest suggestion of serious abnormality. If I hadn't known better, I might have wondered whether I had imagined that single, shocking speech. But I knew I hadn't imagined it.

The behaviour of the Willards confirmed my uneasiness. They were omnipresent. When we went outside to look at the flowers, Jed hovered—raking, pruning, picking up twigs—always within sight. When we went back in, there was Mrs. Willard suggesting a tour of the house. It was logical that she would be the guide; she had been with the family for years, whereas the house and the family history were almost as unfamiliar to Mary as they were to me. And yet . . .

Mrs. Willard confirmed my hunch about

the age of the house. And it was then that I first heard the name that was to assume such ominous meaning to me.

"The Captain built it real handsome," she said. "They tore a lot of the carvings off, later on. Why, they say in his day it was as pretty a house as that Wedding Cake House over to Kennebunk."

I caught Mary's eyes and managed to keep my face sober.

"Oh, yes," I said. "I remember seeing a picture of the Wedding Cake House."

I remembered it; no one who had ever seen it could possibly forget it—much as he might like to. The Kennebunk house had been reproduced in my art-history textbook as a horrible example of American Gothic run wild. But I wasn't about to explain that, not when Mrs. Willard so obviously admired the style, and she took it for granted that I remembered the house because of its beauty.

"It was the Captain's son that did a lot of the damage," she said. Her tone was so actively resentful that it came to me with a shock that the Captain's son must have been dead for almost a century. "They do say he even wanted to tear down the tower. But the builder warned him the whole middle section of the roof might fall in if he did."

"What a shame," I said. "That he—er—damaged the house. But surely this part wasn't built by the Captain? It must be older."

We were on the second floor of the central section, looking down the hall from my room. The major bedrooms were on this corridor and the cross-corridor that connected with it. There were eight bedrooms, and I knew by their proportions and the shapes of the mantels, as well as the beautiful old hand-pegged floors, that they had been built in an earlier and more beauty-loving era than the Captain's.

"Yes, this was the Old House," Mrs. Willard agreed. "The Captain bought it in 1826, after he made his fortune. He had it rebuilt for his bride. She was a Barnes from Boston and she had to have a fine house."

To my shame I had never heard of the Barneses of Boston, but I gathered from Mrs. Willard's tone that they ranked up there with the Cabots. So I nodded, looking impressed, and Mrs. Willard, encouraged by my interest, continued her lecture.

"He had these rooms furnished much nicer than they are right now. The master bedroom—that's the one Ran and Mary have—had a beautiful big carved wood mantel. They took that down in 1930, when old Mr. Max did a lot of remodelling."

I could imagine the kind of overmantel which old Mr. Max had scrapped, restoring the beautifully simple Adam-style mantel with its carved bas-reliefs and French tile facing. It was clear that the house owed its present charm to Mr. Max. He had torn out many of the Victorian embellishments and put back into use the older furniture which his ancestors had relegated to the attic.

"He must have been quite a guy," I said.

Mary nodded.

"He was Ran's grandfather; Ran remembers him quite well. I knew you'd like the house, Jo. I fell in love with it the first time I saw it."

"I never knew Ran owned this place."

"He didn't until recently. His great-aunts lived here. The last of them died in March. There was some kind of silly family quarrel, something to do with his mother's remarriage—the aunts didn't approve. Ran never expected to see the place again after he and his mother left. But the old lady repented on her deathbed and left him the house as a way of healing the feud."

Mrs. Willard said briskly,

"And high time, too. Such nonsense . . . Now down this way is the wing the Captain built on. We don't use it, but I give it a good turning out every six months when my niece comes up."

Mary was beginning to droop a little. Mrs. Willard noticed it, and hurried us through the next eight bedrooms, which were in the Captain's "new" wing. I remember very little about them—only a conglomerate impression of rooms sombre with drawn drapes and most of the furniture swathed in dust covers.

There was one thing I particularly wanted to see, and when Mrs. Willard said she had better go down and start dinner, I protested.

"We haven't seen the tower. I have a strange weakness for towers."

"It's too much for Mary," Mrs. Willard said. "All those stairs."

"I think I will lie down for half an hour or so," Mary said. "But you go ahead, Jo. I know you love exploring. You can't get lost."

I didn't exactly get lost. At any point I could have retraced my steps. But there were times when I'd have been hard put to it to explain exactly where I was. The place was like a badger's warren.

And there was an additional element, one that made the ensuing hour a time I'll never forget. It was a Looking-Glass feeling, a sensation of having stepped through into another dimension or another time; as if there were two houses on that same spot, existing simultaneously, yet separated from one another by an indescribable gulf. The rooms on the lower floors were lovely, charming, warm—inhabitable rooms, where real people talked and ate and slept and did all the normal, real things. The upper floors were cut off by more than a flight of stairs. Up there it was hard to imagine that there was life anywhere for a dozen miles.

I found a ballroom on the third floor—the biggest, dustiest, most echoing vault of a room I had ever seen. Even my imagination, which is pretty good, couldn't people that vast desolation with laughing guests, with music or the swaying forms of ghostly dancers. The other rooms on that floor were good-sized, but not as elegant as the ones below. I assumed that the majority of them were extra guest rooms which had been used only when the family gave big parties. One suite was different. It must have been the children's area—day nursery, night nursery, and the bedroom of the governess or nanny. There was very little furniture left in place anywhere on this floor, but the faded wallpaper in one room had a design of rabbits and ducks, and the battered condition of floors and walls suggested generations of pounding feet, bouncing balls, and crayon murals.

The sight of those rooms made me a little melancholy, and as I went on, still searching for stairs that would lead to the tower, I found myself thinking of the children who had lived in this house over its many years. Ran had been one of them. Surely they hadn't put him up in those dreary rooms, not with the house so empty. Children of earlier eras had not had an easy life; to be seen and not heard was the rule, and upper-class parents made darned good and sure the little darlings weren't even seen any oftener than was absolutely necessary. They lived apart with the servants; sleeping, playing, eating by themselves. Animal crackers and cocoa to drink, with nurse standing by; Mother and Daddy dine later, in state. It sounded delightful—in the poem. Maybe it was. Maybe children really were happier out of the adult world with its incomprehensible demands and strict rules. But the poem hadn't been written by a child, it had been written by a grown-up, under the effect of the useful amnesia that makes adults think of childhood as a happy time—forgetting the loneliness, the uncertainty, the fear.

The fourth-floor corridor was even drearier than the third. Here were the servants' quarters and the vast attics. The drab paint on the walls had been cream-coloured once; now it was mottled and stained by time, and the floorboards squealed as I walked along, leaving the prints of my feet in the dust. The electricity was working, but many bulbs had burned out and never been replaced. They were bare bulbs; no fixtures, not up here, where the lower classes lived. The light they cast was an ugly light, at once sharp and inadequate, leaving great hollows of shadow in between. That long, narrow, barren hallway with its rows of closed doors was a nasty place. I found myself wondering what might be hidden behind those doors.

When I finally found a small stairway going up from the fourth floor, I discovered that it led not to the tower but to the cupola. I had almost forgotten there was one, and I scrambled up the stairs with renewed interest. The steps were narrow and steep but quite solid, and the room they led to was a curious place.

It was small, about ten feet square, and completely empty except for dust. The walls on all four sides were solid glass.

There wasn't much to see outside, only the vast, encompassing darkness of the trees that surrounded the house. In the west the sunset spread bars of bright colour across the sky, but the vault above was already filled with stars. There was no moon; it had not yet risen. I promised myself that I would come up again during the day. The cupola rose up above the trees like a lighthouse out of a waste of water; the view by daylight must be quite spectacular. Possibly I would be able to see beyond the island, out across the rolling water of the ocean. I wondered, romantically, whether the Captain's wife had stood here watching for the first sight of his sails. There were widows' walks in many of the big houses along this coast; this vantage point might have served the same purpose. With sea voyages lasting a year or more, they were lonely times for the wives who stayed behind.

Sometimes the vigil never ended, as some women watched for a sail that had gone down, unseen and without survivors, beneath the stormy waves of another ocean.

Nice morbid thoughts . . . I told myself that I would have one more try for the tower, and then I would go down the first stairs I found. Mary must be wondering what had become of me.

Opening a door at random, I found a staircase I hadn't seen before. There were windows on each landing; I could see a faint glow from the window on the floor below. But there was no glow from above, and when I looked up I saw a solid ceiling. This was the top, the stairs went no higher.

The moon had risen, but it's light was not strong enough to make me want to risk those stairs. I was about to turn back when my hand touched a familiar shape on the wall. It was an electric light switch. I pressed it down, and lights came on. Then I saw the other door, across the landing, and I realized that I had found the tower.

At first I thought the door was locked. I shoved with my shoulder, and the door gave with a screech of hinges and a puff of air, almost as if the room had been hermetically sealed. The air smelled warm and stale.

The first thing I saw were the bars on the window.

They were solid, unrelieved black against the pale silver shine of moonlight, and their shape was repeated in long shadows across the floor. The effect was so startling that I actually fell back a step, my hand still on the doorknob; then I caught myself, with a silent reprimand. No doubt this had once been a child's room. The nursery windows had been barred too. It was a long drop down to the ground.

Unlike the other rooms, this one had a few sticks of furniture. The object that caught my eye, and confirmed my idea that this had been a nursery, was a rocking horse. It was the biggest one I had ever seen; I could have ridden it myself without having to hunch over. It was a rather ghostly sight in the shadows; perhaps, I thought, the darkness made it seem larger than it was.

I couldn't see much more because there were no lights in the room. My fingers explored the whole section of wall next to the door, but failed to find a switch. As my eyes adjusted to the darkness I made out a few more details—a fireplace, opposite the door, and a peculiar structure on the right-hand curve of the wall. I had wondered why the stairs ended on this, the fourth floor, when the tower clearly boasted at least one additional storey. The structure I saw was an iron spiral staircase, like the ones you sometimes see in the stacks of old libraries. So that was how you got to the top floor of the tower. Someone must have liked his privacy. But of all the stupid things to have in a child's room! I had had experience with stairs of this type, and I knew they were extremely slippery. The solid iron knobs on the banisters were an additional hazard if someone should slip.

But then, I reminded myself, old-fashioned houses were dangerous places for children. The fireplaces, despite screens and constant attendance, must have caused many injuries.

The glow from the window was brighter now, a lovely luminous light; the moon must be almost full. I looked at the window. And saw something looking back at me from outside.

I didn't have to remember that the window was forty feet above the ground, on a flat wall; I didn't have to tell myself that nothing human could have reached it. I retreated, with speed. It's a wonder I didn't break my neck. I went down the stairs like a rocket and I didn't stop until I had passed through the door at the bottom and slammed it shut behind me.

I stood there gasping and wheezing, with my back flat up against the door as if I had to press on it to hold it shut. There was nothing behind it—no pressure, no presence. The corridor where I stood was carpeted in soft blue, there were shaded lights and a small table with a mirror above it and a bouquet of wax flowers . . . I recognized the corridor, the first-floor hall that led from the parlour to a small morning room at the back of the house. From another corridor to my left came the seductive odour of roasting chicken; and from the parlour came a voice, calling my name.

I pushed myself away from the door.

"Yes, it's me," I said. "Coming, Mary."

I was back in the real world, back through the Looking-Glass.

II

Ran wasn't home by seven, so we ate without him. By the time dinner was over I felt like a turkey being stuffed for Thanksgiving. I had

49

the absurd feeling that Mrs. Willard might take the spoon out of my hand and feed me if I didn't finish everything she put in front of me. When she finally agreed that we had eaten enough I wasn't sure I could get out of my chair.

After she and Mary went upstairs, I subsided into a chair in the parlour to recuperate. This was a lovely room, with a big bay window along one side and a beautiful panelled fireplace. Furniture design is not my field, but I knew that some of the pieces were valuable antiques. The heavy embroidered material of the draperies looked like eighteenth-century designs. Above all, it was a pleasant room. The soft rose and green and blue of the draperies were restful to the eyes, and so were the simple lines of the furniture. The dark wood surfaces gleamed; Mrs. Willard hadn't been fooling when she said she could handle this place.

After my busy day and abundant dinner I should have been sleepy, but for obvious reasons I found myself increasingly restless. The lamplight cast a mellow glow, the velvet chair was very comfortable, but the copy of *Vogue* I had picked up didn't hold my attention, not even the ad layouts. Pictures and text seemed horribly slick and superficial and fake. I knew why I was ill at ease. I was trying hard not to think about the problem, not yet. Preconceptions are fatal to common sense, and fatally easy to fall into. I had enough prejudices to begin with; but at least I knew they were prejudices, unlike some smart-aleck doctors . . .

I threw the magazine down with a snort of disgust. There were rows of books in the white-painted shelves flanking the fireplace. It was a good collection—classics, old and new, with a sprinkling of thrillers and science fiction and a few new books I had been wanting to read. Ran had catholic tastes and evidently they were hereditary; some of the volumes were cracked and rubbed with years of use. But none of them caught my interest. The grand piano drew me; I don't play well, but I like to play, and I hadn't been able to indulge in a piano of my own, not in my thin-walled apartment and on my thin salary. But my mind shrank back from sound. The house was utterly still. Mary probably wouldn't have been disturbed by my playing, so long as I didn't burst into the "Revolutionary Etude" or one of the more vigorous Beethoven sonatas. But it seemed—

somehow—dangerous to disturb that silence.

With that kind of thought for company, I was relieved when I finally heard the car. It stopped in front of the house with a squeal of brakes and I recognized the driving style. Ran always drove that way, impatient with the time it took to get from the place where he was to the place where he wanted to be. I went out into the hall to meet him. My heart was beating more quickly than it should have done.

The front door opened and there he was. He was almost too handsome—not in the sleek leading-man style, but with a dark, hard leanness that most women find even more attractive. My stomach twisted with the old familiar feeling. I had it under control immediately, but it scared me; I had hoped, and believed, that that weakness was gone for good.

"Jo! My God, it's good to see you!"

He dropped his briefcase and put his arms around me. It was a brief, brotherly hug—nothing more. Then he held me at arms' length and grinned at me.

"You've lost ten pounds. No, make that eight pounds. What are you doing out there, starving?"

"Seven pounds," I said. "Dieting, not starving."

"We've missed you." He put his arm around my shoulders and led me towards the parlour. "I wish you'd give up this crazy idea of earning your own living and—"

"Uh-uh," I said. "No more of that. We agreed, remember?"

"Okay, okay. How was the trip? Will meet you all right? What about a drink?"

"No thanks." I dropped into the chair and watched as a bar materialized out of what had appeared to be a Chippendale sideboard. "Yes, Bill—Will—whatever his name is met me. And told me off, but good. Has he had the gall to tell you what he thinks of your wife?"

Ran stood staring down at his glass, moving it gently back and forth so that the ice tinkled delicately.

"What do you think about Mary? You've had a chance to talk to her."

"I don't know where to start," I said helplessly. I did know; but I couldn't say it, not yet. Not in the comfortable room with lamplight yellow and warm, and the night shut out by flowered draperies. "She's so much worse than I expected. What happened?

I can't believe she would flip over something like—"

"Jo, you are so damned young. Haven't you learned that you don't know Mary—or any other human being—any more than they know you? You see the one tenth that shows above the surface. You never see the pressures, the cracks, and weaknesses that develop underneath."

"Weaknesses, is it? You sound like good old Will. What the hell gives him the right to analyse Mary?"

"He's a damned good doctor. He's here on the island by choice, because he loves the place. He could have had his pick of jobs."

"That's beautiful. It doesn't alter the fact that he's opinionated, antagonistic, and ignorant."

Ran looked at me in mild surprise.

"What did he say to get you so worked up? With me he's humble and definitely sympathetic."

"He says she's spoiled. Neurotic. Weak. Childish."

"Come on, Jo. Will wouldn't—"

"Will did. He doesn't like me, either."

"He doesn't—" Ran's baffled stare changed to a look of amusement. "Oh, Lord, I forgot.

54

I should have warned you. Will is scared of women—young, pretty, healthy women, anyhow. That mask of hostility is a defence mechanism."

"Now, Ran, you don't have to spare my feelings. I don't care what he thinks of me."

"No, it's the truth. Will had a—well, call it an unfortunate love affair."

"Call it anything you like. I'm not interested."

"I knew Sue in grade school," Ran said with a reminiscent gleam in his eyes. "She had red-gold curls and blue eyes. And the way she walked, even then . . ."

"Never mind your lecherous pre-adolescence. I gather Sue was La Belle Dame sans Merci. I hope she gave it to him good."

"She did."

"Ran, I couldn't care less about Will's broken heart. So he's prejudiced against women. That's about as logical as hating Frenchmen because one Frenchman picks your pocket in the Metro. What really concerns me is why you brought Mary here. Wouldn't she be better off in town, with decent doctors close at hand?"

"I told you, she won't see a psychiatrist."

"But at least you'd have them near, so that

you could take immediate advantage of a change of mind. Here, you're hours away from professional help if she should agree to see someone, or if . . ."

I didn't need to go on. We both knew what I meant: or if she got worse.

"That isn't going to happen," Ran said angrily. "And if it should—well, whatever you think of Will's qualifications as a psychiatrist, he's a first rate doctor. He could take whatever emergency measures were needed."

I shivered. The picture was an ugly one: Mary struggling and violent, having to be subdued by an injection before being carried off, an inert, hoarsely breathing bundle, to a padded cell in Boston or New York. Shades of Le Fanu and Wilkie Collins . . . But it could happen.

"But here, of all places," I argued. "Talk about isolation! Don't you ever have storms, times when no one can get off the island?"

"Not these days. You're a hopeless landlubber, Jo."

"Even so . . . I didn't even know you had a house here. You lived here when you were small?"

"Everybody lived here when I was small,"

Ran said, with a faint smile. "My grandfather was still alive; he was the patriarch of the clan, he gathered in loose relatives. Mother came here after Dad died, and we stayed till she remarried. Mary fell in love with the place when we came up this spring to settle my great-aunt's estate. When I suggested we get out of the city, she wanted to come here."

"I see."

I saw a number of things; one of them was the way Ran was drinking. He was on his third now, and all three had been pretty dark. This was a new habit, and one which filled me with disquiet.

"I'm glad you do," Ran said. "Are you willing now to acquit me of kidnapping my wife and carrying her off for my own sinister purposes?"

"I never thought—"

"Naturally you're partisan. I want you to be. I want somebody—somebody who is on Mary's side."

I stared at him.

"I know," he said, not looking at me. "But try to understand, Jo. When two people live as closely as Mary and I do—not just the ordinary closeness of marriage, we've always had more than that—emotions are never simple. I love her. But my ego is so wound up in her that her unhappiness makes me feel guilty and resentful. I can't admit that I've failed, so there must be something wrong with her. Most of the time I feel love and compassion and a desperate desire to help. But there are moments when—when I want to grab her and shake her and yell, 'Snap out of it! Stop acting so childish!' Now tell me what a louse I am."

"I don't think you're a louse," I said. "I think you're a rare bird—an honest man. I know a little something about twisted emotions myself."

He looked up at me, his face a mixture of gratitude and relief.

"Thanks, Jo. I'm sorry; I've let my worries make me selfish. Have you had a bad time this past year?"

"No. No worse than . . . Forget it, Ran. Your worries are my worries, don't forget. We'll work them out somehow."

"What was she like today? What happened?"

"Has she ever spoken to you—has she ever said anything about . . ." It was odd; I couldn't say it.

"About hearing a child cry?" From Ran's tone I knew the subject worried him as much

58

as it did me. But there was a kind of relief in hearing the words said, like the fading of pain after a boil is lanced.

"Ran, she thinks the baby is alive. At least that's what I understood from what she said. 'It is a boy. His name is Kevin'."

"She told you that?" Ran's heavy brows lowered. "My God, Jo, she hasn't said that much to me. Only about hearing the crying. What else did she say?"

"That was about all. Mrs. Willard came in then, and I was too shaken to pursue the subject. I wanted to talk to you first."

"Kevin," Ran muttered. "That's odd."

"The whole thing is odd."

"Not really. It's a predictable delusion for a woman who wanted a child so badly. But I wonder where she got the name. We always thought . . . if we ever had a boy . . ."

There was no break in his voice, no change in his expression of concentrated thoughtfulness; but I sensed that this was suddenly more than he could bear, and I realized with a sharp stab of guilt that his desire for children had been as keen as Mary's.

"Yes, I know," I said. "Randall junior. Elizabeth if it had been a girl . . . Maybe I didn't hear the name correctly. I was, as you might say, taken aback."

"It doesn't matter."

"I'm not so sure," I said slowly.

"What do you mean?"

"I don't know . . . For a second there, when you said it doesn't matter, I had the weirdest feeling . . . of warning, almost."

"Cut it out, Jo. Don't you go psychic on me."

The words were brusque but the smile was not. I laughed self-consciously, feeling that peculiar sense of relaxation that follows an emotional outburst.

"Sorry. The crucial question is, how do I react to remarks like that one of Mary's? Do I accept it? Question it? Contradict it? I can put on any act that's required, but I'm afraid of doing the wrong thing."

"I know what you mean. I don't know the answer, not yet, but I did something today that—"

His voice broke off; and then I heard the other sound.

It was faint, as though it came from a long, long way away—a high, shrill keening sound. The sound of someone crying.

Ran moved so fast that the breeze of his

passage riffled the pages of the magazine lying open on the table. When I stumbled out into the hall he was already halfway up the stairs, taking them three at a time. The sound was still going on, a desolate wailing that tore at the ears. It was real; there was no possible question of that. But I think I knew the truth, even before I saw.

Mary's room was down the hall and across from mine. When I reached the top of the stairs I could see the door—and Ran bent over at an odd angle which made sense only when I heard the click of the lock. He flung the door open and disappeared inside. The sound was loud now, and unmistakable; it came from inside the room.

They stood locked together near the doorway; it wasn't apparent, at first glance, whether Ran's arms were embracing or restraining her. She was still crying, but more normally, with sobs and muffled words.

"Couldn't get out . . . Let me go, Ran, let me go . . . He wants me . . . Couldn't get out!"

The last word rose to a scream, and then she struggled wildly while Ran tried to hold her. I saw her face as she writhed. I don't think I'd have recognized it if I hadn't known who she was. Her eyes, black holes in a white mask, saw me, but without recognition. Then her face vanished behind the heavy shape of Ran's shoulder. I heard him speak, sharply; and then there was a flurry of movement and Mary went limp. Ran gathered her up as she fell. He turned towards me with her body cradled against him. Her cheek lay on his breast. On his cheek I could see the livid marks of her nails. I started towards him.

"Get out," he said. "Get out of here, Jo."

I fell back a step as the door slammed in my face.

3

I WAS lured downstairs next morning by the smells from the kitchen—bacon and eggs and coffee and muffins, fresh out of the oven. The muffins were dark with cinnamon and sticky with warm sugar. I ate three of them, sitting at the kitchen table while Mrs. Willard watched approvingly.

"Don't suppose you usually eat a decent breakfast," she said. "That instant stuff, or dry cereal. That's just like grass. No body to it."

"If I ate like this every morning, I'd gain five pounds a week," I mumbled, through my third muffin. "It might be worth it, at that . . . Where is everybody? Am I late or early?"

"Ran already had breakfast. He's in the library; and he had some work to do this morning."

"What about Mary?"

Mrs. Willard turned away to wipe an already immaculate counter top.

"I take hers up to her. She doesn't sleep too good."

"I know."

Mrs. Willard turned. Her pink face was impassive, but from the cloth in her hand a small trickle of water dripped down on to the spotless floor. Her fingers must have been tightly clenched to squeeze water from a cloth she had already wrung out.

"She was up again last night?"

"Yes. You lock her in?"

"It's Ran's orders."

It is useless to speculate on what would have developed if I had spoken out then and there. Probably it wouldn't have made any difference. We were not ready, either of us, for the kind of confidences that could have changed the course of events. She didn't trust me, and I had reservations about speaking candidly to her. She had known Ran for years, and helped to raise him. How could I tell Ran's old friend and foster mother that I was beginning to suspect his treatment of my sister?

And yet, with my well-known propensity for babbling, I might have spoken, if we had not been interrupted. The shadow fell across the floor between us like a long dark bar, dividing our locked glances as effectively as a wall. Mrs. Willard started, and I turned, half rising from my chair.

"Good morning, all," said Will Graham. Framed by the open door, one long brown hand resting against it, he grinned at us. "You two look as guilty as a pair of thieves. What did I interrupt, some deep dark female gossip?"

"Gossip indeed," said Mrs. Willard tartly. "I know what you're here for, and if you think you're going to talk me out of another breakfast, Willie Graham, you'd better keep a civil tongue in your head."

"How many times have I asked you not to call me Willie?" Will glanced at me; I tried, unsuccessfully, to wipe the grin off my face.

"You mean I can't call you Willie?" I asked. "I would dearly love to."

"Not unless you learn to make muffins." Will sat down across from me. "Women who make muffins can call me anything. I'm very susceptible to muffins."

"You're susceptible to any kind of food," Mrs. Willard scoffed. She handed him a plate.

"I've been up since five," Will said. "If that doesn't rate another breakfast, I don't know what does. And it wasn't your cooking

65

that brought me here, so don't look so smug. I came to ask Jo if she'd like to go for a walk. I thought she might like to see my house."

"It's those beasts you're wanting to show off," Mrs. Willard said. Her voice was so grim I visualized some monstrous menagerie—lions or crocodiles or snakes.

"That's ridiculous," Will said indignantly. "Here I am trying to entertain a visitor and all you can do is insult me." He took a muffin. "I'm leaving. Are you coming, Jo?"

I gave him a suspicious look, which he countered with his famous smile. I told myself it wasn't the smile that made me weaken; if the man was trying, in his clumsy male fashion, to apologize for his outrageous remarks the day before, the least I could do was meet him halfway.

"Okay," I said.

We walked across the lawn in silence while Will finished the muffin he had carried off, and I eyed his lean figure with unwilling amusement.

"Do you always eat like this?"

"I do when I can get it," Will said. "I'm not much of a cook. And—though you may find this difficult to believe—I have a fairly sizeable practice. On the mainland and some of the other islands as well as here. Keeps me busy."

"Does it?"

"I'm sorry about yesterday."

"You're entitled to your opinion."

"But I'm not entitled to foist it on other people so loudly. I—well, to tell the truth, I'd been up all night. Lost a patient. I was in a bad mood."

"I'm sorry. About the patient."

He gave me a quick, sidelong glance and then his sombre face lightened in one of those smiles.

"You really are sorry, aren't you?"

"I'm sorry for the whole sad, sad world," I said. "But at the moment I'm concentrating on Mary."

"Look, let's take the morning off, okay? Forget about Mary for a couple of hours."

"You'd like to forget her altogether."

"I don't provoke," Will said calmly. "Not on a day like this, when I've had a couple of hours sleep. I promise, I will reobserve and reconsider and anything else you want. Maybe I was wrong about Mary—and, by God, you won't get a concession like that from me very often. But this morning I want to relax. Okay?"

67

"Well . . ."

When he said "walk", he wasn't kidding. We didn't follow the road, but struck off into the woods. There was a path of sorts, but it was badly overgrown. Will admitted that it was seldom used; the old ladies hadn't been much given to hiking after they passed seventy, and he usually drove. Even with Will preceding me, fending off the worst of the over-hanging branches, I was winded and dishevelled by the time we reached the edge of the woods.

I understood then why trees and vines had seemed so thick, so twisted together. Without mutual support they could not have survived. Only a few hundred yards away, the ground ended, with breathtaking abruptness, in a cliff that seemed to drop off into empty space. As soon as I stepped out of the woods I could feel the force of the wind. During a winter storm it would howl through the eaves of the forest like a banshee.

The house huddled close to the shelter of the trees. I could see the necessity for that, though I wondered whether I would like living so close to the dark pines.

The house itself was a gem, a classic example of a homegrown architectural style. I knew it must be quite old. The New England saltbox style was at its best in the mid-eighteenth century, which would make this house about two hundred years old. It wore its age well. The silvery grey surface had been weathered by that unique blend of salt sea air that is found only along this coast. Two small one-storey additions had been built out from the back, and a deep porch jutted out to protect the front door. Vines covered its latticed sides, but I could see wooden benches set at right angles to the house. A single massive chimney jutted up from the centre of the roof. The windows were good-sized, and the wooden shutters looked as if they had been designed for use. Even with the woods behind it, the house would endure bitter weather; except for a pair of tall pines by the front gate, it was completely exposed to the wind from the sea.

The only flaw in the scene of picturesque charm was Will's battered blue station wagon, parked at the end of what could only be described as a track. Unpaved and rocky, it curved off to the right and vanished behind the trees.

"How on earth do you get out of here to make house calls in the winter?" I asked.

69

"Oh, I board in town during the worst months. But you could live here all right if you didn't have to answer emergency calls. A jeep with four-wheel drive would get you in and out most days, and I can imagine worst fates than being snowed in for a week or two. With one shed full of firewood and the other packed with canned goods . . . I've got five hundred books I haven't had time to read and a tape recorder I can run from batteries."

I could understand the wistful note in his voice. The picture had a strong appeal for me too. A fire roaring up the chimney while the wintry blasts howled outside . . . Books, music . . . and other equally cosy occupations . . .

"It wouldn't work," I said regretfully. "You couldn't be cut off from your patients."

"I could part of the time, if I could get another man here to share my practice. There's enough work for two, God knows. And I have so much catching up to do. I haven't even time to read the journals the way things are, and you can't give your patients the best possible care unless you keep up to date."

So that was why he wanted to be marooned

70

in his snug little house—to read medical journals in bachelor solitude.

"If that's what turns you on," I said. "Personally, I'd go crazy buried in a place like this all winter."

"It's lucky you aren't then, isn't it? Come on in, and meet the beasts, as Bertha calls them."

Knowing I had annoyed him, I followed him across the lawn. I was curious about the beasts; from Mrs. Willard's tone they might be anything from mice to rattlesnakes. The first of the menagerie was sitting on top of the porch steps. The sheer size of him made me exclaim aloud.

"Heavens, that's the biggest cat I've ever seen! What is it, a lynx or something?"

The cat, a brown tabby, had hair almost as long as that of a Persian; it formed a manelike ruff around the smug feline face. The animal gave me a leisurely appraisal; then it rose to its feet, turned, and brought into view a tail so big, so bushy, and so long that it looked like a Cavalier's plume. My gasp of admiration was the proper response; the cat gave me a coquettish leer over its shoulder and sat down with its back to me, waving the tail.

"What on earth is it?"

"She," said Will reproachfully. "The breed is called Maine coon cats. You can see why, though of course the old story that they are a cross between cats and raccoons is nonsense. The two species don't interbreed."

"I've never seen one like it."

"They are rare, except in New England."

"You breed them?" I sat down on the steps. The cat promptly climbed into my lap and sat down, purring so hard that its sides pumped in and out.

"No, I don't, really. They just keep on having kittens."

"Yes," I said weakly. "I see they do."

Silently and slyly the cats had filled up the yard. There were more coon cats—a red, a silver tabby, a tortoiseshell; two Siamese; a black-and-white shorthair; and an exquisite long-haired creature with blue eyes and dark Siamese markings. Lined up along the path were more commoners—alley cats—in a startling variety of shapes, colours, and sizes. I had barely taken in this display when two dogs came stalking around the corner of the house. One was a terrier; the other, looming over his friend, was a St. Bernard. My head jerked back.

"Good heavens," I said.

Will scooped the purring sycophant from my lap and pulled me to my feet.

"You might as well see the rest," he said, with the air of a man who wants to get a bad job over and done with.

At least "the rest" were smaller than the cats and dogs. Two guinea pigs, a hamster, a squirrel, three snakes—one large, two small—and a parrot who at the sight of me, let out a stream of profanity as colourful as his red-and-green plumage.

"What," I said. "No partridge in a pear tree?"

"The partridge only comes in for chow."

I sat down, after a wary glance at the seat of the chair. My suspicions were understandable, but unjustified. The place was surprisingly clean. Neat it definitely was not, but the clutter was an attractive kind of clutter. There were no dirty socks or unwashed dishes, only piles of records, magazines—and cats. The room was big and low-ceilinged. Three of the four walls had built-in bookcases covering all the surface that was not occupied by windows. The fourth wall consisted almost entirely of fireplace—a huge stone structure whose blackened interior testified to frequent use. There were two doors on that

73

wall, side by side. Will had underestimated the number of books—or maybe, I thought, he actually had read all but five hundred of them. Some of the shelf space was filled by a complex assortment of hi-fi equipment. The twin speakers stood on each side of the fireplace. I glanced at the record albums piled on the table beside my chair. As I might have suspected, Will's tastes were classical.

Will had left the front door open and it wasn't long before the animals filtered in. The dogs flopped down on the rug in front of the fireplace. They fixed mournful eyes on Will. The hamster started running madly around in his wheel; it squeaked. The parrot continued to swear, and, as if on signal, eight or nine cats began to mew.

Looking grim, Will carried the parrot, perch and all, out through a door at the back, through which I caught a glimpse of the interior of one of the annexes—a storage area, filled with firewood and cartons. When he returned, the slam of the door reduced the parrot's voice considerably.

"You don't have to censor him on my account," I said. "I've heard worse at work, when I made a mistake."

"It was the volume, not the content I was trying to control."

"Who did he belong to, a retired sea captain?"

"You're about a century behind the times. No, he belonged to two old ladies—Ran's great-aunts. They liked to hear him cut loose. Said he reminded them of their grandfather."

"They must have been characters."

"They were. An admirable pair, in their peculiar way. After Miss Tabitha died this spring, nobody would take poor old Barnaby. His vocabulary was a little too rich. Bertha always hated his guts."

"So you took him." I studied my host until he began to fidget nervously. "I'll bet most of this menagerie came the same way—abandoned animals that would have been destroyed if you hadn't adopted them. Your bark is worse than your bite."

"I prefer some animals to some people, that's all . . . What about some beer? Or a cup of coffee?"

"I could stand some coffee. If it's ready."

"You'll get instant."

"Fine. What I'd really like is to see the rest of the house. Do you realize what you've got

75

here? I've never seen a gambrel roof on a saltbox before."

"They aren't all that rare." Will opened one of the doors, the one farthest from the fireplace. "Come see the kitchen first. I'll put the kettle on, and then you can inspect the upstairs while the water boils."

The kitchen was a strange mixture of the antique and the very modern, with nothing in between. The four-burner electric stove had been added within the last few years, but its predecessor—and understudy, in case of power failures—was a creaky contraption fuelled by kerosene. You could cook over the fire, though, I thought, inspecting the big fireplace, which was the reverse side of the one in the living-room. You could bake bread—or try to—in the bake oven set into the chimney. The benches beside the hearth would be nice on winter days, with the sleet pounding against the shuttered windows, firelight flickering on the dark wooden flooring . . . Rugs, that was what the place needed. Braided rugs out here, to go with the rest of the room; the plain, white-painted mantel needed a row of ornaments, not the obvious copper utensils, but some good early pottery and maybe a pair of pewter candlesticks . . .

Curtains on the window, something bright, to cheer up the winter gloom. It would be fun to hand-block the material, copying old designs . . .

I turned to meet Will's curious eyes, and felt myself flush slightly. It was a good thing he couldn't know what I had been thinking. Artistic fervour might be mistaken for—something else. Men were so conceited . . .

The other door beside the living-room fireplace opened on to an enclosed staircase. Upstairs, there were only two rooms and a tiny hall. Both the rooms had once been bedrooms, but one had been converted into a bathroom and the potentialities of that room made my mouth water. The same back-to-back fireplace occurred upstairs. Imagine, I thought, a bathroom with its own fireplace; with those panelled cupboards and the sloping eaves . . .

"Hey." Will jogged my elbow. "Talk about crazy things that turn people on . . . You look like Dracula's daughter eyeing a juicy victim. Do you by any chance covet my house?"

"What I couldn't do with it! That bedroom is crying for decent furniture. There are antique shops all over New England. In a couple of years I could . . ."

"Tear yourself away; I think I hear the kettle whistling."

As we went down the stairs he said,

"Ran told me you studied art. But I thought you did—you know, advertising, pop art, that kind of thing."

"You sound as if you prefer that kind of thing."

"I don't care for pop art, if that's what those enlarged soup cans are. But I've never been able to understand the passion some people have for old things. The wormier and more ramshackle the better, I gather. I like functional things with nice clean lines. Something you can sit on without falling through it, and eat off without worrying about spilling the coffee."

"I see what you mean," I said, looking with unconcealed disgust at the kitchen table. "Only a barbarian would put a green Formica table with shiny aluminium legs in this room. It makes cold shudders run down my back."

"It holds coffee cups," Will said mildly, putting them on the tabletop. "What else is a table supposed to do? Milk? Sugar?"

"No, thanks. I don't see how you can live

78

in this part of the world and not be interested in history."

"Who says I'm not interested in history? I can tell you more about the China trade than any man on the island. But what does that have to do with antiques?"

"Why, the art of a period, especially the domestic arts, like furniture and dishes and costume—that's what makes history interesting."

"You'll probably enjoy the local museum, then," Will said. "They've got a lot of junk—excuse me—domestic-art objects. The old ladies—the great-aunts—donated some clothes, I remember."

"I would enjoy it. I'm anxious to see the village; I'll bet there's an antique shop, too."

Will's face went blank.

"Yes, there is," he said; from his tone he might have been admitting the existence of a concentration camp. "You'd be better off at the museum."

I couldn't imagine why he was so annoyed, but I was feeling fairly kindly towards him at that moment, so I decided not to bug him.

"Tell me about the China trade," I said.

He smiled a little sheepishly.

"I was bragging. That was my big hobby

79

when I was a kid. You know it was the East India-China trade that made New England rich, that and the related industries—shipbuilding, the Pacific fur trade, and so on. But I haven't done any reading in years."

"It's such a romantic period," I said. "The clipper ships, beating around Cape Horn . . ."

"The clipper ships didn't come into use until the very end of the period," Will said. "They were not—"

"Oh, who cares?" I waved away this repressive comment. "It's still romantic. I was thinking about it last night, when I was up in the cupola at the house. About the Captain, and his wife watching up there, for the ship to come back after all those months and months and—"

"Captain Hezekiah? You haven't wasted any time, have you? Who told you about the family skeleton?"

"Mrs. Willard mentioned him, but she certainly didn't suggest that there was anything disgraceful about him. According to her, he was the family hero."

"He was very successful," Will said dryly. "But you won't hear any of the good family stories from Bertha. She's been there so long, she identifies with the Frasers. Come to think

80

of it, I believe there is a remote connection, some great-great-great-ancestor in common."

"Really?"

"Oh, we're all inbred," Will said solemnly. He gave me a look of mock alarm. "Don't tell me you're interested in genealogy as well as antiques."

"Why not?"

"Somehow subjects like antiques and genealogy make me think of the Colonial Dames. Sweet old ladies in flowered hats."

I had to laugh.

"Sorry to destroy your image, but I am interested in both. After all, me boy, the McMullens were kings of Ireland oncet."

"They were?"

"No, they were not," I said, abandoning the brogue. "Peasants, that's what they were. And proud of it. But just because my granddaddy came over in the hold of a boat doesn't mean I can't be interested in other people's family trees."

"I think it's very broadminded of you," Will said.

"So do I. You inbred aristocrats, with your receding chins and feeble-minded offspring, are the ones we peasants have to clean up after all the time."

81

Will's hand went up automatically to explore the contours of his chin. Then he grinned.

"Maybe you've got a point there."

"Not about your chin, that was a distinctly weak argument. Hadn't we better be getting back? If I'm late for lunch, Mrs. Willard will glare at me and I'm scared of her."

"We've got plenty of time. There's something I want to show you on the way back. With your tastes, you'll find it absolutely fascinating."

Instead of going back by the path we had taken to reach the house, Will led me down the track—I refused to call it a road. We went towards the cliff, shaking off cats as we proceeded. When we reached the edge of the cliff, only the two Siamese were still with us. Even the splendour of the view could not keep me from glancing uneasily at the animals as they strolled and rolled near the cliff edge. The drop was not sheer, but it was steep and rocky; down below, the green waves dissolved into rainbow-shot lather and amid glistening dark flanks of rocks.

The cats continued to follow us as we walked down the road. Farther down, where the track joined an unpaved but well-gravelled road, Will turned aside into the pines. The gloom cast a corresponding shadow over my spirits. The cats didn't share my feelings; their black tails were cheerfully erect as they prowled. Suddenly one gave a hoarse chirrup and leaped a fallen log, to disappear in the underbush. Its mate was right behind it, ears lifted and hopeful.

"Won't they get lost?" I asked.

"They know these woods better than I do."

An unearthly howl came echoing back through the enclosing branches, and Will shook his head sympathetically.

"She missed that one."

"They have the weirdest voices!"

"You should hear Mitzi when she's in heat. Sounds like a lost child, or a sick baby."

I gave my companion a startled look, but Will's tanned face was as relaxed as his slouched body. So, I thought, he really doesn't know. Why doesn't Ran tell him?

Maybe, after our conversation, I should have been prepared for what Will was leading me into. But I don't see how I could have anticipated the reality; the location of the place was certainly unusual. I came to an abrupt stop on the edge of the clearing, and stared.

The pines around the open space were so

tall and dark that they gave the effect of a surrounding wall. Only when the sun was directly overhead would any but a twilight, diffused light enter here. At this hour the beams fell directly down upon the grass; the contrast was so extreme that the place looked like a stage set, illuminated by spot- and foot-lights.

The trees were not the only barrier. A tall iron fence, painted black, enclosed the plot. It was well tended; the stones stood stiffly erect, despite their obvious age; the scant grass was neatly clipped and the flowers, rosebushes and other perennials showed the work of a gardener's hands.

"What is a cemetery doing out here in the middle of the woods?" I asked.

"It's the Fraser family plot. They aren't buried here any more, of course; but it's consecrated ground, all the same."

"So many of them."

"The Frasers have been on the island for a long time. They had big families in the old days—sisters and cousins and maiden aunts. The servants, too. That's why there are so many graves."

"I'll bet Hezekiah was responsible for that atrocity," I said, indicating the biggest monument in the place. It was more than a monu-

84

ment; massively built of grey stone, it was a miniature Gothic house—a mausoleum.

"Right. How did you know?"

"The general ostentation, and the style. Mrs. Willard said he built his house like the Wedding Cake House—full-blown Gothic revival, in other words. Good heavens, it would be bad enough on a full-sized house; crammed on to that little building it looks frightful."

"Oh, I don't know," Will said thoughtfully. "You have to admit the frightfulness is appropriate to the function."

"I'm not sure that idea appeals to me . . . The place is in excellent condition. Who maintains it?"

"Jed. Who else?"

"And I thought he was lazy!"

"You can't have taken a good look at the grounds around the house, or you wouldn't say that. Jed does more, with less visible effort, than any man I've ever met. But he does like to give the effect of languid disinterest. He's got a funny sense of humour."

"Can we go in?"

"Sure." Will unlatched the gate. "We have to cross the clearing anyhow, to get back to the house."

The cemetery was a microcosm of early American funerary monuments. The epitaphs ranged from curt announcements of the name and the relevant dates to florid home made verses that related the virtues of the deceased or the circumstances of his demise. One or two of the latter were classics of unconscious humour, as worthy of preservation as the well-known examples of the genre which have been so often published. The designs on the tombstones were just as curious. I appreciated the earthy symbolism of the winged skull, which was popular around the turn of the century—the eighteenth century, that is. There was a rising-sun design which struck an oddly pagan note.

After a while Will glanced at his watch.

"Now you will have to hurry if you don't want to be late for lunch. You can come back anytime, you know."

"I'm sorry. This really is a fascinating—oh!"

My unexpected movement caught him off balance, and he swayed backwards under my weight as I threw myself against him. His arms went around me in a completely reflexive movement.

"What in God's name is the matter?"

I made a sound which I would hate to have to reproduce in writing, and then got control of my voice.

"Someone . . . over there."

"Where?"

Still holding me, Will turned in a complete circle.

"I don't see anybody," he said. "And if there were somebody . . . so what? From your reaction I thought you'd stepped on a rattlesnake."

"Over there, by the dead tree, the one that leans at an angle . . ."

There was certainly nothing by the tree now. I detached myself from Will. I will admit that I was not anxious to do so, but I didn't want him to get the wrong idea. It was such a corny trick, the scream and the timid maidenly terror. As my panic subsided, I felt my cheeks get hot. Of course he would think . . . What else could he think? My reaction had been so grossly out of proportion to any conceivable stimulus.

"What was it?" Will asked. "Man, woman . . . monster?"

"I . . . don't know. Something tall and dark . . . Will, I'm sorry. I don't know why I flipped. Just the suddenness of it, I guess."

"By the dead tree?" Will started across the cemetery.

I was grateful to him for pretending to take my foolishness seriously, but I was oddly reluctant to have him search that area.

"Will, don't bother. There isn't anything; it must have been a spot in front of my eyes. Please don't . . . Let's go."

"I'd better have a look." Will didn't stop walking. "This is private property, after all. Ran doesn't mind hikers or nature lovers, but there are some queer specimens wandering around these days. A graveyard might attract some of the real nuts."

It was a rational argument, and it almost convinced me. If a man had been standing there in the shadows, his surreptitious movements could be explained by a theory such as that. All the same, as I went after Will, I was very reluctant to approach the spot. And it wasn't because I was afraid of some harmless, and hypothetical, nut.

The fallen tree was a distinctive landmark. Part of the bark had been stripped away, so that the trunk made a long white diagonal streak that cut across the perpendicular darkness of the other trees. Caught and supported by the lower branches of a big spruce, it seemed to be firmly held, though I wouldn't have wanted to stand under it.

Will was standing by the fence when I reached him, staring at the patch of ground just outside the fence. There was no sign of life or of unusual movement among the trees. There were no weeds or brambles in that spot. The ground was thickly covered with dry brown pine needles.

"That stuff won't take footprints," I said. "If that's what you're looking for."

"I know. There's something funny out there, though. Look—about three feet beyond the fence. It's a squared-off corner of something—stone, by the look of it. Too regular to be a natural boulder."

"It is a stone," I said, in a voice that sounded funny. Like an echo. "A gravestone."

"A grave, outside the fence. That's absurd."

"Maybe. But that's what it is."

"I'll have a look."

"No, Will! Don't—"

He vaulted the fence. It was a darned impressive performance; the thing was breast-high, even for him. But he went over it, long legs and all, in a single neat movement. Hands still on the fence, he looked at me.

"Come on."

"How?"

I didn't want—I most definitely did not want—to cross the barrier and stand in that small, curiously open space.

Will examined the terrain.

"Stand on that stone. I'll lift you over."

"On a tombstone?"

"You aren't superstitious, are you?"

"I didn't use to think so . . ."

But I did as directed. From the stone I could step on to the top of the fence, and then Will lifted me down. His big hands were as strong as they looked. I was ashamed of my vapours by then, and went without protest to help him dig out the stone.

It wasn't as hard as I had expected. The accumulation of needles was inches thick, but it was soft; we could scoop the stuff out with our hands. The object was, as I had known (how?) a tombstone. The upper side was blank. We had to turn it over before we could read the inscription. I rubbed at the encrusted dirt with my hand and then with a stick Will handed me. The inscription had not been deeply cut.

"Miss Smith," I read aloud, not believing it myself. "1846."

Will gave a short, startled bark of laughter.

"It's a joke. Some kid . . . Probably burying his maths teacher by proxy."

"Then why the date?" I frowned, trying to recapture an elusive memory. "I read somewhere about a case, a governess or housekeeper . . . When she died the family realized that nobody knew her first name or anything about her. She was just a piece of furniture, barely human, as servants were in those days. So they buried her under the only name they knew, Miss—whatever it was. Not Smith. I don't recall."

"It's possible, I guess." Will let go of the stone. It fell to the ground with a dead, muffled sound. "Come on," he said, standing up. "We are going to be late now, good and late."

We made our way along the fence to the place where the path continued, on the opposite side of the clearing from where we had entered the cemetery. Brambles and underbrush pushing right up against the iron posts made progress difficult. It was only that one spot that was so peculiarly clear of weeds.

As we trudged along the path, I said,

"What does it mean, Will? A grave outside the fence?"

"Could mean a lot of things. Oh, I get it—you are a morbid little thing, aren't you? Sure, suicides were buried outside consecrated ground. So were other doubtful cases. Heathens and unbelievers—and in puritan New England that included practically anybody who wasn't a Presbyterian. You don't even know that there is a grave there, Jo, it could be a discarded stone. Or if there is—good God, the possibilities are endless and they don't have to be dramatic. It could be somebody's favourite dog."

"Why, yes. I suppose it could. You could call a dog Miss Smith. Or a cat."

"Sure."

And with that, for Will, the subject seemed to be settled. He began to whistle as he preceded me along the path; though it was more often used than the first section, it was too narrow to allow us to walk side by side. I didn't mind his silence; I had plenty to think about.

One thing about the graveyard had struck me, but it was not a subject I wanted to mention to Will—the predominance of a certain name among those on the stones. Perhaps predominance was not the right word; there had been roughly half a dozen occurrences. Yet that was a significant number considering the unusualness of the name. William or James or Robert would have been normal; and also the jaw-breaking names of Old Testament prophets, which seemed to have been popular in this part of the country a century ago. But . . . Kevin?

As the sunlit lawn and white walls of the house appeared through the trees, I found my thoughts reverting to the enigmatic gravestone, and to the transitory and elusive glimpse that had preceded its discovery. The shape I fancied I saw had not resembled those optical illusions which sometimes flicker on the very edge of vision. It had possessed dimension and form. And the form had been human. Somehow I felt sure that it had been a woman's figure.

4

I DIDN'T get a chance that day to talk to Mary alone. Ran was with us all the time, being the perfect brother-in-law and host. He dug up a couple of tennis rackets and challenged me to a game—which I lost. There was a court behind the house; it needed resurfacing, and Ran said he planned to have that done. He was full of plans; he even talked about a swimming pool, since the ocean was too cold for swimming most of the year.

Mary trailed along wherever we went, smiling. That smile got on my nerves after a while. Her feverish activity of the first day was gone, and her behaviour was as Ran had described it—aloof, withdrawn. Yet I had the impression that her listlessness was a façade, behind which something alert and cunning watched. Actually I wasn't anxious for another confidential talk. The first one had shaken me more than I was willing to admit. I told myself to take it easy; we had all summer, there was no need to push.

Famous last words . . .

After dinner Mary declared her intention of going to bed, and Mrs. Willard went up with her as usual. I wondered whether she would lock Mary's door when she left her.

Ran and I took our coffee into the parlour. We hadn't been there long before Will came in. He greeted me pleasantly, but the casual charm of the morning had evaporated. This was a professional visit.

It was a warm evening. With his shirt sleeves rolled up and his tie discarded and his sandy hair rumpled, Will could have auditioned for one of those TV medical shows—the young doctor, exhausted by his selfless services to mankind.

By that type of stereotype Ran didn't come off so well. He had a cup of coffee beside him on the table, but he hadn't drunk much of it, and the after-dinner brandy he was gulping down was his third. Sprawled in his chair, balancing the fat balloon glass between his fingers, he was the image of the idle rich man; the dark smudges under his eyes might have been mistaken for marks of dissipation rather than worry and lack of sleep.

The silence lengthened. I had decided that for once I would try to keep my mouth shut. It wasn't easy; there were so many things I wanted to ask. Finally Ran cleared his throat.

"Have a good day?" he asked politely.

"Lousy," Will said briefly. "I'm going home and hit the sack. I just stopped by to pick up that book you promised me."

"Is that why you stopped by?" I asked.

"Apparently I need a polite social excuse," Will said. He looked directly at Ran. "You were supposed to call me."

"I'm sorry," Ran mumbled. "I've been busy."

"Too busy to report your wife's condition to her doctor? Or am I her doctor? I get the feeling that I'm not exactly the most popular medical man in town around here."

"If you're blaming me—" I began hotly.

"Drop it, Jo." Ran got up and went to the bar. He reached for the brandy bottle. "Anybody join me?"

I shook my head.

"No, thanks," Will said. "You don't need it either, Ran."

"Now you drop it." Ran turned holding his glass. His face relaxed a little as he met his friend's steady eyes. "Sorry, Will. You know I have every confidence in you. I'm just not very efficient these days. What did you want to know?"

For a minute I thought Will was going to get up and walk out. Something stopped him—compassion, friendship, professional ethics maybe just plain curiosity. I don't know.

"Primarily whether those sleeping tablets I prescribed are doing any good. Is she sleeping?"

Ran looked at me.

"Not—not too well," he said reluctantly.

"Did she wake again last night?"

"Yes."

"You're sure she took the pills?"

"Oh, yes."

Will glanced at me. He saw my look of bewilderment, but naturally he misinterpreted its meaning.

"This is the behaviour pattern I find so confusing," he explained. "She's fairly normal during the day; the lethargy and withdrawal are not uncommon, I could understand that. What really throws me are these midnight escapades of hers. Do you know, Jo, that she keeps trying to run away, to get out of the house? Ran assures me that there is no sensible reason—no trouble between them—that could account for it. Even if he's overly optimistic about that, the pattern itself doesn't make sense. Why should she only do this at night? I tell you, Mary is hiding something and it's not the typical defence mechanism of a neurotic."

The description agreed, damningly, with my own observations. But that wasn't what kept me dumb; it was Ran's silence. Why hadn't he told his old buddy and medical adviser about Mary's delusion? It was the key that unlocked the whole pattern of her behaviour, the explanation that made her trouble explicable—and also much more dangerous than Will could possibly realize.

Again Will misinterpreted my silence. I was beginning to feel sorry for him, and the feeling increased as he went on talking—to me, not to Ran, as if he really cared what I thought about him.

"Jo, when I shot my big mouth off yesterday, you were right to get mad at me. I was expressing hostility towards Mary because I hated to admit my own inadequacy. Back in med school I knew I'd never make a psychiatrist, though the subject interested me enormously. I'm too—unimaginative, maybe; too ready to dismiss neurosis as weakness. At least I know my inability, and it's high time you faced it too." He turned to Ran. "I'm out of my depth, Ran. And Mary is no better. You've got to find someone else."

Ran drew a long breath.

"God, I'm relieved to hear you say that! Not that I agree with your appraisal of yourself . . . To tell the truth, I did something the other day and I've been feeling guilty about it ever since."

"What?"

"We agreed that Mary should see a psychiatrist. She won't go to one. So—I arranged to have the mountain come to Mohammed."

"That's why you went to Boston," Will said.

"Right."

"You'll never get away with it, Ran. What are you planning to do, introduce him as an old friend who just happened to be passing through this—this crossroads of the north? Mary will be suspicious of any strange man you bring here."

"Ah," Ran said triumphantly. "That's where the trick comes in. It isn't a man. It's a woman."

"Ingenious," Will said, after a moment. "Also a little ingenuous, Ran. You don't ask people—male or female—to drop in when

99

your wife isn't well. And not even Freud could make a snap diagnosis after an hour's chat over cocktails."

"You haven't heard the whole scheme." Ran went back to the bar. My subconscious was counting; this was his fifth brandy. The only effect it had, however, was to make him look more relaxed and confident. He was smiling as he crossed the room to sit on the sofa beside me, and he leaned forwards, arguing in his old persuasive way.

"The doctor—her name is Anne Wood, incidentally—is going to be a house guest. Now, wait. Naturally I wouldn't invite a stranger to stay when Mary was sick. But if your sister happened to visit you—your hardworking sister, who hasn't had a vacation in years—I'd have to offer her a room, wouldn't I? That shack of yours can't accommodate visitors."

He leaned back, grinning triumphantly.

My first reaction was one of admiration. Mary didn't know Will that well; he might have a dozen relatives she hadn't heard about. I looked anxiously at Will, wondering what objections he would raise next.

"Anne Wood," he said thoughtfully.

"You know her?"

"Read a couple of her articles."

"Is she that well known? What did you think of her work?"

"She's quite well known. I gather that her methods are regarded as somewhat—well—flamboyant by the conservatives in the profession; but that isn't necessarily . . ." He hesitated; and I realized that Ran had put him into a position where he couldn't say anything too critical without sounding jealous. He went on, "No, I'm sure she's sound. Popular, too. May I ask how you persuaded a busy, successful doctor to take a weekend off?"

"Doctor's do take weekends off, I believe."

Ran's voice was cold. He always resented any implication that it was money, rather than natural ability, that got him what he wanted. And in this case, obviously, it was the cash that had turned the trick. He had probably offered the woman a sum that she couldn't refuse.

"Most doctors do," Will admitted. He grinned. "I'm just jealous because I can't. Sorry, Ran. I think it was a brilliant idea and I hope to God it works. When is she coming?"

"This weekend."

101

"Well, I guess we can muddle through till then." Will stood up. "Excuse me, people, but I'm bushed. Maybe that's why I haven't made much sense this evening."

He was drooping visibly as he went out the door; his broad shoulders sagged. I told myself to forget the old maternal instinct; but when I turned to Ran my face wasn't as friendly as usual.

"Why the cold and fishy stare?" he asked. "You were the one who bawled me out for not making Mary see a head-shrinker."

"Oh, I think Dr. Wood is a great idea. It might even help. Why didn't you tell Will about the crying?"

"What's the point? Will's right, and I'm glad he has the integrity and the sense to realize it. I didn't want to be the one to tell him he can't help us."

"You can't judge his ability if you don't give him the data to work with," I said.

Ran's eyes narrowed. He reached out to put his glass down on the table. His hand was unsteady, and I saw then that he was a good deal drunker than I had realized.

"Well, well," he said. His voice was just the least bit slurred. "Could it be that little sister is falling for old William? No—wait—

Jo, I'm sorry, I didn't mean . . . Don't you get mad at me, Jo. I couldn't stand it if you turned on me too . . ."

He reached out for me. Even then, with his arms around me and his lips on my cheek, I felt nothing except the exasperated pity you feel for the unexpected weakness of someone you love. He had held me in his arms before. I'm not trying to excuse myself. But whatever I had wanted from him—it wasn't this, not under these circumstances. I moved my head and my lips brushed his; and then I did try to push him away, my hands hard against his chest. By then it was too late. His unstable weight bore me back down on to the couch.

So it had happened at last—the embrace, so often imagined and guiltily desired during adolescence—and it was nothing, not even passion, because I knew what had brought it on. I couldn't even resent what he was doing. He was no more aware of intent than an animal is when it turns blindly into the nearest shelter. And I knew that when he realized what he had done, he would be sick with guilt. And all the while out of the corner of my wide-open eyes I was horribly conscious of the open door. If Mary came down, or Mrs. Willard . . .

I might have known it would be Will. He called out as he opened the front door,

"Ran? I forgot that book—"

I began to wriggle, ineffectually and frantically. The movement, or the voice, roused Ran. He raised his head, blinking dizzily. I turned my own head in time to meet the full impact of Will's stare.

He stood transfixed in the doorway. It must have made quite a tableau, as he saw it; but he didn't wait to appreciate the details. One stare—a look of the most complete contempt I have ever seen on a man's face—and then he turned on his heel and walked out. I heard the front door close, very quietly.

Ran pushed himself up. He was shocked into sobriety and I found his expression just as painful, in a different way, as Will's had been. I couldn't stand it. I felt sorry for him, but I felt a lot sorrier for myself. I got up and ran out of the room, leaving Ran sitting there looking like Judas.

I could have used a sleeping pill myself that night. When you're young there is nothing, but nothing, worse than humiliation. Torture, tragedy, terror—they may be more painful than embarrassment but at least they have a certain dignity. There is nothing romantic or tragic, or sophisticated, about being caught on the living-room couch with your sister's husband—especially when you are caught by a man whom you are beginning to find somewhat attractive.

It was irrational for me to feel guilty, but of course I did feel just that. The single drunken embrace, ironically, was innocent in itself, but behind it lay five years of a more basic guilt. Worst of all was the simple sordid fact that I had been caught. Will was not the kind of man to shrug off casual immorality even if there had been no complicating factors. And in view of Mary's present mental state, an affair between her sister and her husband was worse than grubby; it was callous and cruel and potentially dangerous.

When I came downstairs next morning, the fine weather had broken at last. The air outside was cool and yet sultry, and grey clouds hung low. It wasn't the best possible weather for a hike, but I wanted to get out of the house before Ran or Mary appeared. I couldn't face either of them.

I took the path to the graveyard, not because I particularly wanted to go there, but because it was the only path I knew. The road led to town—too far to walk, in the time at my disposal—and, in the other direction, to Will's house. I wasn't awfully anxious to see him either.

The cemetery could hardly have looked more dismal. In the oddly clear grey light the stillness of the place held an air of expectancy. The hideous Gothic mausoleum was a unique creation; I had never seen anything quite so awful before.

It was an interesting structure, though. The workmanship was quite fine. The lancet windows were miniature replicas of medieval designs, but I couldn't really consider them a happy thought. They had no glass, of course, only flat panels of stone behind the ornate tracery, but the suggestion of windows in that house of the dead was somehow unpleasant. I began to wonder about old Hezekiah; and then I began to notice other things. The door, for instance. Its heavy wooden panels were set deep in a carved arch which was adorned with sculptured figures, like the saints on a European cathedral. These were figures of Old Testament prophets and patriarchs. But there was a suggestion of something wrong, not so much in the figures themselves as in the details.

Jael, holding aloft the huge spike which she

had driven into the head of Sisera—all right, that was perfectly in accord with the taste of the time. But surely the lady's body was too visible through the folds of her robe, and too voluptuous for that of a Hebrew prophetess. The protuberances on the head of Moses were definitely horns; they came to sharp points. And there was a very peculiar face peering out over the shoulder of another bearded patriarch whose identity was uncertain.

Nor was the door itself lacking in suggestive details. Its ironbound panels were stained with decay, and the heavy padlock reminded me irresistibly of a horrible ghost story I had read as a child. "Count Magnus"—that was the name of it—the story of the traveller who finds the mausoleum with the three huge locks. Returning on successive days, he finds each day that another lock had mysteriously come open. On the third day he flees in terror; but behind him he hears the clang as the third and last lock falls open to the ground.

"Cut that out," I said, addressing my inconvenient imagination. Then I was sorry I had spoken aloud. In the stillness the words came back at me from out of the trees.

Then, as I turned from the door, I saw her.

It was a woman, there was no doubt about that, even though a deep hood of the same black as her enveloping cloak shadowed her features. The cloak hung from shoulder to ground in unmoving folds; so still that the figure might have been a statue carved of dark granite.

My immediate reaction was fright, but not so much because of any quality of horror in the figure itself. The mood of the place, the suddenness of the apparition's appearance, and its utter stillness would have struck even the boldest observer with a shock of surprise—and I'm not that bold. But gradually, as my breath wheezed back into my lungs and the first panic passed I became aware of another, more insidious fear.

She wasn't inside the cemetery. I was glad of that. She stood just outside the fence, leaning slightly forwards towards it. I thought she was about to move, to lift pale hands towards the heavy iron spikes, when suddenly, off in the woods, a bird let loose a flood of liquid notes.

The sound broke some sort of spell; my aching eyes blinked. And when I opened them, she was gone.

Gone, disappeared, vanished. Not even the flutter of a black hem showed that anyone had been there. But I thought I heard a sound, a rustling among the fallen leaves to the right of the path by which I had entered the clearing—as if someone—or something—was making its way towards the gate.

I ran in the opposite direction. Panic made me stumble and trip over obstructions I should have been able to avoid. But the pain of bruised knees and a twisted ankle did not slow my flight. There was only one way I could go, since the path by which I had entered was barred to me—along the other part of the path, which led to Will's house.

I came plunging out of the trees to see the house and the blue station wagon, just starting off down the track.

I ran straight out in front of it. When the car stopped—Will's reflexes were excellent—its hood was so close to me that I was able to collapse on to it. Will didn't even swear as he jumped out of the car and grabbed me; he could tell there was something wrong.

He kept shaking me and asking questions. Finally I managed to say,

"If you wouldn't keep shaking me I could talk."

His hands remained on my shoulders. I thought for a minute that he was going to pick me up and carry me; and the idea was so pleasant that I let myself lean on him. But by that time his professional eyes had inspected me and he had found no serious damage. He propped me up against the left fender of the car and stepped back.

"You're not hurt," he said flatly. "What's the matter?"

"Someone in the woods," I said, wheezing. "In the graveyard. A woman."

"The same person you saw yesterday?"

"I guess so . . . I don't know."

"What are you scared of? Did she threaten you?"

"No, no. She just . . ." I stopped, seeing from his level stare that I was not making a good impression. "She was peculiar looking," I finished lamely.

"How? Wild-eyed, foaming at the mouth, or just plain ugly?"

"I didn't—see her face."

Will sighed loudly.

"I'm in a hurry, Jo. One of my patients is in labour. It's her fourth, so she could have it any second, and she had a bad time with the third. Get in the car. I'll take you home and

110

on the way you can tell me all about your terrifying experience."

He grabbed my arm, none too gently. I
pulled back.

"If you're in that much of a hurry, go
ahead. I'll walk."

"And meet your scary lady again? It's on
my way; get in, I tell you."

This time when he took my arm I didn't
resist. I had enough incipient bruises already.
My offer had been sheer bravado. I wouldn't
have gone back into those woods for anything.

Will was definitely in a hurry; we went
down the track much too fast for comfort, and
when he took the curve along the cliff edge I
closed my eyes.

"Speak up," he said brusquely. "You've
only got about five minutes."

I was in no mood to speak up. I wanted to
sit there like a sulky child, with my lower lip
sticking out. I knew he wouldn't believe me.
He would just decide that Mary wasn't the
only hysterical neurotic in the family. But I
wasn't quite that childish; I told him what
had happened. Naturally, the flat, reluctant
statements failed to convey any of the atmosphere which had made the experience so

terrifying—the only thing that had made it terrifying, for as I heard my own statement I realized how banal it sounded. When I had finished I looked at Will out of the corner of my eye. He was smiling. There was genuine amusement in that smile, but it wasn't a nice kind of amusement. He was laughing at me.

"Annie Marks," he said calmly.

"Who is Annie Marks?"

"Just a poor crazy old lady who likes to dress up in her grandmother's clothes and wander around in the woods. I should have thought of her before. She lives with her daughter and son-in-law, a few miles down the road."

"How many miles down the road?"

"This is a little out of her way," he admitted. "But it must have been Annie. Who else could it have been? Her behaviour is quite characteristic; you probably scared the poor thing half to death when she saw you lurking like a banshee at the door of the mausoleum."

I felt like crawling down under the seat. Will was grinning broadly and humming quietly to himself. The scrap of music acted like a key, opening his thoughts to me, and I could see the scene that was in his mind, the

112

one he found so hilarious. It comes at the end of the first act of *The Magic Flute*, when that arrant coward Papageno, sneaking around a corner, meets his enemy the Moor sneaking around the other side. They stare at one another in horror for a few seconds, croaking out disconnected gasps of musical terror; then, with a Mozartianly blended scream, they both flee in opposite directions. Poor old Annie and poor old Jo must have looked just the same . . .

We stopped in front of the house. Will jammed on the brakes with an excruciating jolt and leaned across me to throw the door open. His smile had disappeared, and the eyes he turned on me told me that he had forgotten the joke and was remembering another scene in which I had recently figured prominently.

"Better put some iodine on those scratches," he said.

After the car had gone off in a cloud of dust I studied my scars. They were hurting now and they looked even worse. There wasn't a square inch of skin on my calves that wasn't scraped, bruised, or scratched. I was going to look a lovely sight in short skirts for days to come. My state of mind was a perfect complement to my legs; it too was bruised, scraped, and scratched.

"Oh, damn," I said.

There was a chuckle from behind me—exactly the sort of noise poor old weak-in-the-head Annie might have made. I whirled around. Mr. Willard—no, it was no use, I couldn't even think of him that way, much less address him by that name—Jed stood there smiling at me.

"Sorry," I said, in some confusion. I wasn't sure how he would react to profanity from a young female. I had watched my language pretty carefully with Mrs. Willard, because I was sure how she would react.

He waved one hand. The other hand held the rake, which seemed to be supporting his leaning form, but I was beginning to know that his shiftless appearance was misleading.

"I'd say it was a pretty mild comment," he said. "Considering . . . Don't mind young Will. The Appleby girl's in labour, and Will takes his job seriously."

I didn't ask how he knew the Appleby girl was in labour when Will himself had apparently discovered that fact only minutes before I ran into him. I was ready to believe

114

that this smiling, vague-looking man and his stolid wife knew everything.

"Nasty scratches," Jed went on, looking me over. "Better put something on 'em."

"I will," I said meekly.

"Yellow soap, too. Bertha has some. Good for poison ivy if you use it right away."

I looked mournfully at my bare legs. I hadn't thought about poison ivy.

"Something scare you?"

I looked up, startled at the accuracy of his guess, and met a pair of very knowing blue eyes. He had, as I have said, an affable face even when he wasn't smiling—one of those faces that invite confidences. And as Mary always said, reticence was not precisely my chief character trait.

"I met Annie Marks," I said, falling into step with him as he headed for the back of the house.

"She wouldn't hurt a fly."

"I know; I probably scared her. But not more than she scared me."

He chuckled again.

"Pretty startling, at that, coming on someone sudden-like. Especially in the woods. They aren't places for people."

The words struck home, they fitted so well

with what I had been thinking. Forests were inhuman places. They were meant for birds and animals, but not for people—unless they were people who were still close to the original primitive origins of man. Quiet people, hunters and stalkers; people who could move as the beasts did, keeping the silence of the shut-in places.

We went into the tool shed and Jed hung the rake neatly on a hook among an assortment of gardening equipment.

"Nature is frightening," I said, half to myself.

"It's unpredictable. But that is why it's so interesting."

"You must find it interesting. You do a marvellous job; I don't see how one man can keep this place in such beautiful condition."

"I like the work. I tried accounting; even got me a CPA." The corners of his mouth twitched slightly at my expression of surprise; but he went on in the same even tone. "I couldn't stand being cooped up. Or the monotony. Some people say that mathematics is exciting. It wasn't to me. Ten digits, that's all there are, and they always act the same way. Two and two always make four—'cept in some of the new mathematics, but bookkeepers don't get into that. But when you work with living things you never know what's going to happen. No two plants are exactly alike. One may die no matter how much care you give it. Another will fight to live through drought and disease and poor soil. Like people."

I sat down—or up—on a high stool by the workbench. I was fascinated by his view of the world, and his even voice and relaxed attitude were soothing to my nerves.

"Why?" I asked. "Why do some live and others die?"

Jed shrugged.

"I don't suppose I'll ever know. Why should I figure it out when all the great thinkers and teachers have failed? But that's the question that keeps me from getting bored."

I was about to speak when something stirred in a darkish corner of the shed. The object lifted and stretched itself, and paced out into the light. It was one of the coon cats, like those Will owned, but it was bigger and plumier than any of his—a big reddish-gold animal, looking like a miniature lion with its ruff and golden eyes. The enormous tail, as long as my forearm, gave it a look of fantasy—a creature out of legend, a storybook lion.

"Isn't he a long way from home?" I asked.

"She," Jed said. "She's not one of Will's. Belongs to Bertha."

"I thought she didn't like cats."

"Oh, she doesn't mind cats. Always room for a good mouser. She just thinks Will goes a little bit too far."

He scratched the cat under its chin and it raised its head, its eyes slitted in ecstasy.

"You've seen Will's place?"

"Yes. I love the house. It must be very old."

"Seventeen thirty. It was the original Fraser house, you know. Wasn't till 1825 or so that Captain Hezekiah moved into the big house."

"You're doing it too," I said.

"Doing what?"

"Looking . . . sideways . . . when you mention his name. Will had the same funny look when he talked about the Captain. What did the man do, for heaven's sake?"

Jed's pale eyes twinkled.

"Heaven had nothing to do with it."

"So I gather. But my lord, I wouldn't think any sea captain would be a very saintly

118

character. What was so particularly awful about Hezekiah?"

Jed picked up an oily rag and began to wipe the gardening tools.

"He sold his soul to the Devil."

"Oh," I said, after a moment. "Is that all? I thought you New Englanders did that all the time."

"Hmmph." Jed seemed to be struck with this idea. "You know, you've got a point there. It does seem to crop up over and over, doesn't it? Captain Ahab, and that young farmer whose soul was saved by the silver tongue of Dan Webster . . . The Hawthorne stories are full of it. Maybe New Englanders are too susceptible to Satan."

"Stories like that must have circulated about a lot of self-made men. People hate to admit that their neighbours are smarter or more successful than they are."

"That's part of it, sure. Natural envy. But they didn't invent tales like that about all successful men. Old Hezekiah acted like a man who had intimate acquaintance with damnation."

When I remembered the carvings on that horrible mausoleum, Jed's phrase was singularly apt. I wondered who had done the carving. No local stonemason, I was willing to bet.

I said, seemingly at random,

"You take care of the graveyard, don't you? Do you know about the grave outside the fence?"

"Sure. I set the stone up every couple of years. Keeps falling down; something peculiar about the subsoil, I guess."

"It's fallen down again," I said.

Like the distant foghorn the stentorian voice of Mrs. Willard floated to my ears.

"Jed! Dinner's ready!"

Jed scooped up the cat, which hung from his hands like a fur piece, blinking affably. I tagged along after him as he walked towards the house.

"Who was she?" I demanded. "Miss Smith?"

The urgency in my voice surprised Jed.

"Why, I don't know as I ever gave the matter much thought. From the date on the stone she'd be from Hezekiah's time, but—"

"A servant," I said. "Governess or housekeeper?"

Jed came to a stop.

"Well, now, that's odd," he said slowly. "I never thought of that. Figured—if I thought

120

about it at all—that she'd be a stranger, a traveller maybe, who got sick and died here, so that all they ever knew about her was the name on her trunk. Somebody from a wrecked ship, maybe."

"Of course, that's much more plausible, isn't it? There must have been many ship-wrecks along this coast . . . And naturally people in near-by houses would take in the injured who were saved or washed ashore. But wouldn't they advertise, or try to notify the relatives if someone died on their hands?"

Jed shook his head.

"It wasn't so easy in those days to com-municate with people. She might not have had surviving relatives who cared anything about her. Or they might have been lost when the ship went down."

"That's true. Why didn't I think of that? I've seen anonymous stones in old cemeteries, memorials to unknown seamen washed ashore after a shipwreck. That must be the explanation."

"Maybe so . . ."

Mrs. Willard called again, and Jed started walking.

"It's a curious thing, though," he said thoughtfully. "Now you've got me wondering about it myself. You know, Jo, there's a pile of old family papers, documents and diaries and such, in a chest upstairs. You just might find something there."

"About Miss Smith?"

"Well, it's not too likely, I'll admit. But there ought to be some papers from Hezekiah's time, since you're so interested in him."

"Maybe I shouldn't pry into private family papers."

"I don't suppose Ran would take you to court," Jed said dryly. "He ought to look through the stuff himself, see what's worth keeping, but I don't suppose he ever will. He never gave a hoot for that sort of thing. He'd probably think you were doing him a service. Keep you out of mischief, too."

We reached the house, so I didn't respond to that last joking comment. Mrs. Willard was at the door looking exasperated, and Jed went off to wash up. The Willards had dinner about an hour before the rest of us had lunch. It was no notion of inferior status that made them prefer to eat alone; they stuck to the old custom of eating their big meal in the middle of the day, and Mrs. Willard thought nothing of cooking two sets of meals rather than succumb to the newfangled notion of dining on soup and salads at noon. So I left them to their meat and potatoes, and Prudence the cat to her dish on the floor, but I didn't escape without a lecture from Mrs. Willard, and a bar of yellow soap, which she ordered me to use—all over.

On the stairs I met Mary. My conversation with Jed had let me forget, for a time, the unpleasantness of the previous night, but the sight of Mary brought it all back to me. I felt so guilty I couldn't look her in the face.

"Good heavens, Jo," she said. "If you aren't a living testimonial to the dangers of exercise. You should have stayed slothfully in bed, like me."

"You certainly look great," I said.

It was true. The sight of her, looking fresh and rested and elegant in her white sandals and expensive little print dress relieved my mind, though it didn't make me feel any less guilty.

Mary didn't seem to notice my discomfort. She caught sight of the bar of soap—it was not inconspicuous, by colour or size—and burst out laughing.

"I see Mrs. Willard caught you. You ought to use it, though, if you've been in the woods.

You used to be horribly susceptible to poison ivy. Remember the time we were camping in West Virginia and you got it on your bottom?"

"Do I," I said. "How old was I, about six?"

"Seven." Mary took my arm. "Come on, I'll go up with you and make sure you don't cheat."

She continued to chat as I got undressed. To hear her talk, you wouldn't have thought she had a care in the world. I even enjoyed hearing her scold me, she sounded like the old Mary.

"I'd have thought by now you would have learned to take care of your clothes," she said, holding up the shorts I had just discarded. "Look at this—a big rip. They look like new shorts, too."

"They were cheap," I said carelessly. "Four-fifty, on sale."

"Oh, Jo."

She looked so distressed that I laughed.

"Now don't start that, Mary. I know I'm just a poor underprivileged orphan who can't afford a decent mink. But you are not going to rush me off to Saks for a whole new wardrobe."

"Your birthday is coming up."

"Coming up! It's in August, my friend, in case you've forgotten."

"There are a couple of decent shops in the village. We'll go shopping this afternoon. Gosh, Jo, do you realize how long it's been since we had a good shopping binge together?"

There are more important things than pride, as Ran had said. I looked at Mary's eager face and I wasn't even aware of a mental struggle.

"Twist my arm," I said.

5

RAN drove us into town after lunch. He said he had some business at the dock—something to do with the boat he had bought and was having fitted up. I thought his behaviour towards me was a dead giveaway, he was so awkward and overly hearty; but Mary didn't seem to be aware of any nuances, though in her normal state she was keenly conscious of other people's feelings. It wasn't a pleasant ride, though; I was too self-conscious. For the first time I was glad to have Ran go away. He dropped us in front of one of the shops Mary had mentioned and asked where and when we wanted to meet him.

"We'll need at least two hours," Mary said with a smile. "You should see this girl's wardrobe, Ran. I'll tell you, we'll meet you at the Inn at four-thirty. You can buy us a drink before we go home."

The shop was small but the clothes were cute. The prices horrified me, after my year of poverty.

126

"Forty dollars for a pair of slacks," I yelped, holding them up. "And this stretch material is completely impractical, Mary; five minutes in those brambles and they would be pulled to pieces."

The saleslady, a sleek elderly person with short grey hair, gave me a nasty look, but Mary just grinned. She bought the slacks herself; the lemony yellow colour and the yellow-orange-rose print of the shirt that went with it looked pretty with her dark hair. I let her talk me into a couple of pairs of jeans and a dress . . . though the price tag on the simple little number set my teeth on edge.

It was fun, though; fun to come out on to the sidewalk carrying shopping bags and parcels; fun to stand blinking in the fresh air wondering what to do next; and knowing that there isn't a single bloody thing you *have* to do.

We sauntered along the sidewalk looking in all the windows. The shopping area was a funny mixture. There were older stores, like the drugstore and grocery and a store with things for boats—practical stores. Mixed in with them were the newer buildings which catered to the developing tourist trade. The Island Boutique, with its fake antique façade,

127

was one of them, and shortly I spotted another—my long-desired antique shop.

Mary laughed when I pointed it out.

"Sure, we've got plenty of time. You know who runs the place, don't you? Will's ex-girlfriend."

"Sue?"

Mary eyed me.

"You remember her name, do you?"

"Yeah . . . So that's why Will looked so supercilious when I talked about antique shops."

"He acts like such a fool," Mary said disgustedly. "This is a small place, people can't avoid one another; but Will behaves as if that poor girl were Medea."

"If she jilted him—"

"Oh, for heaven's sake, Jo, that was years ago. Why can't he forget it? She couldn't have been vicious or cruel, she isn't that kind of girl."

"You know her?"

"I only met her once, briefly; but she's nice. You'll like her."

The proprietress was nowhere in sight when we entered the shop, which seemed dim and shadowy after the street. It was crowded with objects, just as an antique shop ought to be, but as I glanced at the assortment on the front counter I saw that there was an underlying organization behind the apparent clutter. Sue must be competent, whatever her other virtues might be.

The tinkle of the bell over the door produced no result, so Mary called out. After a moment there was an answer from the back of the shop—a call so muffled that it sounded as if it came from a deep cave. This was followed by a scuffling sound, and then a bright golden head popped up above the counter.

People talk about red-gold hair, but you don't see that shade often, especially on an adult. It happens to be the exact shade I've always wanted to have. I tried on a wig of that colour once; it looked so awful on me that I didn't buy it. But I gaped in jealous admiration at the girl who came by it legitimately.

She wasn't really pretty. Her mouth was too big and she had a copious supply of freckles. But no one would have known she wasn't pretty. A woman would respond to the broad electric grin and the lively friendliness in her face. A man wouldn't notice her face at all. She had a gorgeous figure. I don't think she tried to show it off, but the tight, old pants and the man's shirt looked sexier on her than a pair of skintight slacks would look on most women.

She wiped her hand on the seat of her jeans before she offered it to us, and waved away Mary's attempt at introductions.

"Sure I remember you—you don't mind if I call you Mary, do you? I've known Ran too long to be formal with his wife. And this has to be your sister. That's the curse of a small town, girls, everybody knows every blasted move you make. Your name is Jo, you're from San Francisco, and you're an artist."

"Not exactly an—"

"I should have come up to visit you but I haven't had time. Trying to get the place ready for the summer trade. It was nice of you to come and see me. You'll have some coffee, won't you? No, it's no trouble, I always keep a pot on the burner." She winked at me. "It's good for business. Relaxes the customers and makes 'em feel as if they ought to buy something."

"That's a good—"

"They do it in Near Eastern bazaars all the time. I read about it in a book." She led the way to the back of the shop, still talking. "Paper cups, but that's just part of the infor-

130

mal charm. Sit down, won't you? Wait a sec, I'll clear off a couple of chairs."

I caught Mary's eye and glanced hastily away before I started laughing. I knew we were both thinking the same thing. I couldn't visualize Will married to this cheerful chatterbox, he would never have been able to get a word in edgeways. But after seeing Sue I could believe that a man might carry a torch for a good long time.

We took the chairs she pulled up and she sat on a packing case, with her legs swinging.

"Listen, I really am glad you came by. I want to talk to you about something."

"What is it?" Mary asked.

"Maybe I ought to talk to Ran. But to tell you the honest-to-God truth, I'm a little bit embarrassed about it."

Again Mary and I exchanged glances. Sue caught the look and flushed.

"Oh, my gosh, I'm making it sound like some big important thing. Don't worry, it isn't anything like . . . well, like what you might be thinking. The truth is, I've got some things he might like to have back. You know that in the last few years the old ladies—his aunts—weren't too well off?"

"I didn't know that," Mary said, looking

concerned. "And I'm sure Ran didn't either. He wouldn't—"

"Oh, listen, honey, I know Ran, you don't have to tell me he wouldn't have let them starve. They weren't that poor. But there wasn't any extra money, and they were too darned stiff-necked to ask him for help, not after the awful way they acted when his mother got married again. I think they were ashamed."

"But they left him the house," I said.

"Oh, sure. He was the last male Fraser. They'd have left him the house if he'd been an axe murderer. You don't know what family tradition is till you live in New England. That's why Ran has all the money; it came down in a chunk from father to son. Oh, well, what I'm trying to say is that in the last few years the old ladies sold some things. Nothing Ran would even notice was missing, out of all the stuff in that house. But there were a few things I thought you might like to have back."

"You don't mean," Mary said, "that you kept the things you bought from them?"

"I had to let most of them go," Sue said defensively. "I just didn't have the cash—"

"My dear girl. I'm not complaining; I'm

very touched at your kindness, and I know Ran will be too. He certainly wouldn't allow you to suffer any financial loss for the sake of his family. They were his responsibility, not yours."

"Then you'll tell him about it?"

"Right away."

"Oh, there's no hurry. He may not even want the stuff, and if he doesn't, that's fine. But I feel better about it now." Sue smiled. "I guess you think I'm pretty silly, making such a big thing out of it."

"I certainly don't think that."

"As I said, there isn't much left. Just a couple of things I thought—"

The shop bell jingled, and Sue looked up. A frown wrinkled her forehead.

"Oh, Gawd," she said under her breath. "It's that old—Hi, there, Mrs. Cartwright! Be right with you."

The customer was a stocky woman with a chest like a shelf.

"I am in a hurry," she said loudly. "If you don't mind."

"Excuse me?" Sue said to us.

"Go right ahead." Mary stood up. "We've got to run. We're supposed to meet Ran."

"Oh, darn. You'll come back another time?"

"Sure. And I'll tell Ran."

We left Sue in the clutches of Mrs. Cartwright. As we went down the street Mary said,

"She's cute, isn't she?"

"Uh-huh."

"I wonder what happened between her and Will."

"She'll probably tell you if you know her long enough. She talks even more than I do."

The Inn was at the other end of the street, near the wharf. As we went towards it we passed a big white house, set back from the sidewalk, which Mary pointed out as the museum.

"I suppose we don't have time to go in" I said, lingering.

Mary took my arm firmly.

"Not time enough for a confirmed museum hound like you. There will be other times."

We went by, but the sight of the place reminded me of the enigmatic gravestone and the researches I meant to pursue. I almost said something about it to Mary. Ordinarily a mystery of that sort would have intrigued her. We would have speculated about the woman whose life had ended in such obscurity, and we would have gone through the family papers together. Mary would have loved my adventure in the graveyard; her sturdy common sense would have reduced the apparition of Annie Marks to the absurdity it was. But now . . . Well, I didn't need a psychiatrist to tell me I ought to avoid morbid subjects.

Ran was waiting for us in the bar. I wasn't too happy about that, though the drink in front of him appeared to be untouched. I didn't know how many he had had before that one.

Naturally I didn't ask. Ran was so pleased with Mary's good spirits that he forgot to be self-conscious with me. It was pathetic to see how he looked at her, like a parent with a sick child, trying to keep from showing his anxiety but painfully conscious of every word and every gesture the child makes. I noticed, too, that he didn't finish the drink in front of him, despite Mary's teasing. She was in high spirits.

There was one little incident, just before we left. Ran was fumbling for change while the waiter stood by with the check. Mary, whose seat faced the door, gave a gasp of surprise and exclaimed.

"Who on earth is that?"

I turned.

The Inn, recently remodelled, was an attractive old place and the bar was dark-panelled and dimly lit. I couldn't have seen clearly in any case, and the figure Mary indicated was just going out of the door. I caught only a glimpse of a long dark gown and a weird old-fashioned bonnet; but the sight was enough to make me knock over the dregs of my drink.

By the time the waiter had mopped it up Ran had located his wallet and Mary repeated her question.

"Did you see her, Jo? Straight out of *The Scarlet Letter*. Who is she?"

"I'll bet I know," I said. "Five will get you ten. Annie Marks?"

Ran, who hadn't seen the figure, looked baffled, but the waiter gave me a nod and a smile.

"That's right, miss. She's quite a picturesque character, isn't she? The boss doesn't like her hanging around, but she doesn't do any harm."

"The boss ought to pay her," Mary said gaily. "She adds quite a touch of local colour."

I was the first one out of the bar, but I was too late. By the time I reached the street Annie Marks was nowhere in sight. I was sorry about that; I had wanted a closer look. That one unsatisfactory glance had made me uneasy. I had the impression that Annie had shrunk considerably since I saw her in the woods that morning.

II

When we got back to the house Ran went upstairs to change. He was definitely grubby after an afternoon messing about with boats. I had entertained a half-formed notion of finding the chest Jed had mentioned, but I didn't get a chance. Mrs. Willard was waiting for us; she shepherded me and Mary into the parlour and announced that tea was ready. I looked at Mary, who shrugged and smiled. It would have been useless to tell Mrs. Willard we had already had cocktails. When she prepared tea, people drank it.

Mary kicked off her shoes and curled up in a big chair.

"Play something," I said, indicating the piano.

"I'm too lazy. And out of practice. You go ahead."

I was out of practice myself. I never did play as well as Mary. But I wasn't self-conscious about performing in front of her.

I hadn't realized until I started to play how much I had missed making music. If I want to hear perfect Chopin, I put on a record by Rubinstein or Michelangeli. But the satisfaction I derive from playing is only partly related to how well I play. I slashed my way through the first pages of the "Ballade in G minor", got my fingers tangled together after the first measure of the next part, where it gets fast, and stopped on a hideous discord.

"Rubinstein would be lying on the floor crying if he could hear that," I said, turning around towards Mary.

I might have imagined the expression on her face. For several hours I was able to convince myself that I had. She hadn't moved from her former position, feet tucked up under her, body curved into the yielding embrace of the big chair. But now her fists were clenched on the arms of the chair and she was staring at the darkening window with a look of intense longing. Orpheus might have looked like that as he saw his beloved drawn back down into the darkness from which he had almost won her.

"Mary," I said sharply; and she turned a placid, smiling face towards me.

"Why don't you try something a little simpler? 'A Day on the Seashore', or 'The Choo-Choo Train'?"

I let my breath trickle out.

"Never in my life, not even in the first month of piano lessons, did I have a piece entitled. 'The Choo-Choo Train'."

"Really? It sounded so appropriate. I don't care what you play, so long as you have mercy on Chopin and Beethoven. How about some popular music? You always did have a deplorable weakness for that group—what was its name—the Insects."

"Don't ham it up," I said severely. "The lamas in the remotest mountains of Tibet have heard of the Beatles. And they're classics now. You should hear The Who. Or Three Dog Night. Or—"

"You're making those names up."

"You really are square, aren't you?"

"Educate me, then."

"You can't play rock music on a piano," I complained, sounding a few tentative chords.

"You need amplification and a strong rhythm section—"

"And a lot of tone-deaf voices howling."

It was an old argument, dating back to my high school years. For the fun of it we both took extreme viewpoints. Mary denied that any composer after Beethoven was worth listening to, and I expressed a deep devotion to hard rock. I was pounding out a song with a title like "If You Want Me to Love You, Girl, You'd Better Give", when a rattle of dishes made me break off.

The vigour with which Mrs. Willard placed the tea tray on the table expressed her opinion of my music without any necessity for speech; but Mrs. Willard never lost a chance of talking.

"How you can stand that stuff I do not know. Can't hardly find anything else on the radio these days. It makes a person deaf, you know. Science says so. That's what's wrong with the world today. Long hair and short skirts and no morals, and that caterwauling instead of music."

"A very succinct summation," said Mary solemnly. "I see you brought an ally, too. Hello, Will."

He came into the room like one of his cats

encountering an unfamiliar smell—stiff, sidling, and suspicious.

"Wasn't the music that brought him, I can tell you," Mrs. Willard said. "It was the smell of good food. He eats out of cans in that place of his. If it wasn't for the meals he cadges here, he'd have rickets and scurvy and TB."

"Now, Mrs. Willard, Will knows better than that. After all, he is a doctor."

"The shoemaker's children are the ones that go barefoot," Mrs. Willard retorted. She straightened up from the table, where she had been arranging cups and plates. "Don't you know any pretty songs, Jo? That stuff is enough to give a person indigestion."

"What kind of music do you like?" I asked.

"Oh, you know. Music. Irving Berlin, and 'Mary Is a Grand Old Name'. Songs like that."

Will laughed nastily.

"I'll bet Jo never heard of Irving Berlin."

It was such a petty remark that I felt a nice revivifying spurt of anger run through me. After all, who was Will Graham to think he had the right to sit in judgement on me?

I played Mrs. Willard out with a nice medley of George M. Cohan (I saw the musical) and, as soon as she was out of earshot, I gave Dr. Graham the Top Ten pop songs, in order. He hated every note of them.

Before long Ran joined us, and I was interested to observe that relations between the two old schoolmates were slightly strained. I couldn't figure out why Will was sticking around, unless it was for food. He certainly couldn't derive that much pleasure out of recalling his triumphs as a first baseman back in sixth grade, which he and Ran were reminiscing about in a half-hearted fashion. I didn't think even Mrs. Willard's food would compensate William for the presence of two people as disgusting as Ran and I.

Apparently it did. He stayed for dinner. Nobody invited him, he just stayed. And over Mrs. Willard's superb pot roast, I began to get a glimmer of what was on the man's mind.

He couldn't take his eyes off Mary. She was looking lovely, flushed and vivacious, and her conversation had the wit and charm I remembered so well. But Will wasn't charmed. I could read his face like a book by now; it was, for all its reserve, a rather ingenuous face. He was suspicious. As I watched Mary, I began to wonder myself. The change in her was fairly dramatic.

142

It was Mary who mentioned Will's sister, expressing her pleasure at being able to meet her. Will's face went absolutely blank. For a second I was afraid the idiot was going to say, "What sister?"

"Oh," he said, after a long moment. "Yes. Yes, I am looking forward to seeing her."

"How long has it been?" Mary asked.

"Oh. Years."

"What a shame that you can't get together more often."

"Yes. Yes, it is."

"But it's nice of her husband to let her come now, if only for a few days."

Will looked horrified, and Ran said irritably,

"Anne isn't married, dear. I told you that."

"Did you?" The sweetness of her voice should have told me something. "I guess I forgot. Did you tell me what her job is?"

"No, I didn't," Ran said swiftly. Will's mouth had dropped open like a loose trap door. "She's in advertising."

"Just like Jo. That's nice, you'll have something to talk about."

"If there's anything I don't want to talk about, it's my former job," I said. "Maybe we can discuss local history. Is Anne also

143

an authority on the China trade, Will?"

Talk about looks that could kill. Like my own, Will's mental processes seemed to be stimulated by anger. He came back with rather a snappy retort.

"She hates history," he said. "Always flunked it in school."

"Oh, dear, what a shame. I'm so interested in the China trade."

It was stupid of me to bait him; he was a poor enough conspirator at best, and there was a decided risk of his losing his temper and giving the whole show away. Ran realized that too, and intervened.

"I have a couple of books you might like to read, if you're that interested," he said, giving me a warning look. "Well—I talked to Sam today about the boat. He says we can take her out next week. What day is good for you?"

They discussed the boat, safely and dully, for the rest of the meal, and then Will left. When Ran came back into the parlour, after seeing him to the door, I thought he looked more relaxed than he had all day. He gave me a smile which was almost like his old smiles. I wondered whether he had had a talk with old judge-and-jury Graham.

Mary was at the window.

"It's going to rain," she said. "I hope Will doesn't get caught in it."

"He's driven these roads in worse weather than we're apt to get tonight."

"I guess so." Mary let the curtain fall back into place. "What about a drink? Jo?"

"Not for me," I said.

"No, thanks," Ran said.

"What a pair of party poopers. Are you going to let me drink alone?"

She looked young and pretty standing there with her head tilted and her face flushed. I was sorry Will couldn't see her, and see the look on Ran's face as he watched his wife.

So Ran had one drink, and then at Mary's urging he had another; and after a while I got up and went to bed. They didn't need me around. Mary was sitting on the arm of Ran's chair and they were looking at each other in a way I remembered very well. In the past that look had turned me sick with jealousy and guilt. I wasn't jealous, but I did feel a little forlorn as I climbed the stairs by myself.

I was reading in bed when I heard them come upstairs. The two sets of footsteps went past my door; they were slow, and Ran's were unsteady. He stumbled; I heard him swear, and heard Mary laugh.

Maybe it was that laugh that made me . . . not exactly suspicious, the word is too strong for the slight uneasiness that brushed my mind. The laugh wasn't Mary's normal laugh; it was high-pitched, like a child's giggle. I remembered what Will had said about her night-time moods, and my uneasiness grew. I tried to reassure myself. Ran couldn't be drunk; there hadn't been time for him to drink that much since I came upstairs. Surely he would have better sense, anyhow.

When I realized that I was sitting bolt upright in bed, straining to hear sounds that couldn't possibly penetrate two closed door, I closed my book and turned out the light. But I didn't sleep. After hours of tossing, I fell into one of those dismal states of half-consciousness which are worse than pure insomnia. I was just enough awake to know that I wasn't asleep and not enough awake to sit up and turn on the light. I don't know how long I lay there, listening to the rain drip, and hearing every squeak of settling floors and walls. Old houses are noisy at night. I kept telling myself that, but my unconvinced muscles tautened at every new sound. Finally, in sheer exhaustion, I dropped into deeper slumber. But part of my mind was still alert. The subconscious trains itself that way; a nurse can sleep through a thunderstorm and waken at the slightest change in her patient's breathing.

That part of my mind heard the footsteps, soft and careful as they were, but I was so groggy that it took me several precious seconds to believe what I had heard. By the time I had crawled out of bed and opened the door, there was nothing to be seen. I stood swaying and blinking, cursing my overactive imagination; then I heard the sound of the front door closing.

I had sense enough not to go howling down the stairs in pursuit. The walker in the night might have been one of the Willards, on legitimate business. Instead, I went to my window, which overlooked the front porch.

It was hard to see, with rain streaking the glass and heavy clouds cutting off moon and starlight. But the expanse of lawn was lighter than anything that moved on it; after a few moments I made out, not one dark figure, but two. One stood at the foot of the drive. The other was moving. It was Mary; she was walking quickly, almost running as she crossed the lawn.

Then I realized who—or what—the other dark shape was; and simultaneously it hit me, a wave of terror so intense that my knees gave way under it, and I would have fallen but for the grip of my fingers on the window frame. The emotion had nothing to do with Mary. It was pure terror, complete in itself, requiring no cause and no rational excuse. I took one more look at the still, dark shadow standing so motionless at the foot of the drive; and I thrust myself away from it as I might have fled from an approaching tidal wave or avalanche. The terror subsided as I burst out of my room into the dim hallway; it left me shaking and staggering, with my nightgown clammy with perspiration. I went into Ran and Mary's room without knocking and switched on the light.

She was gone, of course. Her side of the bed hadn't even been slept in. The covers were turned back but there were no wrinkles on the pillow. Ran lay motionless, his back to me; my rude entry hadn't disturbed him. His breathing was so stentorious it sounded like snoring.

I pushed at his shoulder and he rolled over

on to his back. His face was slack, its fine lines blurred by sleep—and something else. Drunk, I thought. Contempt and anger rose to such a pitch that I slapped him across the face. He stirred but did not waken; and a new, uglier suspicion replaced the first. I slapped him again, and again; no longer in anger, but deliberately. Finally his eyes opened. They stared at me with no sign of recognition and then closed again; and I whirled, snatching at the telephone on the bedside table.

I didn't know the number and didn't have time to search for a directory; but the operator got it for me in a hurry. She was probably used to frantic voices asking for that particular number. When I heard Will's voice I didn't even take time to identify myself.

"Mary's gone," I said. "I saw her leave the house and go into the woods. I can't wake Ran, he acts as if he might be drugged. Did you prescribe sleeping pills for him too?"

"No. How bad is he?"

"He opened his eyes and looked at me. I had to hit him several times."

"Wake Bertha. She'll know what to do for Ran. You and Jed go after Mary. I'll start from this side of the woods, meet you at the house in an hour, whether you find her or not."

"Whether—"

"If we haven't located her in an hour we'll have to get the police. Any questions?"

"No."

"Get moving, then."

I went down the stairs at top speed. Mrs. Willard responded to my knock so promptly I wondered if she ever slept. Certainly there was no drowsiness on the round face that stared at me through a modest crack in the door, and when I had told my story she nodded calmly.

"Get some clothes on," she said, surveying my scantily clad shape disapprovingly. "Warm clothes, you'll need them. I'll be right up."

"Meet you in the kitchen in five minutes," called Jed. I could hear him moving around.

By the time I had scrambled into slacks and sweater and sneakers, Mrs. Willard was on her way up. I met her in the hall; she carried a steaming coffeepot in one hand and a bowl of ice in the other. I wondered how the Hades she had got water to boil so quickly, and I spared a shiver of sympathy for Ran. Drastic measures were in order, and Mrs. Willard was the girl who could administer them.

Jed was waiting for me, a big flashlight in each hand. He was fully dressed, even to high-laced boots.

"Which way did she go?"

We went to the door and I pointed out the direction.

"No path there," he muttered. "And no way of telling which direction she took once she was in the trees. I'll head off that way. You'd better stick to the path, no sense in getting you lost too. You aren't scared, are you?"

"I'm scared. But I won't panic; don't worry."

He nodded and handed me one of the flashlights.

"Keep an eye on your watch; Will is right about the time. But don't lose your wits. Slow and cool, that's the way. We'll find her."

He didn't wait for an answer, but went striding off across the grass. I headed down the driveway, trying not to run; I knew if I didn't keep my movements slow and deliberate I would start yelling and darting mindlessly. He was right, we would find Mary—eventually. But even if she encountered no other perils, in her weakened condition the damp and exposure could be fatal unless we found her soon.

I had assured Jed I wouldn't panic, and I didn't. But I hesitated under the eaves of the trees, and only the need that drove me that night could have sent me voluntarily into those stygian shadows. I thought I knew the path, but in the uncertain light it looked different; once I lost my way and blundered into a man-high clump of brambles before I realized that I was off the path. My stumbling progress made a hellish amount of noise, or so it seemed in the quiet of the night. From time to time I stood still, listening and calling and flashing the light off to each side among the tree trunks. The torch was a big heavy model, but it didn't carry far; the darkness swallowed it up like a hungry mouth. After a time I began to lose confidence in my sensory apparatus. The crack of a branch sounded like a surreptitious footstep, and the wail of a night bird might have been a weak human voice calling for help.

My progress was slow because I wanted to inspect as much of the surrounding terrain as I could without actually leaving the path. Mary might have fallen, fainted, or hit her head; she could be huddled unhearing behind any tree trunk or fallen log. She might even be hiding. It was a nasty thought, but it was probable. Yet my main reason for delay was one I was reluctant to admit to myself. I didn't want to search the graveyard.

I kept telling myself that there was no special reason why Mary should have gone there, but I knew there was. It was a crazy reason; but Mary's present actions weren't exactly sane. Throughout the ages the bereaved have tried to call back the dead. No part of Mary's flesh and blood lay in that isolated clearing in the woods; the thing she wanted had never been hers to lose. But I didn't know what mad logic ruled her mind, and there was a pull, an attraction, from that place. If I felt it, God only knew what Mary might feel.

I had to cross the cemetery in order to follow the path to its end and circle around back to the house. It was the only part of the terrain I knew well enough to search without running the risk of adding myself to the list of those missing. So I had to go to the cemetery in any case; but I shrank back from it with every nerve in my body.

Almost half the allotted time had passed—about twenty-five minutes—when I heard sounds behind me. My first thought was that it might be Mary; I turned and started back along the path. My torch was held low, so that I could avoid obstacles underfoot and at first, when I saw the dark form come around a turn in the path, my heart leaped with relief. Then I realized it was too tall and bulky to be Mary and at the same moment I saw the flash of the light it carried. The light struck me full in the face and I stopped, putting my hand up to shield my eyes.

"Jo. It's you."

"Ran?" I knew why his voice had that flat defeated sound; he had hoped I might be Mary. "How did you get out here? You were dead to the world the last time I saw you."

"Bertha. She's a devil, that woman . . . No sign of Mary?"

"Not yet. But it's so damned dark . . ."

"I know. She could be three feet away and you wouldn't see her."

"Ran, let's get help. Now. Twenty or thirty men combing these woods . . ."

"Not even a posse can do much before morning," Ran said flatly. "Come on. We're wasting time here."

I hesitated, resisting the pressure of his hand on my shoulder.

"You have no idea where she might have gone?"

His hand fell away. In the diffused light I saw his eyes narrow as he stared down at me.

"Why do you ask that? Don't you think, if I knew anything . . ."

"I didn't mean that. I don't know what I'm saying."

"None of us know." Ran passed his hand over his face. He looked sick, physically as well as mentally, and I knew that despite the efficacy of Mrs. Willard's methods he was driving himself to the limit of his endurance. "Let's go on, Jo. If I don't keep moving I'll lose my mind."

We searched the graveyard together, circling it from opposite directions, flashing our lights behind every stone, and under the dark eaves of the mausoleum. I couldn't see Ran after we separated, but the glow of his flashlight was reassuring. I wasn't alone.

When we met at the farther gate, neither of us had anything to report. Ran was hatless and his face was shining with rain. Under the intertwined branches the drizzle was reduced to a drip, but here in the open it was hard enough to soak us. I thought of Mary, perhaps lying unconscious in the cold rain, and my stomach twisted.

"Nothing here," I said. "I'll follow the path, Ran. Why don't you go some other way?"

"Time's getting on." Ran consulted his watch. "Maybe we ought to get back to the house."

"But you said—"

"Maybe I was wrong. We need an army and searchlights. She might not be in the woods. She might be on her way to town, or . . . We're wasting time, Jo!"

I couldn't blame him. I felt the same way myself, wanting to rush off, beating at bushes, flattening all obstructions. As I hesitated, I saw his nostrils flare. His head turned sharply. My senses were duller, but I heard the next sound, a slither and soft crackle, as if some walker had slipped on the mud of the path.

Ran was off without speaking, moving at a speed that was reckless on the narrow way. I pelted after, almost as fast, and it wasn't long before the inevitable happened—a crash, a curse, and a fall; and I jumped a tangle of leaves and dead branches to find Ran sprawled on the ground, head and shoulders propped at a crazy angle by the trunk of the tree whose low-hanging branch had knocked him flat. He wasn't unconscious, for as I dropped to my knees beside him, he groaned and sat up. There was a trickle of blood just starting from a cut above his eye.

"You heard her," he gasped, and tried to stand. At the movement his eyes fogged and he fell back against the tree.

"Yes. Wait a minute. You're stunned."

"Can't wait—she'll get away—"

"I'll go after her, just sit till you get your wits back. I'll go—"

His hand caught at my arm as I stood up.

"Not there, she left the path—that's why I ran into this damned tree; she's out there somewhere—"

Before the silence of the twisted darkness he indicated, we both fell silent. Ran shook his head frantically, as if trying to clear it; a small red drop fell on to the back of my hand and I stared at it as if mesmerized.

And then, through the silence, came the sound that, once heard, could never be mistaken for any other sound. Soft but oddly distinct, it was a child's voice—the voice of a small child crying.

It was pitiful and yet horrible; the most pathetic sound I had ever heard, and the most dreadful. When it died away, in a last tremulous wail of misery, Ran and I were both on our feet. My hands were so numb I couldn't feel them; and then I realized that we had clasped hands and that his grip on my fingers was hard enough to leave bruises.

"What in God's name?" I gasped.

"Not—God's," Ran said oddly; his voice broke in what might have been a hysterical chuckle. "That's what Mary hears. That's what she is following."

"No wonder," I said, shakily. "Let go, Ran, you're hurting me. She can't be far ahead. We've got to find her."

I left him standing there, swaying and white-faced, with blood streaking down his cheek and dissolving as the rain mingled with it. The blow on the head had been damaging, but I couldn't stop to look after him then; Mary's need was more urgent.

After a time I heard him stumbling along behind me. When I stopped he bumped into me; I turned on him with a fierce demand for silence. Even his ragged breathing made too much noise. I couldn't sympathize with him, my thoughts were too concentrated on Mary.

158

To be so close, so close that we had heard her, and to lose her now . . . Then I saw her, on the very edge of the light—only a flicker of movement, quickly stilled, but I knew.

"Mary! Please—Mary, don't run away."

Only silence answered, but that was encouraging; I would have heard her if she had moved.

I called again. I willed Ran to silence. He said nothing. Even his heavy breathing slowed.

"Mary," I called. "Please, Mary, come back. I'm wet, and I'm so tired . . ."

A flicker, a shadow stirring, furtive as some trapped wild thing . . . Motionless, barely breathing, I realized that the rain had stopped and that a rising wind was breaking up the heavy clouds. Straight ahead, above the trees, a star flickered and was obscured and shone out again steadily. We must be on the edge of the woods. Straight ahead was Will's house, and the cliff . . .

And the cliff.

"Mary!"

Perhaps it was the shrill new note of alarm in my voice that broke the spell I had been weaving—with, I think, some success. Or perhaps it was the ghost of a sobbing cry, mingled with the murmur of the wind.

159

Whatever it was, the shadowy shape at the outer limit of the flashlight beam moved away. After the first second I couldn't see it any longer, but I heard it, crashing through the underbrush with the careless disregard of quarry that sees safety within easy reach.

I went off down the path as if I had been shot from a gun, and I came crashing out of the woods in time to see—too much. There was light now, it seemed brilliant by comparison to the dark woods, for a half-circle of moon was free of cloud and the coarse grass between the house and the cliff edge lay pallid under its rays.

I saw Mary right away. She was on the road, almost halfway to the cliff. She wasn't running, she was walking steadily and quickly towards the edge.

While I hesitated, remembering stories of potential suicides who had been sent over the edge by a shout, Ran came bursting out of the trees behind me. Simultaneously, another figure appeared on the road to the right, where it dipped around to join the wide road. The figure was Will's; his height and walk were unmistakable.

At the sight of Mary he stopped short, held, probably, by the same reasoning that

160

kept me silent. But Ran was beyond coherent thought. He went staggering past me, evading my outflung hand, calling her name.

Mary stopped. She glanced back over her shoulder, and for a second I thought Ran had been right and I had been wrong. Then, for the last time that night, the crying came again.

It was softer this time and still unlocalized. It might have been the weeping of the night itself, if the night had had a human voice. It turned me sick with pity and cold with terror; and on Mary it acted like a goad and a spur. She started to run. I took a few frantic, running steps, and then stopped; it was obvious that she would reach the cliff before Ran could stop her, and I was even farther away. Will was no closer.

Will crouched and straightened up. I saw his arm move. And on the very edge of the cliff Mary staggered and swayed and fell—safely on to the grass, five feet from the edge.

6

"I STILL say you were taking a terrible chance."

"For God's sake, Jo," Ran said angrily. "He saved her life."

"If that stone had hit her in the head—"

"But it didn't," Will said. "It hit her in the midriff, which is where I meant it to hit her. It didn't even knock her out. She fainted. If she'd gone over the cliff . . . Oh, hell, this is beside the point. Why should I defend myself from the hysterics of a female? You're the one I blame, Ran. Why the hell didn't you tell me?"

"I don't know." Ran's hand went to his forehead, and the square of bandage that covered a three-inch gash. He looked terrible. Like the rest of us, he had changed into dry clothes, but he kept shivering. "I couldn't believe it myself, I guess. Or—maybe I was scared to admit that I did believe it."

"You didn't use to be that stupid," Will said.

He crossed to the bar and poured a stiff jolt

162

of brandy into a glass and carried it over to me. I was huddled on the rug by the fire; I felt as if I'd never be warm again. But I didn't want any brandy. Will ignored my scowl and shake of the head. He forced the glass into my hands.

"Medicinal purposes," he said. "God knows you need something to clear your brain. Ran, you'd better stick to coffee. I suspect you may be slightly concussed and even if you aren't, alcohol doesn't mix with that sleeping prescription."

"I can't figure out how she got it into me," Ran said dully.

"You never even imagined that she would try; why should you have been suspicious?"

That had been hard for me to face, though I had suspected it when I saw how Ran slept— that Mary had deliberately spiked one of his drinks with several of her sleeping pills. Her flight had not been the result of a sudden uncontrollable urge; she had been planning it all day. Her improved behaviour must have been part of the plan, to throw us off guard.

I began to feel better—physically—as the brandy and the fire warmed me. I was thinking about offering to make some coffee when Jed came in with a tray.

"Bertha's upstairs," he said. "That shot you gave Mary seems to be working, Will, but Bertha thought she'd better stay, just to be on the safe side."

"Right," Will said. "I don't want her left alone for a minute. Coffee or brandy, Jed?"

"Coffee keeps me awake this time of night," Jed said gravely, and accepted a glass from Will. He took a chair, and Will looked at him suspiciously.

"Did you and Bertha know about this—this quest of Mary's?"

"You mean did we know about the crying?" Jed drank brandy. "Bertha suspected."

"Well, of all the dirty tricks—! What was this, a conspiracy of silence?"

"Mary never said anything definite. And," Jed pointed out delicately, "it wasn't our business to tell you, Will. I thought you must know."

"He knows now," I said. "If he'd quit harping on how terrible we all are for not confiding in him, maybe we could proceed to some constructive conversation."

"You, too?" Will demanded.

"Now, now," Jed said calmly. "Stop fighting. That isn't going to do a bit of good."

164

He was sitting in one of the brocade arm-chairs. Against the delicate fabric his shabby overalls and thick boots should have looked out of place, but Jed was at ease wherever he happened to be. He looked as suited to his environment as a squirrel in a tree.

"Okay," I said. "I'm sorry, Will. You did save Mary's life tonight, and it was unforgivable of me to talk the way I did. I'm just not at my best."

Will looked sheepish.

"None of us are. We've got a lot to talk about, but maybe this isn't a good time. Ran ought to be in bed."

Chin sunk on his breast, hands dangling, Ran looked as if he could have fallen asleep in his chair. But when he heard his name spoken he looked up, and there was a look in his eyes that made me forget the weary lines in his face.

"We've got to talk now. Have you forgotten who's coming tomorrow?"

"Oh, God," Will muttered.

"The psychiatrist," I said. "So? Why the consternation"

"Psychiatrist?" said Jed.

Ran explained. As he spoke, Jed's face grew longer and longer. He shook his head.

"I wish you'd told us, Ran. I don't like to sound as if I'm making excuses for me and Bertha; but if I'd known what you were planning I'd have persuaded Bertha to talk to you."

Will was right, we were all sodden with fatigue. It took several seconds for the import of Jed's comment to sink in. Will was the first to understand.

"You mean—are you trying to tell me that you and Bertha have heard that sound too?"

"That's right."

"When?"

"It's been—oh, I'd say almost thirty years ago."

"Both of you?"

"I only heard it once," Jed said "Bertha heard it several times."

"I'm really flattered," Will said heavily. "You all have such a lot of confidence in me."

"Now, Will, be reasonable. The first time it happened you weren't even born. This time—well, now, what did we actually know? It took Bertha a long time to make the connection between Mary's trouble and that long-past thing that happened to her; even up to last night she wasn't really sure. And it

166

isn't the kind of thing you can speak right out about."

"That is true," Ran said. "Don't you think I would have told you, Will, if I could have brought myself to do so? I thought I was going crazy. There is such a thing as collective hallucination."

"How many times, before tonight, have you heard it?"

"Once. I guess that was what sent me haring off to Boston. I began to have visions of both of us, Mary and myself, prowling the woods every night like a pair of ghouls." He shivered. "The thing . . . pulls at you, Will. I don't know whether you noticed it tonight. But the . . . pull is very strong."

"You didn't tell all this to your Dr. Wood, did you?"

"No. I just couldn't do it." Ran looked up. "Will, it wasn't that I didn't trust you. But sometimes it's easier to tell these things to a stranger; you know what I mean? At least I thought it would be. I was wrong. I've made a mess of it, Will."

"Stow it," Will said. His voice was brusque, but it seemed to tell Ran something he needed to know. The two of them exchanged a long, unsmiling look, and some of the sick despair left Ran's face.

"You ought to be in bed," Will muttered. He shook his head. "There's so much I need to know, and so little time. I don't suppose we can head that damned woman off now?"

"She's already on her way. She said she planned to stop over along the way, and get in sometime tomorrow afternoon."

"She didn't mention where she planned to stay tonight? No such luck . . ." Will ran his fingers through his hair. "Why couldn't she fly, like a normal person?"

"She's nervous about flying," Ran said.

I laughed. They all looked at me as if I'd cut loose with a string of obscenities, and I said helplessly,

"It just struck me as funny, a psychiatrist who's afraid of flying . . . All right, I'm sorry. But I don't understand why you're all so appalled. What difference is it going to make if she does come?"

The three men exchanged one of those glances that women find so maddening. Jed, always charitable, took it on himself to explain.

"You're worn out, Jo, or you'd be thinking clearer. This lady is a doctor. She's going to

168

be looking for signs of a nice simple nervous breakdown, or whatever fancy name they call it nowadays. She won't find any, because that's not what we've got here. Do I have to spell it out? Seems to me we're all afraid of saying the word."

"A ghost," I said experimentally. The word felt funny in my mouth.

"Now wait a minute," Will said. "I'm not saying I don't believe it. What I am saying is that I'm thoroughly confused, and I'd like a couple of days to reappraise the situation. That's why I'm not happy about having a stranger come in, someone we'll have to lie to and deceive. Of course we can't tell her about the—the crying. She'll think we're all crazy."

"It's been thirty years since I heard it," Jed said. "But nobody who ever once heard it could forget it, or mistake it for any other sound on this earth. And you're not convinced?"

"My God," Will said. "You're asking me to throw overboard a whole lifetime of rational thinking. I—I just don't know, Jed. I don't know what to think."

"What else could it be?"

Will shook his head.

"Jed, there are a dozen possibilities. Some

169

freak combination of wind through a natural crevice in a tree or cliff . . . A night bird, an animal . . ."

"Wait a minute," I said. "Will, those cats of yours. You told me that a Siamese in heat sounds like a lost soul. Or a baby crying."

Ran sat up straighter, with a half-voiced expletive, and for a moment Will's face lit up. Then gloom settled on it more heavily than before. When he shook his head I could see how he hated to abandon the idea.

"You've never heard a Siamese in heat. I have. It's a God-awful sound, but not as bad as what I heard tonight."

"Add one teasponful of imagination, mix with a generous pinch of sheer funk . . ."

"No. Look, Jo, I made damn good and sure that both the Siamese were locked in tonight; I didn't want extraneous animals crashing around in the underbrush while I was listening for Mary. Not to mention the fact that my female is not in heat."

"Go on, Will," Jed said. "Jo doesn't know this, and maybe Ran has been away from the island too long. But you and I both know every species of bird or animal or insect that has ever lived in these woods. Neither of us is going to get all worked up about an owl or a possum. There's only one animal I know of could make a sound like that one. A human animal, a young one. A child."

I couldn't argue with that even if I had wanted to. He knew what he was talking about. I was three-quarters convinced; Jed was right, no one who had ever heard that sound could mistake it for any normal noise. The thing that held me back from complete conviction wasn't logic, it was, as Will had said, the accumulated thought patterns of my whole life. It is very hard to reverse every rational conviction you have ever held, overnight.

It was even harder for Will because he didn't have my knowledge of Mary to reinforce belief. In a crazy way it was easier for me to believe in a ghost than to believe that Mary had cracked up. But people have the most amazing ability to fight truth, even when it's staring them in the face, if it disagrees with their cherished preconceptions. Out there in the wind-racked night, I believed. If I hadn't been so busy running, I'd have been down on my knees. Here, surrounded by the comforts of civilized doubt, scepticism fought back.

I had plenty of time to meditate on these

things; there was a long silence after Jed's speech. Finally Will said stubbornly,

"Jed, I'm not saying yes or no. All I'm saying is that we have to consider all the possibilities, no matter how far-fetched."

"A lot of pretty smart people have believed in survival after death," Jed said.

"I tell you, I'm not denying that as a possibility. But it's only one possibility among many."

"Such as?"

It had become a debate now between the two of them. So far, Jed was ahead; it seemed to me that he had pretty well knocked out Will's first two suggestions. Will took a deep breath, marshalling his next attack.

"For one thing, that there really is a child out in those woods. All right, I know it's virtually impossible; we'd have heard if a local child were missing. But we ought to check. Then there's the chance of some exotic animal or bird, escaped from a zoo, maybe."

Ran made a wordless sound of disgust.

"No, Will is right," Jed said calmly. "His ideas strike me as even wilder than the one he's fighting so hard, but it's true, we've got to check every possibility. And there's another one Will hasn't mentioned."

172

This time the silence had a different quality. Ran looked as baffled as I felt, but Will knew what the other man meant. And he didn't like it.

"Might as well say it," Jed went on. "We've had enough trouble already with people keeping quiet about what they were thinking. The other possibility is a mechanical device of some sort."

"Oh, no," I said involuntarily. "It was a human voice. Nothing mechanical could sound so pitiable."

"Machines reproduce sounds," Jed said. "Including human voices. A radio, for instance. Or a tape recorder."

Will nodded reluctantly. I began to be aware of a peculiar sensation at the pit of my stomach. I said slowly,

"Are you suggesting that somebody is deliberately producing those sounds? To draw Mary out of the house, or—or drive her crazy?"

"Not necessarily," Jed answered.

I was definitely feeling sick to my stomach. Ran didn't seem to get the point; he didn't have my evil mind.

"My God," he muttered. "When I think of

the time we've wasted! If I had only had sense enough to speak up . . ."

"Probably wouldn't have made any difference," Jed said. He stood up. "Folks, it's too late to do anything more tonight. We'll get to work first thing in the morning. Goodnight."

When he left the room I followed, practically on his heels. My departure resembled flight. Ran might be too stupefied by drugs and sleeplessness to understand, but the implications of the last hypothesis were only too clear to me.

Of course it was the hypothesis Will must favour, even though he couldn't say so. The other theories were too wild. There couldn't be a living child out in those woods; the entire island would have been alerted to search for it. The idea of an animal, any animal, was equally preposterous. And Will—rational, scientifically trained—couldn't possibly accept a supernatural origin for the sound.

So that left only one explanantion. The pitiful weeping, by Will's logic, must be a recording. The effect of the sound on Mary had been sinister and dangerous. Tonight she had almost lost her life. At best she risked losing her reason or her physical health. And who had a reason for wanting Mary out of the way? Who else but Mary's sister, who was—as Will had seen for himself—in love with Mary's husband.

II

Basically I must be an optimist. It takes so little to restore me to an idiotically hopeful view of the universe—little things like some sleep, sunshine, and the smell of coffee. I slept like a log, out of sheer exhaustion; and when I woke up next morning the first thing I saw was sunlight pouring in the window. The heavenly odour of Mrs. Willard's coffee came in through the same aperture, and by the time I had got dressed I was able to reappraise my grisly night thoughts.

Not even Will Graham could seriously believe that I was capable of hurting Mary. I even had an alibi if—which God forbid—it should ever come to that. I had been three thousand miles away when the trouble began.

There was another suspect, of course. But I wouldn't let myself think about that. I didn't believe it.

Which left me face to face with the sole remaining hypothesis.

I was brushing my teeth when I reached that point in my meditations; I remember very clearly seeing the grim amusement in the reflected face that stared back at me out of the mirror. It seemed like such a weird thing to be thinking about on a bright spring morning, in the midst of a humdrum process like tooth brushing.

The face was not the face I had seen so often in the mirror in my San Francisco apartment. The brown hair and the turned-up nose were the same, but almost every other feature seemed to have altered. There were hollows under the cheekbones, and a new droop to the mouth—and a line where there had never been one, across the forehead.

Experimentally I tightened my mouth and stuck out my chin. It was a pugnacious chin anyway—suitable, as I had often told Mary, for the descendant of bull-headed Irish peasants. Maybe it was time I displayed a little of that fighting spirit instead of feeling sorry for myself. A fine state of affairs that would be, a McMullen letting herself be intimidated by a few ghosts.

In that fine mood of belligerence I marched across the room and flung the door open, ready to proceed and do battle.

I found myself facing Will Graham. For a second my new-found courage faltered; I wondered whether he had been lying in wait for me. Then I realized that he had probably just been passing by, and I got a grip on myself.

"Oh—good morning. I didn't know you were planning to spend the night."

"I didn't. I got back here at six."

He looked tired. But I refused to let myself feel sorry for him. We were all tired. A man shouldn't be a doctor if he expected to get his sleep every night.

"How is Mary?" I asked.

"Amazing. The way that woman bounces back . . . She's asleep again. But according to her she hasn't the faintest recollection of doing anything last night."

A door opened softly and Ran came tiptoeing down the hall. Will frowned at him.

"I don't want her left alone, Ran."

"I'll go right back. I heard you two talking and there's something I want to say to Jo. In front of you, Will."

"Now, Ran," I said unhappily.

Physically Ran wasn't in top condition. His skin had a sallow pallor and the scratches on his face stood out shockingly. But his eyes were clear and hard.

"I'm sorry if it embarrasses you, Jo, but from now on I'm sticking to Jed's policy of candour. I owe you an apology and so does Will. I told him the other night that you were in no way responsible for that stupid performance of mine. You know how I feel about Mary—I've never looked at another woman—"

"Uh—" I said; and a reluctant grin touched Ran's mouth.

"All right, so I've looked. And maybe I've had a few ideas. But that's all. As for you, Jo, you're not only my kid sister, you're my friend; at least I used to hope you were. I guess I never realized how important that relationship was to me until I messed it up. Do you think I'd destroy a rare feeling like that for some cheap suburban affair? I wouldn't have insulted you, or Mary, in that way if I'd been in my right mind. You believe me, don't you? You believe it will never happen again?"

"Ran," I said. "You don't have to do this."

"Yes, I do, and I've got to do it in front of

178

old Cotton Mather here." He indicated Will, who was looking as uncomfortable as I have ever seen a man look. "There's nothing stuffier than the combination of puritan New England and Scottish Presbyterian. This so-called New Morality everybody talks about may have trickled into Massachusetts, but it never got past the borders of Maine. I want Will to get down off that pulpit of his and apologize to you. If there's any blame attached to anyone, it's one hundred per cent mine. You never thought of me as anything but a brother. I hope to God you can go on thinking of me that way."

He had never looked more handsome. The dark bruises of fatigue and the rakish bandage, half hidden by locks of black hair, only increased his appeal. But there was a difference; and it was in my mind. Poor Ran, flagellating himself, had never suspected that morally I wasn't as innocent as he believed. And he would never know; it wouldn't relieve his conscience, it would just make him feel worse, to find out that I had adored him from afar in the past. Because now it was gone. Gone, as if it had never been.

I believe in candour too. But there's a limit to everything.

179

"You're an old Calvinist yourself," I said. Deliberately I stood on tiptoe and kissed him lightly on the corner of the mouth. That was the final test; not that I could kiss him casually, as a friend, but that I could do it in front of Will without the slightest twinge of self-consciousness. I added, "Go back to Mary. I'll ask Mrs. Willard to bring you up some breakfast."

"That would be great." But Ran didn't move. He looked at Will; and Will, red as a brick and rigid with embarrassment, muttered something which, if you strained your ears, might have been, "Sorry."

"That's all right," I said, and walked away, with dignity.

He trailed after me. I wasn't sure whether he believed Ran, or whether he even cared. Being Will, he would have to act like a gentleman even if he had his doubts. But I no longer cared whether old Cotton Mather believed in my virtue or not. Ran was right. We had all been skulking, verbally and physically, for too long.

Breakfast was always an informal meal and that morning Mrs. Willard covered the kitchen table with an assortment of food that would have fed an army. Food was more than nourishment to her; it was a form of emotional expression. The worse things got, the more she cooked.

The kitchen was a good place for taut nerves. I've never seen a warmer, friendlier room. One end of it had been thoroughly modernized, with the latest in gleaming kitchen gadgetry and a table set in a curved bay window. The other end still had the huge brick hearth of the original house. The Willards used this part of the big room as their sitting-room; there were oak settles flanking the fireplace together with a few comfortable chairs, and a beautiful handmade rag rug covered the hearth. The seats of the settles were piled with cushions; most were covered with cotton or corduroy, but one seemed to be made of the long-haired fake fur that is becoming popular for bedspreads, covers, and cushions. It didn't seem the sort of thing Mrs. Willard would care for, and when I studied it more closely I recognized Prudence the cat, curled into a ball, adding the final quintessential note of domestic comfort.

Mrs. Willard took a tray up to Ran, and Jed came in and sat down with us. I won't say I wasn't glad to have him. The tension between Will and me was still pretty thick. But I had intended in any case to speak my own little piece and contribute my bit to general knowledge.

"How's the ghost theory this morning?" I asked Jed.

Will scowled: I gathered that he did not care to have the subject treated so flippantly. Jed was more tolerant. He finished his mouthful of pancakes—he ate as fastidiously as one of Will's cats—before he answered.

"As of now, it's a hundred to one on the ghost."

"Have you been out in the woods this morning?" Will asked.

"Since it was light."

"You didn't find anything?"

"No child, no strange animal."

"Are you sure?"

"Nobody could be sure," Jed said patiently. "Not unless he tore up the whole blamed thirty acres by the roots. But I think I would have seen signs—tracks or spoor—if there had been anything to see."

"If anyone would, you would."

"Well?" I said to Will.

He gave me another scowl and spoke to Jed.

"Have you had a chance to check around the town about a missing child?"

Jed grinned. He indicated his wife, who had just come back into the room.

"Now, Will, do you think there could be a child lost in the entire state without Bertha knowing about it?"

"What are you all jabbering about?" Mrs. Willard turned from the stove.

"The crying," Jed said.

"Oh." Mrs. Willard flipped a pancake. She snorted. "Willie Graham, are you still harping on that? You don't have any sense. Do you think there was a child lost now and another one lost thirty years ago when me and Jed heard the crying? Use your brains."

I beamed at Mrs. Willard.

"She's got you there."

"Oh, hell," Will said. "Don't you glare at me, Bertha, I'm not going to apologize for one little 'hell'. You drive me to it. Come here and sit down and tell me all about your experience."

"All right." Mrs. Willard placed another pancake neatly on the heaped plate and turned off the stove. "But you'll have to keep quiet, Will. If you start sneering in your smart-alecky way, I'll lose my temper."

183

"At least keep an open mind," Jed added. "We've eliminated your other theories pretty well. And you know what Sherlock Holmes used to say."

"Eliminate all the impossibilities and whatever is left, however improbable, is the truth," I quoted inaccurately.

Will shook his head disgustedly.

"Conan Doyle had a good mind," Jed said. "And he came to believe in some of the things you're doubting, Will."

"He lost his son," Will said stubbornly. "When people are bereaved, they crack up. It's pitiful, but it's understandable that they should."

"Mrs. Willard hasn't lost anything," I said; and then I could have bitten the tongue right out of my mouth. "I'm sorry," I stammered. "I didn't think—"

"What are you sorry about?" Jed asked reasonably. "You didn't know."

"I knew," Will muttered. "My mother told me about the little girl. But I didn't realize . . ."

Unexpectedly, Mrs. Willard laughed. I think it was the first time I had ever heard her laugh out loud and the quality of the sound

184

amazed me; it was the merry, high-pitched laugh of a young girl.

"Good gracious," she said. "You're all making such a to-do of this. It was thirty years ago, and people don't suffer any tragedy that long." She looked at me. "In those days, Jo, the island was pretty cut off in the winter and there wasn't a doctor living here. They didn't vaccinate you for diphtheria back then, least not around here. She was the only one we had—the only one we ever had. But, like I say, it was half a lifetime ago. And I know I'll be seeing her again. Not too many more years to wait now."

She said it in the same tone in which she might have said, "I'm going to Boston next week to visit her."

"Course," she went on calmly, "right after she died I was pretty near out of my mind. I was sick too, couldn't even get out of my bed; and it was that week, during one of the worst blizzards we've ever had in these parts, that I heard the crying. I heard it for four nights, and on the fifth night I couldn't stand it any more. I got up out of my bed and tried to go after it."

She glanced around the table. "Isn't

anybody going to eat those cakes? They'll go to waste if not; I can't keep 'em.''

"Cut that out, Bertha," Will said. "You know you've got us on the edges of our chairs. What happened? I hope you didn't go out of the house during a blizzard."

"The storm was over," Mrs. Willard said. Her face had gone blank, as if she were seeing something far off—in time, not in space. "I got the back door open without waking Jed; and the world outside was like some place I'd never seen before; some place out of a book. It was so still you could hear the branches creak under the weight of the ice on them. Everything was white and black. The snow was deep, and there'd been sleet after it; the whole surface shone like glass in the moonlight. The moon was small and bright like a little tiny silver coin, and the stars were like points of ice, so cold . . . I could hear the crying just as clear; it was the saddest sound I ever heard, and I can still remember how it dragged at you. I thought how cold it was, and how deep the snow lay; and how dark and lonesome it would be for her out there.

"Then I saw somebody standing out on the lawn. I never did see her face, on account of the hood that was attached to that black cloak—"

This time when she stopped speaking it wasn't for dramatic effect. She looked at me in alarm; the noises I was making must have sounded as if I were strangling.

"What's the matter, Jo?"

"You saw it," I gulped. "You saw—her—too? I thought—I was going to tell you—"

Jed sat up straight and banged his hand down on the table.

"Annie Marks!" he exclaimed. "Good Lord, I must be getting thick in the head in my old age. I knew perfectly well that morning when you told me about seeing the woman in the woods that poor old Annie never gets this far away from home. But I never connected that . . ."

"Bertha," Will said; there was a note in his voice that I'd never heard him use to her before. "On your honour, tell me the truth. Did you ever speak of this experience to Mary or Jo?"

"Will!" I exclaimed. "Of all the outrageous—"

"No, no," Jed said coolly. "It's all right, Jo. He knows better than that; but naturally he's got to ask. I would myself." He glanced

187

at his red-faced, spluttering wife, and went on, with a smile, "First time I've ever seen Bertha speechless. So I'll tell you, Will. Neither one of us ever said a word to another living soul. Not even to the old gentleman—Ran's granddaddy. There's no way either of these girls could have heard the story."

"I'm sorry," Will said, with an apprehensive look at Mrs. Willard. "Bertha? You all right?"

She recovered herself.

"Just wait till the next time you come around here cadging a meal," she said ominously.

"I said I was sorry!"

"Oh, do shut up, Will," I said. "You keep interrupting, and ignoring all the important things. Mrs. Willard, I've seen that woman too. Just as you did, not too clearly; she wears a long black cloak and the hood hides her face. I saw her in the cemetery in the woods—twice, in the same spot. Did you—"

"No." She shook her head. "She was outside the house the one time I saw her, near the edge of the woods . . ."

Her voice trailed off. I nodded impatiently.

"Yes, I've seen her there too. But there's

something else that's more important to me right now, and I'll be damned if I'm going to let myself be diverted. Maybe you won't want to answer it, but I've got to ask. It's Mary I'm asking it for. You survived this thing. How? How did you fight it?"

"Well," Jed said. "We talked about it."

He looked at my rebellious face and he smiled rather sadly.

"Jo, don't you think if we had a magic cure we'd be upstairs right now giving it to Mary? All I can tell you is that, in my opinion, the two cases aren't the same. Bertha and I didn't know then that there wouldn't be more children. I think too, though I can't prove it, that some kinds of mind are more susceptible to this sort of influence. Maybe Bertha wouldn't ever have heard it if she hadn't been sick and weakened. I only heard a far-off echo of that sound myself; and it came to me through her. I never saw the woman she described. There's another thing. I don't quite know how to say it . . . Mary is a Roman Catholic, isn't she?"

"She was. For the last few years neither of us has been anything in particular. I don't think Mary ever forgave God for taking Mother and Dad."

"Well, that's what I mean," Jed said. "Your generation doesn't have it. I'm not saying our kind of faith was a purely good thing. It can be awfully narrow and cruel. But it can also be a rock to lean on. I don't know what it was that roused me, that night; but I got to the door in time to stop Bertha from going out, all barefoot she was, into the snow. And when I heard what she'd been hearing . . .

"I was young and simple in those days. I knew my Scripture, and it seemed to me there was only one place that sound could be coming from. So Bertha and I—well, we wrestled with Satan for the next three nights. Then it was over. You see why I can't tell Ran about this? It probably wouldn't work for me any more, I've read too much and raised too many questions. It surely wouldn't work for Ran and Mary. And, as I say, I think Mary's case is a lot worse than Bertha's."

"It's not a case, it's a nightmare," Will said, with a groan. "I'm even more confused than I was before. What is this thing, anyhow?"

"I don't know what it is," I said. "But its name is Kevin."

The remark created all the sensation I could have desired.

"Mary told me that," I went on, "the first day I was here. 'It is a boy; his name is Kevin.' That has to mean something, Will. All these years she's wanted a baby, she had the names picked out. A boy would have been named after Ran."

"Kevin is a good old Irish name," Will said.

"But it's not one of our family names, don't you see? It was a Fraser name; I found it on half a dozen of the stones in the cemetery. Why would Mary come up with that name unless this business has something to do with the family or this house?"

"Now we're getting down to it," Jed said with satisfaction. "Didn't Ran tell me that it was Mary's idea to come back here this summer? That she took a violent attachment to the house after they were here a couple of months ago?"

"That's right," I said. "Of course! It's in the house—something here, that only comes to women who have lost a child. An only child. That's why it hasn't been heard or seen more often."

"Shades of Charlotte Brontë," Will muttered. "Family curses, yet . . . But that would explain why Mary is getting the full treatment. She is the last Fraser wife in the direct line, whereas Bertha, being only distantly related, got a milder dose . . . Oh, damn. It sounds absolutely demented."

"No," I said. "It sounds right. The thing that bothers me is the connection between the woman and the crying. It is odd; the child has never been seen and the woman makes no sound. The two must be related, mustn't they? They couldn't be separate phenomena?"

The theory was beginning to get to Will. He was succumbing to its fascination as he would have done to an intellectual game . . . fitting the pieces together.

"I can accept one set of impossible phenomena more easily than two separate sets," he said. "And if we agree that the two are connected, we've got another piece of evidence. A date and a name."

"I'm glad you saw it all by yourself," I said.

"I wasn't with Jo the second time," Will said, half to himself, half to the Willards. "But I gather she saw the apparition in black in the same spot where it appeared the first time; and that was how we happened to find the grave. Suppose the apparition is . . . Miss Smith."

192

"A lot of help that is," I said. "We already agreed that it would be impossible to find out anything about her."

"That was when we thought she was only a mysterious stranger," Jed pointed out. "If she's so fond of the family that she feels she has to haunt them, there must be a closer relationship than we thought."

"You two," said Will, looking from Jed to me, "have a sick sense of humour."

I ignored him.

"We also know the date," I said. "It was 1846, wasn't it—the year she died?"

"Yep. You know," Will said, "that would be in Hezekiah's time, wouldn't it? Somehow that strikes a chord."

"In what way?"

"Just the combination: mysterious woman, weeping child, and a man who is popularly supposed to have sold his soul to Old Nick. Suggestive, wouldn't you say?"

"You have a lot of nerve criticizing other people's reasoning," I said. "I see what you're driving at. But you haven't got a shred of evidence."

"The time is right, though."

"That's true. And I know what I'm going to do this morning." I got up. "Jed, you mentioned a trunkful of papers. Where is it?"

"Up in one of the attics. I'll fetch it down, you don't want to sit up there in the dust. Where do you want it, your room?"

"That would be fine. Thanks."

"Saturday morning," Will said. "Hey, this is my day off. It says here. I think I'll go home and take a nap."

I glanced out the window.

"I think you won't," I said.

"If I'm not entitled to a nap—"

"You may be entitled, but you aren't going to get one." I pointed. "You're going to be entertaining your long-lost sister."

I thought for a minute that he was going to fall out of the window.

It might have been the car that affected him. I don't know much about cars, but I soon learned that this was a Maserati, because people kept mentioning the name with the same kind of reverence they might have displayed towards Saint Peter. All I saw that first day was that it was a convertible, azure blue and low-slung. And the girl who got out of it was the kind of girl you automatically associate with a car like that—the girls that appear in TV commercials, long and slim and golden-haired.

She wasn't a girl, though; she was a woman, and when you were close to her you could see the tell-tale lines around the mouth and neck which make-up can never quite conceal. At least I could see them. Most men probably never looked.

She wore a white linen trouser suit, but because it was warm she had the jacket slung over her shoulder. A red-and-white-striped shirt moulded the upper part of her body like a second skin. I knew who she was, but it didn't seem fair—that kind of looks, and that many brains, in the same woman.

She didn't seem to be in any hurry to come into the house, so I decided I'd better go out to greet her. I knew she must have seen the faces gaping at her from the window. I glanced at Will. It would be an exaggeration to claim that his eyes were really bulging.

Will followed me out. The woman met us halfway, with a pleasant smile and a brisk professional handclasp. But her manner didn't fool me; I saw the way she eyed Will's face and his impressive height. She was even taller than I, five feet ten or eleven; a woman as tall as that doesn't often meet attractive men who are taller.

"You must be tired after such a long drive,

Doctor," I said. "Wouldn't you like some coffee? Have you had breakfast?"

"Not 'Doctor', please," she said competently. "Unless Mr. Fraser has changed his mind about letting his wife know who I am. Anne would be better, don't you think? I'll skip the coffee, if you don't mind. This is a good opportunity for me to clear up a few points about the patient before I meet her as my hostess. I had hoped to have an early opportunity of speaking with you, Doctor—there, I'm doing the same thing! I must say 'Will', mustn't I?"

"There's a bench under the rose arbour," Will said. "Maybe it would be a good idea if I briefed you on a couple of things."

It was pretty obvious that I wasn't invited to the conference, but I wasn't going to let a little thing like that stop me. I was very curious to hear what Will was going to tell the lady. That was why I trailed along—no other reason—and though Anne didn't look pleased, she didn't quite have the nerve to tell me to get lost. As for Will, I don't think he noticed I was there.

The bench wasn't big enough for three of us, so I sat on the grass. I could see their faces more easily from that position. And there were still violets there, in the shady dampness under the arbour—big fat purple violets and white ones with delicate purple streaks shading out from an amethyst heart.

Anne had apparently been told about the general situation by Ran. She kept nodding as Will talked. Only one detail surprised her. It surprised me too; I hadn't been sure that Will was going to tell her about the crying.

"Is this specific delusion a recent development?" she asked. "Mr. Fraser hinted that his wife refused to accept the loss of the foetus, but he didn't mention actual auditory hallucinations."

Under any other circumstances it would have been funny to watch Will squirm. He hadn't had time to figure out a sensible story, and he wasn't a good enough liar to overcome that handicap. When you lie, or avoid the whole truth, you often fail to see the corner you're talking yourself into until it's too late to get out of it.

"I didn't—er—learn of them myself until last night," he mumbled. "But I believe they have been—um—occurring for some time. In fact, Mr. Fraser has—uh—heard sounds also."

Anne didn't seem to notice his embarrassment. Maybe she was accustomed to having men get red and start stammering when she was around. She nodded.

"Collective illusion. Not surprising, considering the amount of emotional strain."

"Count me in," I said cheerfully. "I've had a collective illusion too."

Anne glanced at Will. The look finished Will; it was a sidelong, significant look, as meaningful as a wink. It linked the two of them, the pros, against the nuts. After that look only a saint would have had the guts to admit that he was one of the nuts.

"That's very interesting," Anne said. "What was it, Jo?"

"It sounded like a child crying," I said.

"I see." She was silent for a moment. Then she said, "I'm theorizing without sufficient data, which is unforgivable; but have you considered the possibility that there may be actual sounds, auditory illusion rather than a genuine sensory hallucination? Not a child, of course; but some—oh, some animal or other cause—that might sound like a child to someone with Mrs. Fraser's particular problem. If that is so, this may not be a very healthy environment for her. I shouldn't stick my professional neck out this way—I may be

198

completely off base—but you might want to consider taking her away from here."

My jaw dropped. It was such an obvious solution, and yet it hadn't occurred to any of us. I hated to admit it, but the lady was not stupid.

Will was so impressed he was practically inarticulate.

"My God, Doctor—Anne—why the hell didn't I—"

She interrupted him with a deprecatory little laugh.

"I may be all wrong, Will. It's easy for me to jump to these conclusions. And of course I'm emotionally detached from all this. You say you only learned of the auditory hallucination last night? You haven't really had time to assimilate it. And—I have a feeling that the information came to you as something of a shock."

It wasn't that brilliant a deduction. To a doctor, the physical signs of fatigue and distress must have been plain on both our faces. But Will, that gullible male, looked at her as if she had just accurately read his palm.

7

WILL took his "sister" to town for lunch. It was a perfectly reasonable thing to do; we hadn't expected her for lunch, and Will had to make some gesture of brotherly affection. But as I watched them glide off in Anne's car, I wanted to spit or stamp or do something equally childish.

I turned to see Jed behind me. As usual, he was leaning on his rake, and his eyes were amused.

"That the doctor?"

"Yes."

"Good-looking woman."

"Yes."

"Don't worry," Jed said. "You've got at least ten advantages."

"What are they?"

"Ten years."

I laughed unwillingly.

"Four or five, maybe."

"Unless she started medical school at the age of twelve, she's got to be well over thirty.

But I guess that's not so important. What do you think of her? As a doctor, I mean?"

"She's good," I said. "I hate to admit it, so that probably means she's even better than I think. She made one suggestion that absolutely floored me because it was so sensible. If Mary hears things here that distress her, maybe we ought to take her away. Go back to New York."

"Hmmph." Jed's eyebrows drew together. "To tell the truth, I was surprised one of you hadn't brought that up before this."

"You thought of it? You would . . . I don't know why I'm so stupid."

"You aren't stupid, you're worried. Sure, I thought of getting Mary away from here. I still think it would be a good idea. Only it won't work."

"Why not?"

"She won't go," Jed said.

He went off, to do something to the roses—mulch them or feed them or prune them—whatever it is you do to roses in the spring—and I wandered aimlessly around the grounds for a while. I felt depressed. All my fine resolutions about clever plans seemed hopeless. I kept thinking about the two professional sceptics, admiring each other over the Inn's lobster bisque and, no doubt, laughing themselves sick over the superstitious stupidity of the rest of us.

When I finally forced myself back into the house I found Ran in the kitchen, with Mrs. Willard standing over him trying to make him eat. I joined them, not because I was hungry but because I didn't have the strength to argue with Mrs. Willard about eating.

"How's Mary?" I asked.

"She threw me out," Ran said. "Okay, I know she isn't supposed to be left alone. But what am I supposed to do when she pretends she doesn't remember a thing about last night? Maybe she isn't pretending. I tell you, Jo, when she looks at me with those big brown eyes I start to wonder whether I'm the one who's imagining things."

"You aren't," I said. "Believe me, you aren't. I'll go up to her."

"I wouldn't. She says she wants to rest this afternoon to get ready for Will's sister."

"The lady has arrived," I said, and told Ran about the conversation with Anne. He didn't seem to be much interested, he was too preoccupied with the change in Mary.

"I've never seen her like this," he said helplessly. "She keeps saying she's tired, but she doesn't look . . . You'd think, after a night like that one, that she'd be a wreck, physically and every other way. But no. I tell you, Jo, it's like five different women in the same body. You don't think—"

"No," I said firmly. "You're on the wrong track. Maybe I'd better tell you what we discussed this morning. Mrs. Willard—you don't mind . . ."

"Such a fuss about nothing." Mrs. Willard sounded grudging, but I noticed that she followed my recital with poorly concealed interest. When I had finished, Ran's first reaction pleased and touched me. He reached for Mrs. Willard's big work-worn hand and squeezed it.

"Bertha, I'm sorry. I never knew."

"I keep telling you, you're all making a big thing out of it," she said gruffly. "The question is, what are you going to do now?"

"It's a good question," Ran said wryly. "I'm not quarrelling with your conclusions, Jo, but I'll be damned if I can see what they lead to, in terms of action."

"Anne suggested we take Mary away from here," I said. Ran's face lit up. I hated to spoil his hope, but I had to. "I'm not sure she'll go, Ran. Or that, if she does, it will solve the problem."

"It's worth a try," Ran said.

"Maybe." I stood up leaving my barely touched plate. "In the meantime, I'm going to delve into your family secrets via some old papers. Do you mind?"

"Trying to lay the ghost?" Ran smiled at me. "Just don't get your hopes up. I don't remember anything in the family history that could account for this."

"Anyhow, I can sit up there with my door open and keep an eye on the hall."

"That's good," Mrs. Willard said. "And I think I'll give that linen closet a good cleaning. It's been needing it for a long time."

"And you can watch the other end of the hall," Ran said grimly. "Thanks. Both of you."

"Why don't you go out and get some fresh air," I suggested. "You look like a ghost yourself."

"Maybe I will. I might go to town and see if I can find the doctors. I'm curious as to what wild tale Will is telling the lady."

"Me, too," I said.

Ran drove off, and I went upstairs. As Jed had promised, the trunk had been brought to my room. It was a squat, dark, leather-bound box about three feet long by a foot and a half high. There was a brass trim, now tarnished, around its top. I felt my sagging spirits lift at the very sight of it squatting there, and when I sat down on the floor beside it and lifted the lid I was conscious of a prickle of anticipation.

I don't know what I expected to find. Or rather, I do know, but I hate to admit it—one of those documents so popular in the sensational fiction of the last century. The "manuscript"—they were almost always "manuscripts"—appeared in chapter fifty and cleared up all the miscellaneous mysteries that had filled the first forty-nine chapters. They had titles like *The Strange Experience of Mr. W——B——*, or *The Confession of Lady Audley*.

Consciously, of course, I wasn't that naive. But I was disappointed as the time dragged on and I found nothing that seemed to have the slightest bearing on our problem.

It was an interesting collection, in its way. Everything was thrown in helter-skelter; there were letters, baby books, albums, and even a recipe book, its yellow pages filled with recipes that started out "Take twelve eggs and a pound of butter". They were indeed the good old days.

There were photographs of grim-faced men and sour-looking women, standing or sitting stiffly—all, I suspected, more or less unidentifiable by now. It was sad how quickly people's memories faded; I remembered going through an old album of Mother's with Mary, and hearing her puzzle over the snapshots of pudgy babies and laughing girls in flapper costume.

Not a cheerful thought . . . I put the photographs to one side; they were all too recent to come from the period I was interested in.

I found one useful document; a family tree, which looked as if it might have been drawn up by one of the great-aunts. Ran's was the last name on it. I thought, Mary will be interested in this; and then I realized how it might strike her, with Ran's name at the bottom of the sheet, the last of the Frasers, and likely to remain so. It made me feel rather bad for a moment. And then I felt a stir of annoyance, not only at myself for thinking that way, but at the stupid sentimentality of the whole idea. The last of the Frasers—and so what if he was? It was the first time I had considered Mary's desire for children as anything but pathetic. Now I found myself thinking that she had a lot of other things to be thankful for; and that if she was really that keen on kids there were a lot of nice babies who didn't have parents and whose assorted genes had potentialities just as desirable as the sacred genes of the Frasers. All this mystique about old families and blue blood and William the Conqueror . . . What was so great about William the Conqueror anyhow? He was just a bloody-minded illiterate killer like all the other antique kings people are so anxious to add to their family trees. How many people do you know who brag about being descended from Chaucer or Erasmus?

The Fraser family tree was useful, though. Without it I'd never have been able to understand some of the other material. There was a sheaf of letters from a girl named Angela, to a Prudence Fraser, and I found Prudence on the chart. She was Hezekiah's granddaughter, the child of his eldest son Jeremiah. They were entertaining letters, full of gossip about beaux and pretty clothes and parties, and a social historian might have found them fascinating. But they were of no use to me.

Most of the other letters were dull. I found several that dated to the years between 1860 and 1864. They were addressed to a woman named Mercy, from her daughter-in-law in Providence. I felt a stir of interest when I realized that Mercy was Hezekiah's wife. What struck me about those letters, though, was the fact that there were so few references to the war. To most of us those dates immediately conjure up a single overwhelming historical event; and though Mercy and Abigail mentioned bandage rolling and hospital duty, they discussed these things in the same tone in which a modern woman might describe her bridge afternoons. I decided that they must have been very dull women. Then I remembered the letters I had written to Mary during the past year. How often had I discussed current events?

I did wonder about the dates. If Mercy was still alive and kicking in 1864, I thought she must have been a pretty old lady. But when I consulted the genealogy I found that she wasn't all that old. Her husband had been born in 1800 and had died in 1846 . . .

That date made me wonder again. It was the same as the date on Miss Smith's tombstone. Did the coincidence mean anything?

Maybe, but I couldn't even begin to guess what it might mean. It was interesting, though, to realize that "old" Hezekiah had only been forty-six when he died. I had been thinking of him as doddering, with long white whiskers down to his knees. But he had been vigorous and, no doubt, virile, up to the moment of his death. I wondered how he had died. Certainly not of old age. Maybe his wife had poisoned him. If he had been the reprobate his descendants seemed to think he was, she might have had good reason.

Mercy, *née* Barnes, had been born in 1811. I stopped to figure it out, and realized that she was only seventeen when she married Hezekiah in 1828. He had been twenty-eight. It seemed rather late in life for a man of that era to marry. I recalled someone's telling me that the Captain had been a self-made man, and I began to see him more clearly. Proud, arrogant, even; determined to make his fortune and establish his name before he took a wife; able, at that stage in life, to woo and win a bride from a respectable old family. He hadn't wasted any time once he got going; his son Jeremiah had been born in the year following his marriage. Mercy had been eighteen.

I thought of the gently bred girl from Boston, only seventeen years old, coming to this remote place to live as the wife of a man like Hezekiah. Twenty-eight doesn't sound old; but by that time he had been at sea for at least ten years, probably longer, and the reputation that lived on as a family legend could not have described a gentle person. I found myself feeling rather sorry for Mercy. Her first baby at eighteen, and then—I glanced at the genealogy—more babies at two-year intervals thereafter. If the Captain hadn't been gone so much, it probably would have been every year. Nine children, all with good solid biblical names like those of their parents. Five of them had survived infancy. Not a bad average for those days; but it wouldn't help, as you watched a baby die of diphtheria or measles, to know that you were still ahead of the average. No wonder the women of the letters had sounded stilted and cold. They had to be, to survive.

I was romancing a little, by that time. But it's amazing how much you can get out of a few bare names and dates.

I was well through the loose top layer in the trunk by then, and I hadn't found a thing. Then, on the bottom, I saw a pile of books.

There were over a dozen of them, and they half filled the trunk. I reached eagerly for the topmost book. It looked like a diary.

It wasn't a diary, it was a ledger, tall and narrow, bound in red cloth which had faded badly. My spirits sank as I opened it and scanned the entries. "One yard of cotton cloth for a bonnet for Hepzibah, ten cents." "Two pounds of tallow candles for the servants, seven cents." It went on in the same vein, page after page of it, and not even the date—1837—at the top of the first page could arouse my interest. These were Mercy's account books. Young she may have been, but she was not the fragile little piece of fluff I had pictured; she had sailed right into the housekeeping and had done it with vigour. Every penny was tabulated, and the entries showed that she was a woman of a saving disposition. Tallow candles for the servants—wax for the gentry.

I restored the ledger to the trunk and got to my feet. I was stiff after squatting on the floor for so long. It was later than I had realized. I went to the door. Mary's door was open now, and I heard her moving around.

I went down the hall and looked in. My face must have mirrored the uncertainty I felt; she turned, and seeing me, laughed aloud.

"You look like a chipmunk peering nervously out of its hole to see whether the cat is around. Come on in. I don't bite, I just bark a little. You ought to be used to that, Jo."

She was dressed in a long hostess gown that had a bright full skirt of flowered print and a low-cut peasant-style blouse. Sitting at the dressing-table, she was working on her face.

"Wow," I said. "You're giving them the full treatment, aren't you? I love that dress."

She turned, lipstick brush in hand, and looked me over.

"I wish you'd let me get you that trouser suit we saw."

"What for? There's nobody I want to impress."

"And here I thought I was providing you with a nice eligible bachelor."

"You mean Will Graham? Can you see me snowed in half the winter in that cabin of his, up to my elbows in cats?"

"I'm not suggesting that you marry him," my sister said mildly.

She turned back to the mirror and I stood in the doorway watching her. It was the craziest feeling, carrying on this light chatter that had no bearing on what either of us was really thinking. But I knew, instinctively, that I had to play it this way. I couldn't even mention the things Mary didn't want to talk about. I don't know whether she felt schizophrenic; I know I did. And I wasn't sure how long I could keep it up.

Since Ran hadn't returned, I assumed he had located Will and Anne. He had, and obviously they had all found plenty to talk about, because it was late before they got back to the house. Mary and I were in the parlour. She wasn't as cool as she pretended to be; I saw her colour when the front door opened.

She put on a good show, however, as she greeted Anne and offered to show her to her room. They went up the stairs together. Ran followed, carrying Anne's bags.

As soon as they were out of sight I turned to Will.

"Well?"

"Well what?"

"What did you tell her?"

"Yell a little louder, why don't you?" Will said disagreeably. "Then Mary will be sure to hear you."

He stalked into the parlour and I trailed him like an obedient puppy. When I tried again to interrogate him he shrugged irritably.

"Jo, let's not have any whispering in corners, shall we? If anything will increase a patient's delusions of persecution, that's it."

He was right, I guess, though I wouldn't give him the satisfaction of admitting it. Ran and Mary both came down shortly and it wasn't long before Anne joined us. I had seen her glance at Mary's long skirt, so I wasn't surprised when she appeared in an equally glamorous outfit. It was trousers again; the trouser suit fad suited her tall slimness and I imagined she wore them often. This costume, consisting of tunic and trousers, was cocktail wear; it had glitter around the hem of the tunic and across the breasts. The high Chinese collar was plain. The colour, a luscious pale blue with the faintest touch of green, was very becoming to her blonde elegance.

It was a strange evening. There were so many cross-currents in that room that I could almost see them woven like ribbons from wall to wall, crossing and intersecting and tangling as conflicting motives met. It seemed to me that we were all concealing things from one another. The rest of us were trying to

214

deceive Mary, and she certainly was not being candid with us. Will was thinking God
knows what about me and Ran; as for Anne, I
don't think I'd have enjoyed hearing her
private thoughts about any of us.

One thing surprised me, and that was
Mary's reaction to Anne. Several times in the
past few days I wondered if Mary hadn't
somehow found out the truth about Will's
"sister". Now, watching the way the two
women talked together, I realized that it
didn't matter. Mary had responded instantly
to the other woman's charm; they were getting along like old pals. Of course, I told
myself, that was a psychiatrist's business,
winning a patient's confidence. And yet it
made me a little uneasy to watch them.

I thought at first that was why I felt uneasy.
But gradually, as the windows darkened with
twilight, I realized that my growing discomfort was unrelated to anything that was going
on inside the room. It's hard to describe that
sensation; the nearest analogy I can come up
with is the onset of seasickness or flu, the first
stages, when you feel funny but you don't
know why. But this wasn't physical discomfort, it was purely mental. It grew to a point

215

where I couldn't sit still any longer. I got up and went to the window.

It was the loveliest time of day, the soft grey time when the world looks relaxed and at peace but there is still enough light to see clearly. To the east the sky was deep indigo, with a single bright star shining like a beacon; in the west the sunset colours lingered. The light dulled the natural colours of objects but left their outlines clear. So I saw her plain, without any possibility of error.

She was standing on the edge of the paved terrace, not five yards away—closer than she had ever been. I still couldn't make out her features. The hood of the cloak cast a pool of shadow where her face should have been. One thing I knew, if there had been the slightest lingering doubt—the figure was not that of Annie Marks.

The glass I was holding fell from my hand. I was numb with terror, and with a freezing cold that had nothing to do with the temperature of the room. My lips were so stiff I could hardly move them.

"Look," I croaked. "Oh, look. Will!"

It's a sign of how far gone I was that I should call his name. He came; and he put his hand on my bare arm. His hand was warm,

216

warm and living and human, and the touch spread through my chilled bones as brandy spreads.

"Look," I chattered. "Look at her standing there. Will, make her go away, find out what she wants. It gets worse every time, every time she's a little closer . . ."

Will's fingers tightened on my arm with such intensity that the bones felt as if they were grating together. I let out a yell of honest agony. Ran came rushing up thoroughly confused by the whole thing, seeing only that Will was hurting me. He got us untangled and put his arm around me. My eyes were filled with tears of pain, but I twisted my head around so that I could look out of the window.

Shadows on the lawn; but only normal shadows. She was gone.

"That hurt," I said, weeping.

"I'm sorry," Will began.

"It doesn't matter. You saw it. I know you did."

His face was a flat brown mask.

"I didn't see anything," he said.

Anne had come to join us at the window; standing to one side, as if dissociating herself from the fuss, she was lighting a cigarette.

Her eyes met mine, and I knew she was wondering which of the sisters was sick in the head. Both, maybe.

"What was it, Jo?" Ran asked. "What are you talking about?"

"The woman! I told you this morning. The woman in the—"

And then, almost too late, I remembered Mary. I turned. From the depths of the big chair where she sat she watched me with affectionate concern. The mildness of that concern was a bad sign; ordinarily she'd have been fussing over me, demanding to know what had frightened me. I swallowed all the words that were boiling up in my throat, though the effort almost choked me. I hated to imagine the effect a macabre description like the one I was about to make would have on her.

"Just imagination," I said slowly. "Twilight is such a spooky time of night."

I don't suppose anyone believed me. Ran didn't; I could tell by his face that he realized what I was talking about. He looked terrified. And in his fright and concern for Mary he spoke with brutal directness.

"It's not the twilight. It's this damned house. We're getting out of here. Mary,

218

Jo—we'll leave Monday, go back to town. Maybe later on we can go abroad for a few months. It's the wrong time of year for Switzerland, but in June—"

I tried to stop him, but it was too late. Mary came up out of her chair as if propelled by a spring.

"Go away from here?"

She looked as if she were going to faint. Ran went to her, his arms outstretched, but she put him off with a convulsive movement of her hands.

"I won't go, Ran. I won't leave. I like it here. I feel better here. If I go I'll be ill. Really ill."

It was a threat, and Ran knew it. His arms dropped heavily. He stared at Mary with naked fear in his eyes.

Her face softened a little at the sight of his distress. She knew she had won; she could afford some compassion.

"You don't understand, Ran," she said pleadingly; it was as if the two of them were alone in the room. "You must bear, or lose; there is no other way. Just give me a little more time."

"Mary," I said hoarsely.

Mary looked at me.

"No, Jo," she said. "I can't talk now. I have too much to do. Now why don't you sit down and relax? I must—I must speak to Mrs. Willard about something."

She left the room. After a moment Ran followed.

"What was that all about?" Will demanded.

"Blackmail," Anne said coolly. She put out her cigarette. "She's threatening to break down completely if he forces her to leave."

"Oh, that, sure. But what did she mean when she said—"

Ran re-entered the room. Will glanced inquiringly at him and he nodded wearily.

"She's with Mrs. Willard. I just wanted to be sure. You ought to hear her, chatting about *hors d'oeuvres*." He looked at me. "Jed was right, wasn't he? He warned you she wouldn't leave."

"I believe I also mentioned that possibility," Anne said waspishly. She wasn't so pretty or so charming when her professional pride was challenged. "If you hadn't been so abrupt, Mr. Fraser—"

Ran looked like a whipped dog, and I said angrily,

"It wouldn't have made any difference. We knew it probably wouldn't work, but we had to try it. Sure Jed was right; he always is."

"Jed? Who is this Jed you all keep quoting?"

"Somebody call me?"

There he was in the doorway. He must have been there for some time waiting for a chance to interrupt. As Will had said, he had a funny sense of humour. I suspected he was enjoying the look on Anne's face as she compared his lanky overalled form with the expert she had visualized from our respectful comments. She probably expected another psychiatrist.

Ran, who was so totally without snobbery that he never sensed it in other people, introduced the two of them to one another. Jed nodded politely.

"Did you hear what happened?" Ran asked.

"I gather Mary refused to leave the house."

"She said something odd," Will said. "What was all that about 'You must bear or lose'?"

By that time I shouldn't have been surprised at the breadth of Jed's acquaintance with the classics; but I really didn't expect anyone else to recognize that obscure quotation. He did; I could tell by his face. His eyes moved inquiringly from one bewildered face to another, and stopped when they came to me.

"You know it too," he said. "You and Mary must have read the same books."

"There were books all over the house," I said. "In every room, even in the hall. Memory is a funny thing. I couldn't remember my mother's face without the pictures; but I can close my eyes, and see that set of Kipling. It was in a bookcase in the dining-room. Brown cloth bindings stamped in gold. *The Just-So Stories* and *The Jungle Books* were the first, and then *Puck of Pook's Hill*. From the time I was three or four, somebody read to me every night. They took turns—Mother and Dad and Mary. After I learned to read I was insatiable. I tried everything, from Dad's old Hardy Boy books to Shakespeare. A lot of it I didn't understand. But nobody controlled my reading; they explained when I asked questions, and suggested books I might enjoy, but they never . . ."

I stopped, realizing that they were all staring at me. Memory *is* a funny thing. It can rise up, alive and hurting, after years of indifference.

"So," I said. "That's why I know the story. It isn't one of his best-known tales. And nobody reads Kipling these days, do they?

He's too sentimental for modern tastes. This is a particularly sentimental story."

"Wait a minute," Will said. "I knew it was familiar. Sure, it's the story about the blind woman who keeps her house open, furnished with fires and toys—for the ghost children. She can hear them; but the only ones who can see them are the bereaved parents."

"'You must bear or lose'," I quoted. "The narrator of the story was a father. I always wondered if it wasn't semi-autobiographical. Didn't Kipling lose a little girl?"

Anne lit another cigarette.

"Naturally I am aware of the form Mary's delusion has taken," she said. "She believes that the spirit of the child she never had is lost in the dark and is calling to her. Your description of the story fits in very well. But I don't believe it adds anything to what we already know."

She looked so smug. I was rather upset anyway.

"You know, we know, everybody knows," I said. "But you don't know, not really, not with your blood and bones and guts. Damn it, Doctor, you can't help Mary if you won't face the fact that people are sentimental and primitive and uncritical. Our sophistication is a veneer; when trouble strikes, we revert to the emotional patterns of the Middle Ages, or before. I don't know what you think about the soul, or survival after death, or anything like that; the important thing is what Mary believes. I know how she feels because I have the same weakness. The idea of death as a journey—it's only a figure of speech, to describe a transition that is otherwise incomprehensible. But it isn't just an academic description; it has a more complex meaning to some of us. And then when we think about the children . . . It must be terrible to see them start out on such a long, long journey, when we never let them out of the front yard alone. In the dark nights, with rain or snow falling, the thought is unbearable. And no matter how fine a place Heaven may be, we can't believe that they won't feel strange and lonesome there."

"Neither the harps nor the crowns amused,
    nor the cherubs dove-winged races,
Holding hands forlornly, the Children
    wandered, beneath the dome,
Plucking the radiant robes of the passers-by,
    and with pitiful faces

Begging what Princes and Powers
refused:—

'Ah, please will you let us go home?'"

There was a long silence after Jed had finished.
He broke it himself, with an incredibly
cynical chuckle.

"The old boy sure knew how to wring out
the pathos, didn't he?"

I wasn't going to let him get away with it so
easily.

"Don't forget the ending," I said. "'Shall I
that have suffered the children to come to Me
hold them against their will?'"

"This," Anne said, with fastidious distaste,
"is not really a good idea."

To my surprise, Jed nodded vigorously.

"You never said a truer word, Doctor. But
that's the point Jo is trying to make. This
whole subject is emotionally overloaded. A
person can't hardly think about it at all
without these images coming to mind, and
such thoughts can break you to pieces if you
let them. It's like that story, that has such a
grip on Mary. To somebody who doesn't
have that particular weakness it's just a piece
of sentimental foolishness. But what's folly to
you may be life and death to somebody else.

225

That's what Jo is saying—isn't it, Jo? You don't dare sympathize too much, or you end up wallowing in grief. But you can't ignore these things either, or pretend they don't exist. It's awfully hard to avoid falling into one extreme or the other."

I beamed at Jed. He almost had me convinced that that was what I was trying to say. I hadn't realized how smart I was.

II

The hands of the clock moved on towards midnight, and past. My room was in shadow except for the circle of light cast by my reading lamp. The silence and the cool breeze that stirred the white curtains should have made me sleepy, particularly after my activities the night before.

I wasn't sleepy, although the book I was reading was decidedly soporific. It was a history which Ran had pressed upon me, reminding me that I had once, in a moment of mania, expressed an interest in the China trade. The subject had come up at dinner. I think we were all groping rather desperately for something safe and detached to talk about. Although I was becoming convinced that the

226

trouble in the house was bound up with Hezekiah and his family, I didn't see that there was any danger in talking about him so long as Mary didn't suspect any connection.

We actually worked up a certain amount of merriment on the subject of old Hezekiah; I kept teasing Ran about his reluctance to discuss his ancestor's weaknesses, and he finally told us some of the riper stories. I could see why the family hadn't taken any pride in the old boy's exploits. Even in Victorian times there was a certain admiration for a virile, tom-cat type of man; but Hezekiah had an unpleasant weakness for very young girls, and seduction was too kind a word for his sexual techniques.

"Still," Ran said—giving the devil his due—"he was a damn fine seaman. He must have been pretty good to command his own ship at nineteen."

"It wasn't unusual in those days." Will grinned. "The case that impressed me was that of the captain's wife who took over when her husband came down with brain fever. The first mate was in irons for insubordination and the second mate didn't know any navigation. So Mrs. Patten, who had taught herself navigation on an earlier voyage, took command of the ship. She not only nursed her husband through brain fever, but she navigated that clipper ship with its rough, tough crew from Cape Horn to San Francisco. She was nineteen at the time."

"Oh, well, sure," I said feebly. "I'm sure I could have done a little thing like that when I was nineteen . . . You know any more stories to make me feel inferior, or do you want to talk about Hezekiah?"

"I don't think I do," Ran admitted. "Let's stick to his good qualities, shall we?"

"Did he have any?"

"If you consider ambition and ability good qualities. He came up the hard way, through the hawseholes, as they used to say; that means he rose to command from being a foremast hand. By the time he was nineteen he had his own command; by twenty-six he was building his own ships at Bath and had bought this house. That doesn't necessarily mean he was unscrupulous; if you were good enough you could get rich quick. Salaries weren't all that high, but an officer had the privilege of several tons of cargo space on the return trip for his private investment, and also a primage, or commission on the proceeds, after the cargo was sold. Hezekiah bought into a ship-building firm when the trade was expanding enormously and he went on sailing his own ships . . . Anne, you look bored. I'm sorry this is so dull."

She had hidden her yawn behind a well-manicured hand. Now she leaned forwards, her eyes sparkling with amusement.

"Tales of virtuous accomplishments are always dull, aren't they? Let's get back to his vices. He must have been a handsome dog to cut such a wide swath."

"Oddly enough, they say he was an ugly devil."

"They say? Isn't there a portrait of the family hero anywhere about?"

"You'd think there would be. I seem to remember one, but I don't know what's become of it. But he wasn't handsome; he was short and stocky, bowlegged and hairy. He must have had sex appeal, or something; they used to lock their daughters up when Hezekiah's fore-topgallant sails rose up over the horizon. He calmed down a bit after he got married; his wife was the daughter of a Boston shipping family, and he needed her money and connections. Of course he wasn't home much. He had plenty of time and opportunity to indulge in his favourite habits while he was on his travels."

"The old male boast," Anne said. "Enough tall sons of the same age to provide pall-bearers."

"I think that's repulsive," I said.

"It depends on the point of view," said Will.

"Be that as it may," Ran said hastily, "Hezekiah could have done it. They usually stopped at Hawaii on the way out; the ladies of the Sandwich Islands had quite a reputation for beauty and accessibility. Then the big shipping families maintained permanent quarters in Hong Kong, and some had fancy summer homes at Macao. I can see Hezekiah living it up out there in more than oriental splendour. On the homeward voyage they went to Java and Madagascar and the Cape. Not to mention the red lights of New York and Boston."

"Whooping it up around the world," I muttered. "While the wives sat at home scrubbing and baking and nursing sick kids."

Anne laughed.

"Possibly Mrs. Hezekiah was happy to get him out of the house. Really, though, Ran, I don't understand why the family has made such a big thing of his sins. They sound pretty normal."

"It depends on the point of view," I said, glancing at Will. "As to what's normal, I mean."

"The stories that have survived are the expurgated versions," Ran said. "But what really bothers his descendants was the cargo Hezekiah specialized in. He started with tea and silks and the usual things; but there wasn't much demand for European imports in China, so my admirable progenitor turned to opium."

"Oh, great," I said. "A pusher in the family."

"He carried opium to China, not back to New England from China," Ran said. "Maybe I'm being a little hard on him; if we're going to make moral judgements we have to consider the mores of the period. The British had been pushing Indian opium into China for decades. When the Chinese objected, the highly respectable merchants of London and Bristol went to war to make sure they wouldn't lose their profits."

"You mean that's what the Opium Wars were all about?" I asked incredulously. "I've heard about them, but I never realized . . . I had the vague idea that the British got mad because the Chinese were trying to monopolize the trade."

"Quite the contrary," Will said. "The people who want to legalize various forms of cheap euphoria these days don't seem to realize that other countries have tried it and found out that it doesn't work. Even before 1800 the Chinese made the importation of opium illegal. But the good Christian merchants of Europe found the trade too profitable, and by bribing dishonest Chinese officials they kept the stuff coming in. Finally the Chinese government cracked down, and the Europeans rammed drug addiction down the throat of an entire nation by bloody force. Oh, I guess historians will give you a long list of other causes; but that that motive could enter in at all . . . Most New England merchants refused to deal in opium. Maybe their motives weren't all that noble; they were wary of a trade that, being illegal, carried some risks. The fact remains that Hezekiah was the biggest American dealer in opium, and some of his methods for running the stuff in sickened his contemporaries. And they weren't noted for weak stomachs."

That conversation had interested me

enough to make me want to find out more about the subject—hence the book I was now reading. It was a terrible story. Reading history has one therapeutic effect; you realize that we aren't any worse than our ancestors—maybe we've even improved a little. But the book was dully written and after a while even the tragedy of the Opium Wars couldn't keep me interested.

I got up and went to the window. I'll be honest; it took some courage for me to look out. But there was nothing on the lawn except moonlight and the shadows of trees and shrubs. I thought how beautiful it could be here if the terror that haunted Mary could be exorcized—and if I could ever get a good night's sleep. I hadn't done very well with sleeping in this house.

After a while I began to feel drowsy, but still I sat there, arms folded on the sill, looking out into the still beauty of the night. I wished the window weren't screened. I would have liked to thrust my head and shoulders out into the chill air and the moonlight, which looked like crystallized water.

The feeling came on so gradually that I wasn't aware of it for some time. By the time I recognized it, it was too late. I tried to take a deep breath, and couldn't; my chest felt as if it were bound by an iron band.

Then I staggered to my feet, grabbing at the curtains for support, because I heard a certain sound. And it was not outside, defiling the crystal moonlight. It was in the house.

The breeze from the window had not been cold before that, only pleasantly cool; but it was cold now, the air that blew around me had an Arctic chill. My teeth began to chatter. I couldn't move at first, my legs were so numb with cold. Then the crying came again, louder now, and I turned and stumbled towards the door.

My fingers were stiff; they fumbled with the knob. When the door opened there was no rush of warmer air, the hall outside was filled with the same polar cold. Another feeling filled it: a demand, wordless and peremptory, pulling as strongly as gravity pulls a falling body to earth.

I turned left, without hesitation or thought—away from the other inhabited rooms on the corridor, towards the stairs at the end of the hall. There was a dim light in the corridor, but it seemed dimmer than usual, the warm orange of the bulb diminished by the cold. On the enclosed stairs there was no light at all. I felt my way up, my bare feet aching. The rest of my body was shaken continually by shudders.

Perhaps the worst thing about that experience was the fact that beneath the surface compulsion my mind was working normally; and that meant I was aware of the horror that pulled at my limbs, and my helplessness to resist. My brain felt like a captive animal, twisting and biting at the invisible cords that held it.

I came out on to the familiar landing, and there was light again, from the small window on the wall. It was a chilly, pallid light, the visible emanation of the cold that numbed me. The crying was all around me now, it filled my head with a buzzing agony of sound. When my obedient body stopped before a certain door, my mind knew it, and was not surprised. The captive hand reached for the knob and turned it; and the door swung open.

Moonlight cast the shadow of the barred windows out across the dusty floor. Thicker shadows clustered batlike in the gaping mouth of the open fireplace. The room was not empty. It was filled with sounds and movements. Mice, said the last desperate voice of sanity inside my beleaguered brain;

mice, the sounds when an old house settles . . . With a creaking shiver, the white bulk of the rocking horse swayed. A chiming echo, almost too dim to be heard, might have been the ghost of a music box, sounding faintly across a century.

The cold was savage here, this was the core from which it came. I stood as if frozen to the floor, incapable of movement. The crying had stopped when I opened the door, but the shifting hints of movement were worse than the sound. Then I turned my head and saw her standing by the cupboards in the farthest corner.

I saw her take shape. If I had ever hoped to deny her nature I could no longer do so; she formed her body out of the shadows themselves, wrapping them around her like garments. There was a ray of moonlight, I think; or perhaps she shone by her own pale light. I saw her face plainly now. The hood was thrown back . . . No, the hood and the cloak were gone. Of course, I thought; she is inside the house. One does not wear a cloak or coat inside. I felt my unwilling feet move, carrying me through the door and into the room.

Her dress was dark, as the cloak had been,

236

but there was a suggestion of white at throat and wrists—or was it only the moonlight shining through her? The hair was dark, pulled smoothly back. The eyes . . . My eyes dropped, affronted by those pits of darkness. Her other features were uncannily distinct—the long tight mouth and narrow nose, the uncommon breadth of the cheekbones and the way the face narrowed abruptly to a pointed chin. There was a mole near the corner of her mouth—the left corner.

I thought at first that her absolute stillness was her most terrifying attribute. It was horrible because it violated the normal categories of experience. No statue could counterfeit life so expertly; no living thing should be so still. There is some movement, however slight, in any living creature—the lift of the breast, the beat of the pulse in the throat. No pulse, no breath moved the creature that stood before me.

I was wrong, though. Her stillness was horrible, but motion would have been worse. I knew, because she tried to move.

I saw the hideous effort before I heard the sound that must have prompted it; but that sound was perhaps the only thing that could have broken my paralysis. With an effort so great that it felt like muscles snapping, I turned away from the writhing white face and pushed my resisting body into position across the doorway. The footsteps I had heard were running; and as my arm went out, barring the door, Mary threw herself against it.

I was stronger than she was, even then. The cold that sapped my strength weakened her too, I heard her teeth chattering. It seemed to me, though, that the cold was slightly less; or perhaps it was my need that warmed me, the need to keep Mary, by any means, from seeing the thing that stood in the corner, fighting to break whatever bonds held it motionless. I forced Mary back out of the doorway; and then my numbed throat relaxed, and I yelled at the top of my lungs.

The sound was horrible in that ringing silence; I was appalled myself at the crash of it. It did seem to crash, and it seemed to break something. I knew, without looking behind me, that the shadowy form was gone. Mary drooped forwards over my arm, and simultaneously I heard voices and pounding footsteps below as the others woke and came after us.

8

"I DON'T know why we don't just give up," Ran said, and grinned feebly at me as I turned a startled face towards him. "I mean, give up trying to keep a normal schedule. We could sleep all day and face the fact that we're going to be up all night."

Will was not amused.

"This can't go on much longer," he said. "It's too hard on all of us physically—not to mention the other effects. And I can't stay here every night. I've got my little responsibilities at home."

"You're being here didn't make any difference tonight," I said.

"No." Unoffended, Will studied me with interest. "You were the heroine tonight. Now that the pandemonium has subsided, would you care to tell us what happened?"

"Oh, for God's sake," I said wearily. "Let's not have another conference now. I'm dead tired."

That wasn't the reason why I didn't want to talk. Anne was with us. She hadn't ap-

239

peared until most of the excitement was over, and her impeccable coiffure and make-up filled me with fury. I didn't blame her for not wanting to appear in the curlers and night cream I was sure she used, but any doctor who puts her appearance ahead of an emergency is a lousy doctor.

She was wearing a gorgeous pink robe which flattered her complexion. She crossed her legs and looked at me.

"It must be nearly dawn," she said.

"It's two a.m.," I said crossly, swallowing a yawn. "I haven't been to bed at all."

"Then you were awake when Mary left the room," Ran said. "I wondered why I didn't hear her and you did."

"I didn't hear Mary. I heard the crying." I had stopped worrying about Anne and what she thought. "It was the same sound we heard that other night, only it came from inside the house. I followed it, up to the tower, to the room that used to be the nursery. She was there—the woman. I saw her face this time, saw it so plainly that I'd recognize her in the middle of a crowd. Mary followed me, or else she heard the crying too, I don't know. When I heard her I knew I had to keep her out of that room—"

"Why?" Anne asked. She didn't sound critical, only curious. The question irritated me, all the same—probably because there was no reasonable answer.

"I don't know why. I just knew she shouldn't go in there. It was wrong. Bad."

"I see," Anne sat back in her chair and reached for a cigarette.

"You didn't see, that's just the trouble. Unless you've experienced something like this personally, you can't believe it." I turned to Will, who was watching me with a face as unreadable as Sanskrit. "I don't blame you either, but I'll be damned if I can understand why you didn't see that—that thing—on the terrace this evening."

"I did," Will said. He added, "Why do you think I almost squeezed your arm off?"

I gaped at him, torn between relief and anger.

"You son of a gun," Ran said. "Why the hell didn't you speak up?"

"In front of Mary?" Will hesitated. "Okay, I'll be honest. It really threw me, that's why. I didn't know what to say, so I just kept my mouth shut."

Anne cleared her throat and got up.

"Mr. Fraser. I'm not trying to put you on

the spot. But—it was you who came to me, if you recall; if you have decided to dispense with my services, that's up to you. However, if you want me to stay on, I think you ought to be candid with me. All of you."

Will crossed the room and put his hand on Anne's arm. They made an odd couple standing there together, she in her immaculate elegance and Will with his hair standing straight up on end, wearing a robe that most tramps would have sneered at. But his smile was persuasive. I wasn't surprised when her stiff face relaxed and she smiled back at him.

"Sit down," Will said. "You're right, Doctor, we owe you an apology and an explanation. After you've heard it, you'll probably walk out on us. I wouldn't blame you."

It was a masterful exposition that he gave, accurate and impartial. The last shred of Anne's antagonism vanished as she listened. When he had finished she said thoughtfully.

"I—honestly, I don't know what to say. You've missed your calling, Will. If anyone else had told me a story like that one, I'd have laughed. Or, as you said, walked out."

"It's true," I said. "Every word of it."

"Jo." Will glared at me. "I know exactly how Anne feels. You see—" He turned back

242

to Anne, and I saw the way his eyes shone, his anxiety to convince her. "You don't know, Anne, how we have been literally forced into this explanation. You don't know Bertha Willard. I do, and I tell you, it's easier for me to believe in ghosts than to think Bertha would imagine something like this. Nor have you heard the weeping; it is indescribable. Without that background it's no wonder you're sceptical. I would be too."

"And neither of you knows Jo the way I do," Ran said. "She isn't subject to hallucinations either. Nor does she lie."

"Thanks," I said. "I needed that."

"You are all convinced, then," Anne said briskly, "that the phenomena are supernatural?"

She looked soberly and inquiringly from one to the other. No one spoke; I guess the word still embarrassed us. She nodded.

"I see. Well, in that case—excuse me if I put it badly—but I don't understand what you want with a psychiatrist. Shouldn't you consult the SPR, or a medium?"

I didn't realize, at first, why the idea shocked me so. I turned to Ran and saw the same repugnance in his face. Will said violently,

"Good God, no. That's the last thing we need!"

"That's interesting." Anne got out another cigarette. She glanced at Will, but he was lost in an unpleasant reverie, frowning at his own thoughts; and after a moment she shrugged, smiled slightly, and reached for the table lighter. She went on, "Why does the suggestion rouse such consistent and violently negative feelings?"

"My patients up here don't go in for séances," Will said. "But I've read of cases of people getting hooked on spiritualism. A fraudulent medium can prey on the patient's emotions and worsen the fixation."

"Oh, certainly," Anne said. "And many, if not most, of the practitioners are frauds. Even a sincere stupid hysteric could do considerable damage. But they aren't all frauds, you know. The Society for Psychical Research is a reputable body."

"No," I said. "No séance. Good Lord, no."

"Why not?"

I knew that sooner or later she was going to ask "why" once too often, and I was going to blow my top. But I hadn't quite reached the boiling point yet. And damn it, it was a fair question.

Why not?

"Oh, I know the answer," I said gloomily. "And I'll bet Ran and Will feel the same way, even if they are too chicken to admit it. I'm not afraid of a fake medium, or a séance that flops. I'm afraid of one that might succeed."

Ran nodded in silent agreement. He looked disturbed, but I knew he couldn't possibly be as revolted by the idea as I was. He hadn't seen the thing that would come in answer to such a summoning.

"Why should you be reluctant to admit that?" Anne asked in her dulcet professional tones. "Given your basic premise it's a perfectly reasonable fear. But let's pursue this argument one step further. If you are, in fact, dealing with a—what did Hamlet call it?—a perturbed spirit, then surely there is only one thing you can do. If the spirit is earthbound and unhappy, it ought to be laid to rest. Isn't that right?"

She had selected me as her opposite in the discussion, and as her cool, intent eyes fixed themselves on my face, I felt the way I used to feel when debating with a more skilful opponent. I was being backed into a corner by logic even while I knew, with a sense that transcended logic, that I was right. I always had a sneaking sympathy for Socrates' opponents in those dialogues.

"Yes," I said reluctantly. "I guess so."

"No, you mustn't agree with me out of politeness," Anne cooed. "If you have reservations, speak up."

I gave myself a mental shake.

"If the spirit is human and earthbound," I said, "then—well, according to the stories I've read, you call in a priest or minister and exorcize it. There's a procedure, isn't there?"

"No," Anne said decisively. "I mean, there is a procedure, but you don't want that. You've never heard the service, I don't imagine. I have. It casts the spirit into outer darkness. 'I exorcize thee, thou foul spirit . . . in the name of our Lord Jesus Christ be rooted out and put to flight from this creature of God.' And so on."

"How the hell did you know that?" Will asked.

"One of my patients thought he was possessed," Anne said briefly. "I hardly think the effect on Mary would be beneficial."

"You are so right," I muttered. "Good heavens . . . So why did you bring it up?"

"You brought it up," Anne said, with a

246

slight snap in her voice. "I didn't mention exorcism. I was thinking of another procedure entirely. Modern spiritualists don't exorcize an unhappy spirit, they try to reassure it and, if you'll pardon the expression, push it over the threshold into Paradise."

We were all silent, thinking this over; then Will cleared his throat.

"What exactly do you have in mind?"

"It's only a suggestion; I'd certainly have to consider it from several angles before proposing it seriously," Anne said. "But if you insist, Doctor—I am thinking of a ceremony during which Mary's ghost could be re-assured—and could reassure her."

"A dramatic performance, in short," Will said in a peculiar voice. "With a record of the Sistine Chapel choir at the end fading off into celestial silence. Where would we get a ventriloquist at such short notice?"

"I know it's unorthodox therapy," Anne said tightly. "But sometimes shock treatment is necessary. Mary's case is extraordinary. I've never seen anything quite like her behaviour, and I can assure you I've had a great deal of experience. I also have a feeling, although I can't justify it logically, that she is approaching a crisis of some sort. Rapidly."

"I have the same feeling," Will muttered. "Oh, hell, I don't know what to say. I'll tell you frankly, Anne, the idea of a fake séance repels me. I know, I know, it might work. But I don't like kidding my patients."

"You'd lie to a child, wouldn't you, if the truth would hurt it beyond endurance?"

"Just a minute," Ran said. There was an authority in his voice that stopped all discussion. "You two are the experts, I know; but I'm the one who has to make the final decision, isn't that right? Anne, I want to apologize to you for putting you in an awkward position. All I can say in extenuation is that we didn't see this thing taking shape until after I had consulted you. Of course I'm hoping that you'll bear with us. We need your expertise, and your scepticism; maybe we're all a little bit crazy. But at this time I am definitely against a séance."

"You're a very honest man," Anne said, giving him a charming smile.

"Me, too," Will said quickly. "I agree with Ran."

She transferred the smile to him and gave him her hand as a bonus.

"Let's be friendly opponents, then," she said. "All open and aboveboard."

They gazed into each other's eyes over their clasped hands. I stood up. I had to move to keep myself from saying something disagreeable.

"I'm honest, too," I said. "But I'm not open-minded. I'm a mass of prejudices, and what I want to do right now is talk to Jed. He's the only one in the house who knows what he thinks, and why."

I had heard his footsteps in the hall, so his appearance wasn't the conjuring trick it appeared to be. Standing in the doorway, he greeted us with a collective nod.

"Mary's asleep," he said. "Bertha sent me down to report."

"Good," Ran said. "Jed, we've been levelling with Dr. Wood. She thinks we're all out of our minds, but she's being very tactful about it."

"That's fine." Jed sat down. "You know how I feel—the fewer lies the better. We're going to have to start making some progress on this thing. I don't like the way it's moving in on Jo."

"Neither does Jo," I said. "It isn't just getting closer, it's getting clearer. I saw the face as distinctly as I see yours."

"That plain?"

"Down to the mole on her cheek," I said, and shivered involuntarily. "It was fantastic, Jed; like a life-sized photograph, that was how it was."

"Describe it, then," Will said. "While it's fresh in your mind."

Jed coughed

"Didn't somebody tell me Jo was an artist?" he inquired of the room at large.

"I'm not thinking," Ran said ruefully. "Jo, can you do it? Can you sketch the woman?"

"I'm not sure. Portraiture was never one of my strong points, I'm just a hack . . ."

Jed got up and began to ransack the walnut escritoire by the window. He came back with a handful of Mary's stationery and an assortment of writing materials. I found a pencil that wasn't too hard, though I really needed something softer for those shadowy outlines; but after the first few tentative lines the picture took shape with a speed that scared me a little. It was almost as if some outside force were controlling my hand.

They all watched, peering over my shoulder. Anne had forgotten her scepticism, and leaned over the couch breathing down the back of my neck as I sketched the pale face, wide at the cheekbones, narrowing to the small delicate chin; the fine shape of the nose, and the smooth black hair. I couldn't do much with the eyes; I shaded the sockets and smudged them with the ball of my thumb, and then went on to fill in the body, increasingly absorbed as the pencil moved, producing details that seemed to come from some other source than my conscious memory. When the sketch was done I sat back and looked at it, and was amazed at what I saw. There was no doubt about the costume. It was a plain dark dress, high-necked, with long tight sleeves and a skirt gathered at the waist—a full, bell-shaped skirt, but without hoops. The white I had observed at the neck and wrists were collar and cuffs—plain, without lace or ornament. Even the hair style was distinctive, drawn back from a central parting in sloping wings across the temples and ears into a heavy knot or chignon at the back.

I glanced at the others to see how they were reacting; and found Will looking at me with respect.

"You're good," he said.

"I'm not really that good," I admitted. "I'll cast modesty to the winds and admit that this is the best portrait I've ever done. And there are things in it I don't remember seeing. Do you suppose I'm inventing—filling in, restoring?"

"I think you're doing just that," Jed said, without looking up from the drawing. He scratched his chin reflectively. "Restoring. That doesn't mean you're inventing anything, but your trained muscles dredge up details you think you've forgotten."

Ran was staring at the drawing.

"You didn't say she was beautiful."

Startled, I glanced at the drawing.

"Beautiful is not exactly . . . Oh. Well, the bones are good, aren't they? But the mouth, I don't remember it as being quite so—so soft. Damn it, Ran, you're right. She is beautiful in a strange, haggard sort of way—and the thing I saw wasn't, believe me. So I haven't got it right."

"Wait a minute." Jed's long fingers caught my hand as I reached for the pencil. "It is right, Jo. Don't start messing it up."

"Jed, do you recognize it? Do you know who she is?"

"No, I don't know who she is. But I've

seen that face somewhere. I know it. That's how I know it's right."

"What about you, Ran? Maybe she's an ancestress."

"No . . ." Ran sounded uncertain, though; and Will said,

"Jed, are you sure it isn't the general appearance of the lady that's familiar to you? I've seen dresses and hair styles like that—even the pose—in old daguerreotypes. I had that same feeling of half recognition myself, till I realized what it was."

"Yes," Ran said. "That's right, Will. That was why I hesitated."

Jed shook his head.

"No, I've seen that face. If I could only remember where!"

II

It was a nice day to spend in a graveyard—grey and cool with ground mist gathering among the trees. I don't think I'd have had the nerve to go by myself. The wisps of pale vapour coiling among the dark tree trunks were too suggestive.

Not that Will was the most cheerful companion in the world. I assumed he was sorry he was with me instead of being back at the house admiring Anne's professional brilliance and her blue stretch trousers. But I really didn't care. I was tired and depressed, and the weather made me feel mournful, and I didn't believe in happy endings.

Mary's condition was as ambiguous as it had been after the other midnight adventure. She was still pretending not to remember. Will was ready to admit that she might be suffering from a form of amnesia. He said that when people found it impossible to accept something, they just cut it out of their memory. Mary's fixation could affect her that way, because her rational mind must know the illogic of what she wanted. I suggested tentatively that maybe this was a good sign—that part of her mind, at least, was still able to distinguish fantasy from reality. Will said he was damned if he knew what it was.

"You may not like this," he said gloomily, pushing a dead branch out of the way as we went along the narrow path, "but I have the feeling that Mary is putting on a big fat act. I get glimpses of something sly and furtive in her expression. I never felt that way in the beginning."

"I feel it too. Some hostile mind looking out at me through Mary's eyes."

"For God's sake, Jo, you aren't suggesting—"

"Possession? No. That's the worst of it. There's nothing alien about the look, it's Mary; but it's as if something had concentrated all the nasty side of Mary, all the meanness and hatred we all have in us somewhere. She's baiting Ran; I wouldn't have blamed him if he'd socked her one this morning."

"You mean those cracks at breakfast about the way he's been drinking?"

"Yes, and all expressed in the sweetest, most solicitous terms. He's not an alcoholic, Will; he used to be almost abstemious. But to hear her, you'd think she had to pour him into bed every night."

"It's partly defensive, I think," Will said. "She wants to make the rest of us look bad so we can't criticize her. She's not openly hostile towards you, but she's not precisely forthcoming, either. That's a disappointment. I was hoping she'd talk candidly to you."

I kicked at a stone in the path.

"I goofed," I said, without looking at him. "I had a chance and I muffed it."

"What do you mean?"

"The very first day she was trying to reach me. When she appealed to me not to let you and Ran take her away, she was sounding me out. I was so dumb; I thought she meant—oh, well, I might as well get all my evil thoughts out in the open. I thought you two were planning to have her committed, shut up in a mental institution."

"You thought Ran would do a thing like that?"

"But it might have been necessary. I did have some doubts about Ran; you aren't the only one who considered ordinary human wickedness as the only alternative to the supernatural."

"*Touché*," Will said dryly. "So long as we're indulging in an orgy of self-recrimination, I'll admit the possibility did pass through my mind."

"I thought it did. That Ran and I were conspiring to get rid of Mary."

Will stopped so suddenly that I bumped into him. He turned.

"You and Ran? I thought of Ran, but . . ."

I stared up into his face, warmed by an absurd wave of pleasure; and then Will proceeded to spoil it by adding coolly,

"You were in San Francisco when the

trouble began. Oh, hell, Jo, it was just a passing thought; I know Ran too well to take it seriously. I was surprised—is that a good word?—when I came on you two the other night, but I didn't need Ran's explanation to understand what had happened, once I had time to think it over. That's true, Jo."

"Will, you don't think Mary could have seen us, do you?"

"I didn't see any sign of her. Oh, I suppose she could have; or maybe she suspected something from your behaviour . . . Why? Do you think that's why she stopped trusting you?"

"I don't know. Something happened; or maybe it was just my response, or lack of response, to her statement about hearing the crying. If I had only tried . . . Well, it's futile to think about that now. I've lost her. The only one she seems to want around is Anne. And I don't like that."

I regretted the words as soon as they were spoken. I sounded as if I were jealous of Anne's influence with Mary. And maybe I was.

"You ought to be pleased," Will said reproachfully. "If Anne weren't baby-sitting Mary, the rest of us couldn't be out pursuing our no-doubt futile research."

"Do you really think its futile?"

"Oh, today is one of those days when I think everything is futile. Don't mind me. We have to do this, so let's not argue about whether it's worth doing."

"You did show Mrs. Willard the drawing?"

"Yeah. Same reaction Jed had; it's familiar but she can't remember where she saw it."

"Too bad the old ladies donated so many records and pictures to the museum."

"It's less convenient having them there, but Ran won't have any trouble getting at them, even today. The old guy who runs the museum fawns on Frasers."

The path broadened out as it reached the graveyard, and Will waited for me to catch up with him. He had preceded me because of the obstructed condition of the path. Instead of entering the clearing he leaned against the fence and reached for his cigarettes. In silence he offered me the pack and in silence I took a cigarette and waited for him to light it. I was no more anxious to enter the cemetery than he was. In fact, I wasn't sure why I had wanted to come.

"I don't know what we're doing here," Will said, breaking the silence. The thought was so akin to my own that I started a little.

"We're on our way to feed your cats, I think," I said.

"And pick up the car."

"Why did you leave it at home yesterday?"

"It had a flat tyre, and I was late."

"So you'll have to fix the tyre now."

"Yep. Cheerful thought."

Off in the woods there was a rustle and squawk, as some bird expressed annoyance. The sound was distorted, mournful. I shivered.

"Horrible day. Isn't the sun going to shine?"

"We may be in for one of our fogs," Will said. "This is the area where the expression pea-souper originated. Maine has more fog-bound days per year than any other state in the union."

"You're probably just bragging. Though why that should be anything to brag about . . ."

He didn't respond, and I let the words trail off, too dispirited to talk. There was a melancholy peace about the scene; but the hideous Gothic mausoleum with the fog around it was like something out of a stage set for *Dracula*.

"Well," my companion said, after a time. "I guess she isn't going to show up."

"Don't," I said, glancing over my shoulder at the mist-shrouded spot where the grave lay.

"Wasn't that why you wanted to come this way?"

"Certainly not."

"Really? I was hoping she would materialize. I'd like to get a good look at her."

"That's what you think now."

"That bad, hmmm?"

I shivered. Will said thoughtfully, "That's odd. The face you sketched didn't convey that feeling."

"It wasn't the look of it," I said, groping for words. "It was the atmosphere. The cold, the whole feeling—"

"I know. Like a nightmare in which the events themselves are quite prosaic. It's hard to describe something like that. Why did you want to come to the graveyard then, if the idea of seeing her bugs you so?"

"I had some vague idea of looking at the stone again, to make sure there was nothing else on it."

"There wasn't. I saw it too, remember?"

"Well, if you say so. I don't particularly want to go near the place."

"Okay." As we stood side by side, his shoulder touched mine, and I let myself lean, just a little. It felt so solid and supportive. He went on, "I thought maybe you were going to ask me to dig up the grave."

"Will!" I stared at him in horror. "Of all the awful ideas . . . Why would I want to do that?"

"It's not such a crazy idea—after you've accepted our original crazy premise, I mean."

He went on smoking placidly, leaning on the wet black iron bars; and I thought about the idea. It was still horrible, but it had a grisly attraction.

"Why?" I asked. "Could you tell anything, after all this time? From just—"

"Just bones? Not much. Signs of foul play? Poison wouldn't leave a trace, neither would a knife or a bullet unless it nicked a bone. Even supposing we found overt signs of violence, that could be caused by a number of things. A fractured skull might be the result of a fall."

"No one has even suggested the idea of—of murder," I said. "But that's one of the conventional reasons for a ghost walking, you know. For vengeance, or to right a wrong, or . . . Will, would you mind very much if we continued this discussion in your living-room, with all the lights on?"

He didn't answer or turn his head. He was staring out across the clearing. Finally he said, in a muted voice,

"Look at the way the fog gathers, there beyond the stones. You can see how ghost stories begin, when you watch fog; that patch over there is the right size and shape, and the way it moves with the breeze almost suggests—"

"Stop that!"

"Sorry." He turned his head and looked at me. His eyes shone with amusement. "That wasn't bad, was it? I really scared you."

"You aren't at all superstitious, are you?"

"Not at all." He rested his elbow on the fence and studied me quizzically. "But I think I know what your trouble is."

"What."

"You're hopelessly sentimental. A sucker for every corny cliché and every hackneyed emotion in the book."

"Why fight it?" I said listlessly. "You're absolutely right. You name it, I'll cry over it. 'Danny Boy', with lots of violins; all the songs ever written about hopeless love and angel children; 'The little toy dog is covered with dust, But sturdy and staunch he stands';

the statue of Nathan Hale; the Blue and the Grey, and *Uncle Tom's Cabin*—"

"How about 'Up the hill to the poorhouse I'm trudgin' my weary way'?"

I laughed unwillingly.

"Oh, well, I guess there's a limit. But it's far out, and I don't mean that as slang. Some of my friends have taken up old movies and books, as camp and chic. When Shirley Temple pleads for the life of her soldier daddy, guess who's the only one crying?"

"Anne would say you're too suggestible to be a reliable observer," Will said.

"But that's just it. I know I'm susceptible, and that's why I'm especially sceptical of my own feelings. Look, I can read *Gone with the Wind* and feel my heart bleed for the beautiful gallant South, but even while the tears are running down my face, I know that the gallant South is a fiction and that its position was morally indefensible."

"All right, all right," Will said. "I believe you. And in deference to your sensitivities, we'll postpone further discussion till we get home."

On the cliff edge the fog wasn't bad; the sea breeze whipped most of it away. But Will predicted worse to come.

"The wind won't hold," he said. "By late afternoon this stuff will have closed in, and you won't be able to see your hand in front of your face."

"I wonder . . ."

"What?"

"Oh, nothing." I was wondering whether the weather would keep Anne from leaving as scheduled. The thought of her staying on filled me with a depression which, I preferred to believe, had nothing to do with my personal feelings towards anybody at all.

Will had thoughts of his own about the practical difficulties of fog.

"I think I'll stay at the house again tonight."

"Why?"

"Oh, I've no reason to anticipate anything. I was just thinking that I'd hate to have Mary get out tonight if the fog does close in."

Which was another cheerful thought.

Fortunately the activities of the next half-hour were practical enough to cancel the effects of fog and pessimism. Will's house grew on me. Even when it was dark and unheated it was a warm place; the walls closed in and shielded the inhabitants. I realized for the first time that day what comedians cats are; in some ways they're funnier than dogs because they're not trying to be entertaining or ingratitating. The performance the Siamese put on for Will would have done credit to Duse; they all but fainted at his feet, trying to suggest emaciation, starvation, and heartless neglect. The coon cats were more direct. They shrieked in various keys, from soprano to tenor, but the burden of the refrain was the same—abandonment and agonizing hunger. If I hadn't known that he had made a special trip home the night before to feed the wailing felines, I'd have thought they hadn't eaten for a week. The dogs just sat and drooled, with their big sad eyes focused on Will. From the next room came various other animal signals of distress. The only ones who weren't yelling were the snakes, and they would have if they could.

I made coffee while Will was opening cans for the crowd, but we had to drink it standing, so to speak; Will was anxious to get to town. His patients had been considerately healthy for the last twenty-four hours, but there were a couple of them he wanted to check up on.

"On Sunday?" I said incredulously. "House calls? Nobody makes house calls."

"I do," said Will. "Have another cup of coffee while I change the tyre."

"I'll help you."

"Hah," said Will.

The phone rang just then, and I gathered from Will's end of the conversation that he was going to have a new patient when he got to town, so I went out and started on the tyre. I had the car jacked up and the wheel ready to come off by the time he came charging out; and although he shouldered me out of the way with hardly more than a grunt of thanks, I did get one of those rare looks of approval from him. I wondered what a girl had to do to be rewarded by, say, a hearty "Well done", or a slap on the back. Build a log cabin, maybe, or take out a tonsil. Not that I wanted a slap on the back . . .

As we bounced off along the track, he asked, "Where did you learn to change a tyre? Not from Ran; he hasn't done anything to dirty his hands since he was a kid."

"I've learned to do a lot of things this past year. I couldn't afford to pay a mechanic or a plumber or a maid every time some little thing went wrong. So I learned to change my own tyres and sew on my own buttons.

What's so strange about that? Millions of people do."

"Millions of people don't have a millionaire for a brother-in-law."

"I'm just trying to impress you," I said flippantly, "with my pioneer virtues and strong muscles. What's the matter with the newest patient, the one who called just before we left?"

He took the hint.

"Probably just a belated virus. Tommy Meservey was what they call a ten month's child, and he's been a month late for everything ever since. But his mother is the nervous type. She reads medical journals in her spare time. Which is more than I do."

We stopped at the garage to leave the tyre and then Will dropped me in the centre of town while he proceeded on his rounds. We had arranged to meet in an hour at the drugstore. I was supposed to join Ran at the museum, where he was presumably buried in the family records. But as I turned away, after watching the old blue station wagon turn the corner, I found myself in front of Sue's Antiques. The face peering at me through the window, Sunday morning or not, was indubitably that of Sue.

The door of the shop opened and she called to me.

"Jo? If you aren't going any place in particular, come on in and have some coffee." I walked towards her and she added, with her wide grin, "You looked sort of bereft standing there. Maybe it's the fog; it makes everything look lost and dreary."

"I don't feel especially dreary," I said.

"Oh, you know what I mean."

"Sure, I know." I returned her grin; there was no point in finding offence where none was meant. Malice, I felt sure, was not one of Sue's vices. "I'm supposed to meet Ran. But I don't have to be there for an hour."

She closed the door behind me but did not lock it; and I asked,

"Are you open on Sunday? I don't want to interrupt your work."

"I'm open any hour of the day or night that anybody wants to buy something. Trade isn't so brisk that I can afford to pass up a customer. I've been accused of dragging them in off the street."

She grinned again, and brushed back a lock of shining hair with smudgy fingers that added another streak of dust to features already liberally covered. I accepted the coffee she poured, though I was dubious about it. My hunch was right, the liquid was as black and bitter as medicine. Sue swallowed hers down, and wiped her hands on her shirt-tail.

"I'm going to go on working, if you don't mind. I picked up a bunch of miscellaneous junk on the mainland the other day—had to take it to get a terrific old spool bed. I want to get it sorted before tomorrow. Are you interested in old prints? I have a few, on that shelf back there by the books. Look 'em over if you want to."

I didn't expect to find anything rare; Sue was too competent to be unaware of the value of the stock she handled. But some of the drawings were pretty and amusing. I found one that really appealed to me. I was holding it up, admiring it, when Sue came wandering back, carrying another cup of coffee.

The print was of a sailing ship, caught in motion by the artist. The waves peeled crisply away from its prow, and every yard of sail was up.

"Isn't it beautiful?" I said.

"Should be. That's the *Flying Cloud*, the most beautiful clipper ever built. And the clippers were the most beautiful things that ever sailed the sea."

"I wonder if Ran's ancestor, the Captain, sailed ships like this."

Sue snorted.

"You're way off. First clipper wasn't launched till 1845. First real clipper, I mean; the *Anne McKim* wasn't a true clipper, she was square-rigged on all three masts and her plan makes her a ship, not a clipper; I don't care what you say—"

"I don't say anything," I said respectfully. "You know a lot about ships, don't you?"

"Should. My family's from Bath. Most of the fortunes in this part of the world were made from shipbuilding and/or the East India trade. The way Bostonians talk, you'd think none but Massachusetts ships ever crossed the Pacific. That's Massachusetts bull. The Maine captains knew Canton as well as they knew Portland a century and a half ago. Hey—that reminds me."

She ducked down out of sight under the counter. There was an interval of muttering and scrabbling, and then she reappeared, with dust in her bright hair and a grin on her face.

"Look at this."

It was a box, about eight inches square and six inches high. Made of some light-reddish wood, it was completely covered with carvings in bas-relief. Dragons and flowers and twining vines, butterflies, snakes, beetles—every form except the human had furnished an inspiration. It sat on four small feet carved with claws, and it had handles and a clasp of tarnished silver metal.

"Chinese?" I asked. "It's charming. Is this one of the things your Maine captains brought back from Canton?"

"Not just any old Maine captain. This is one of Hezekiah Fraser's treasures. Remember I told you and Mary about the things the old ladies sold me?"

"That's right, I'd forgotten. But how do you know this belonged to Hezekiah?"

"He was the only sea captain in the family," Sue said. "Didn't Ran tell you about him? His son didn't follow in his footsteps; he took over the family business, and the Frasers have been businessmen ever since. So I assume this is one of Hezekiah's imports. His carryings-on in the Orient have made local legend, you know."

"I did hear about that. He must have had a regular harem out there."

"Well, I don't know about that, but I do know this box has been worrying me. There are a few chairs and an inlaid table in the back, and if Ran wants to drop by and look at them, I'd be pleased. But this—it seemed to me Ran might want it if it really was one of the old Captain's souvenirs. It's a nice piece of work, too. Can you take it along now, or is it too heavy?"

"No." I lifted the box experimentally. "It isn't heavy, and the car should be right down the street. No problem. Ran will drop in one of these days and reimburse you."

"He can have it for what I paid for it." Sue smiled. "Plus four per cent. I'm a businesswoman."

"And a very nice gal." I picked up the box. "I'd better get going."

Sue peered out the shop window.

"Is that Ran, looking for you? It's so hard to see in this fog . . . No, it's not Ran. It's Will Graham."

"I imagine he's on his way to meet Ran. Nobody knows I'm here, so I'd better run."

She put her hand on my arm.

"Hey, Jo. One more thing."

I glanced at her. She was smiling broadly.

"What is it?"

"You've heard about me and Will? No, don't be polite, I know you have."

"I understand that you were engaged once."

"And that I broke his heart?"

"Well . . ."

"Honestly, the people in this town." She sighed. "And Will is the worst of the bunch. *He* jilted *me*, Jo, that's the honest-to-God truth. You know Will—or maybe you don't. He was very fond of me; I think he still is. But he knew marriage wouldn't work for us, and he's not the type to go nobly into some dumb fool thing when he knows it's a mistake. In order to save my face here in town, he told people that I had broken the engagement; it's better to look like a hard-hearted flirt than an unwanted woman, you see."

"But . . . the way he acts . . ."

"Act is the word. It's partly conscience, too; the darned fool still feels guilty."

"He doesn't need to." I was suddenly quite sure of that.

"No." Her eyes—clear and blue and smiling—met mine. "Oh, I wasn't very happy for a while. But I realized he was right. I'm too bullheaded and independent to get along with a man as domineering as Will is. Now I'm not sure I ever want to marry. I'm enjoying my freedom. But it would be nice if Will and I could be friends again; I'd enjoy talking to him now and then."

"I know what you mean," I said. "But sometimes I think men come from a different species altogether. They have the weirdest ideas . . . Except Jed, of course.

"Jed Willard? I'd propose to him tomorrow if I weren't scared of Bertha."

"Me, too. He's a fantastic guy."

"Will is going to be just like him in another thirty years," Sue said.

I really believed, then, that she was telling the truth about her feelings for Will. Women are instinctive matchmakers—I wonder why?— but no woman tries to fix things up for an old boyfriend unless she is thoroughly through with him herself.

"Will doesn't have Jed's Olympian calm," I said, peering out of the window. "Look at him, pacing like an expectant father. Ran told him we'd meet him at the drugstore, and he's probably furious because we aren't there. I really must go."

Ran was waiting when I reached the store; it was my absence that had sent Will into fits. I let him rave on for a few minutes and then I said,

"Oh, cut it out. You haven't been here five minutes. I saw you arrive."

"Where were you?" His eyes fell on the box, which I had placed on the counter. It certainly wasn't inconspicuous. "You were *shopping*?"

"You make it sound as if I'd been headhunting." I turned to Ran. "Sue gave me this, for you. She bought it from your aunts."

I told him the whole story. He looked amused.

"That sounds like Sue. She always did have an overactive conscience. I'll have a look at the other stuff and pay her back for all of it. I imagine she only took this as a tactful way of giving the aunts a loan. Who would want such a monstrosity?"

He was chatting on, carefully not looking at Will. I was thoroughly out of patience with the pair of them; such a fuss about a casual boy-girl romance that had died a natural death years before. But I couldn't ignore the slur on the Chinese box, to which I had taken rather a fancy.

"It's not a monstrosity," I said. "I don't know anything about oriental art, so I can't tell you whether its worth anything, but it's certainly attractive. The metal is silver or I'll eat my diploma, and the carving is exquisite. Look at the lock. I've never seen one like it. How does it work?"

Strictly speaking, it wasn't a lock; at least there was no visible keyhole. On the centre edge of the lid there was a grotesque animal head; from its open mouth a tongue of tarnished silver came down over the front of the box. Clearly there was a catch of some kind connected with this appendage, but my fingers moved back and forth over it without producing any results. Ran got interested.

"Let me try. It must be this metal whatnot. Press on it . . . No, that doesn't work. It doesn't seem to move at all."

"I should have asked Sue," I said. "It would be a pity to force it."

"There may not be anything inside. Wait a minute." His thumbnail found a minute crevice under the tip of the tongue. "So much for that famed oriental subtlety," he said triumphantly. "Look, it just pulls up."

He suited the action to the words. The silver tongue lifted, and Ran raised the top of the box.

For a full thirty seconds we stood there, stupefied and staring.

The box was lined with crimson velvet,

now worn and dusty. There was only one object inside. It was a miniature set in an oval gold frame—a portrait of the head and shoulders of a woman. The shoulders were draped with some light fabric, in the manner of an old-fashioned evening dress, and the white throat was bare except for a locket on a chain. But the face was the face I had seen take shape out of the shadows of the tower room.

9

RAN was the first to move. He slammed the lid of the box down as if the contents had been alive and liable to escape.

"Let's get out of here," he said, and headed for the door with the box under his arm.

We crowded into his car, which was parked at the kerb. Ran turned the interior light on and the fog shrouded the windows like curtains; we were much more private here than we would have been in the store. I understood Ran's need for privacy. This might be the first breakthrough we had had. It was also unnerving, in a very specific way. Will was the one who put this feeling into words.

"Let me go on record," he said, staring as if mesmerized at the painted face. "I'm resigning as group sceptic. Do you realize that this almost constitutes legal evidence? Sue will testify that this box and its contents have been in her possession since the old ladies sold it to her. Jo couldn't possibly have seen it

278

before today. Mary hasn't seen it. So how did Jo produce a portrait of this woman?"

"Somehow I find the differences between the two portraits even more convincing than the similarities," Ran said. "The dress isn't the same and neither is the hair style; the face is younger, happier. Yet it is unquestionably the same woman."

He had caught the two essential differences in two words: younger and happier. This girl couldn't have been more then twenty. The smiling face had the rounded softness of youth, and the dark hair was set in loose ringlets. The contrast between this unmarred face and the haggard visage I had drawn was extreme; and yet there was no mistaking the identity of the two. My drawing showed this girl as she would have looked after years of living—unhappy living. As Will had said, it was virtually conclusive evidence, at least to us who knew that the people involved were not in collusion.

"She was beautiful," I murmured. "Ran, look on the back. Maybe there's a name . . ."

But there was no writing on the back. There was something even more startling— another portrait. The face of a young child.

The face itself had no remarkable qualities.

It's very difficult to do good portraits of small children; they all look alike, in a way, with their round faces and buttony noses and fair, smooth skins. They haven't lived long enough for experience to mould their faces. This was a typical vapid baby's face, with the golden sausage curls and rosebud mouth that painters of the nineteenth century liked to put on their cherubs. But it was a baby's face; that in itself was enough to make me catch my breath.

Ran turned the miniature over and over in his hands as if he wanted to dissect it.

"This is almost worse than nothing," he said, between tight lips. "Who the hell are these people? There's no name, not even a date."

"Yes, but it is evidence," I said eagerly. "The two go together, don't they, the woman and the child? Ran, it's the kind of thing a woman would have done for her husband—the father of the child."

"Or a father might have it painted of his two children," Will said repressively. "Jo, you're jumping to conclusions again. The girl could be as young as sixteen; the baby, a year or two. They could be the children of the same father."

"Oh, you're hopeless," I said. "Don't look so discouraged, Ran. If you took this to a city museum—there ought to be one in Portland—an expert could tell you a lot about it. The date, maybe even the name of the painter, if the style is distinctive enough."

"I'll do it tomorrow." Looking more hopeful, Ran closed the box. "We'd better get back. It's lunchtime, and I don't want Mary thinking we've run out on her."

"I'll see you later." Will reached for his bag. "I have to take a patient across to the hospital this afternoon. I just stopped by to tell you that, and to ask whether you made any discoveries at the museum."

"Nothing as spectacular as this. In fact, you'll probably say nothing at all. There was only one odd little fact; I got it from Hezekiah's obituary. He died as a result from a fall; tumbled down a flight of stairs and broke his head open."

"What's so odd about that? " I demanded. "He was probably drunk."

Will looked thoughtful.

"No, that is slightly peculiar, Jo. I wouldn't think a man of his age and presumed toughness would fracture a skull so easily. It must have been quite a tumble. After all, the stairs at the house are fairly wide, shallow, and carpeted; and the banisters, though they're heavy, are just wood, with no sharp protruding carvings. Unless he—"

"Wow," I said suddenly. "Hey, I wonder . . . It didn't say which stairs he fell down, did it, Ran?"

"I get the impression that he wasn't at home when he fell. There was something about an iron staircase. There's nothing like that at the house."

"Oh, yes, there is," I said. "Yes, there is, too. Up in the tower, in the nursery—the room where I saw her last night."

"I didn't notice any stairs," Will said. "But I guess I didn't even look inside the room; I just grabbed up the wounded and left. You must remember those stairs, Ran."

"You know, I don't believe I ever saw those rooms in the tower," Ran said, frowning. "When I was a kid, the upper floors of the tower were kept locked. I remember once trying to pick the lock on the fourth-floor door. I was nosy, like all kids, and a locked door was a challenge. I didn't succeed, though. And one of the aunts caught me up there one day and beat the hell out of me. I got the point; that part of the house was out of bounds."

"I can see why they wouldn't want you roaming around there," I said. "I remember thinking how dangerous that stair was, and wondering why they would have it in a child's room."

"Why do you keep calling the tower a child's room?" Ran asked. "I remember the old nurseries very well; I used to go up there and thank God I didn't have to live in them."

"The tower room was also a nursery," I insisted. "The windows are barred, like those of the main nursery; and there's a rocking-horse up there."

"A rocking-horse?" Ran stared. "There was no such object in the house when I was a kid, that I know. Jo, I'd better have a look at that room when we get back."

"There is a pattern developing," Will said. "A rather interesting pattern. It's still vague, but—"

"It's too darned vague," I said. "Nothing we find ever answers any questions; it just raises more questions. I keep thinking we'll find something clear-cut, like a diary."

"Wouldn't that be handy," Ran said. "There certainly wasn't anything of that nature at the museum; most of the material was what you might call public records. The aunts wouldn't hand over personal papers, especially if they showed the sacred Frasers in a bad light. Hey—you said you were going to look through that trunk, Jo. I gather you didn't find anything."

"No. Just forty of Mrs. Hezekiah's account books. Talk about dull."

"Dull?" Will swung around to face me; I was sitting in the back seat while he and Ran occupied the front. "It's obvious you've never done any historical research. How detailed were the accounts?"

"Detailed is not the word. The old bag wrote down every cent she spent."

"I gather you took a dislike to the lady."

"I hate people who keep account books," I said. "No, really, she was an iceberg. I didn't examine the books in detail, I just skimmed through one to see what it was; but I'll never forget one of the entries. She had nine kids, and lost four—"

"Not a bad average," Will said.

"Yes, I remember thinking that myself. But, Will, that woman listed the expenses of their funerals, right down to the cost of the black crepe armbands for the servants. I tell you, it made me shiver to see that neat precise

284

handwriting record items like, 'Coffin for Baby Jonathan, four dollars'."

"My God," Ran said. "I'm on your side, Jo."

"You aren't being fair," Will objected. "New Englanders pride themselves on their fortitude. And believe me, you appreciate that quality after you've had a series of hypochondriacal patients who howl about a scratch on the knee. Mrs. Hezekiah may have been torn to pieces inside, but she wouldn't show it, not even to an account book."

"I still pity her poor children."

"What were their names?"

"Oh, names like Jeremiah and Jonathan and Patience . . . No Kevin. I'm sure of that; I found a genealogy."

Will swore.

"A genealogy and those account books, and you say you didn't find anything? Jo, you are the most . . . If I didn't have a sick kid and a hysterical mother on my hands, I'd come back now and go through those books item by item. Don't you realize that books like that are an absolute mine of information—impartial, unbiased information, because there is no attempt to mislead a reader? Look up the year Hezekiah died. Look for the names of servants and their wages. I don't know about this portrait, but all the other evidence we've got suggests that the woman was a governess or housekeeper. She'd have to be paid, wouldn't she? Good God, when I think of all the time you wasted—"

"Time," I said coldly, "is what I have not wasted. We don't have enough of it, that's all. Do you know how long it's going to take to go through one of those blasted books?"

"I don't care how long it takes." Will opened the car door and a long white tendril of fog moved in like a groping arm. "I'll be back as soon as I can. Certainly in time for dinner—"

"That," I said, "I expected."

Ran was excited and animated as we drove back to the house. I made suitable responses, not wanting to ruin his mood; one of us might just as well be happy. But what I had said earlier was true; it seemed to me that instead of solving problems we were just getting more problems to solve. All we had were theories. They might make sense, but they didn't lead to anything.

I remember the rest of that day as chaotic. A number of incidents stand out in my mind, separated by periods of aimless wandering around. The fog didn't help.

One thing I remember vividly is the conversation I had with Anne after lunch. I have excellent reasons, now, for remembering it.

When Ran and I got back to the house we found Anne and Mary in the library with an enormous jigsaw puzzle spread out on the table. Jigsaws were one of Mary's favourite dull-day activities; I don't know how Anne had wormed this fact out of her, but she had; and there they were, the two of them, matching pieces and looking as cosy as a basketful of kittens. Ran's face lit up at the sight of them, in the pathetic way it did whenever he saw Mary seemingly better; and after lunch he invited her to a *tête-à-tête* with the puzzle. They went off arm in arm and as they left the room Ran turned his head and gave me a meaningful glance. I nodded reassuringly. Then I asked Anne to come upstairs with me, saying I had something to show her.

We had agreed on the way home, Ran and I, that Anne ought to be told about our latest discoveries. He said we owed it to her. Maybe we did. I didn't think it would make any difference one way or the other; so I agreed to take on the job of showing her the miniature.

She was impressed. I didn't have to tell her who the subject of the portrait was, she recognized it immediately; and she listened in silence as I narrated the circumstances of its discovery.

"Of course it isn't as conclusive as Will thinks," I said flatly. "I could have seen another portrait somewhere in the house—although none of the people who have lived here for years remember any such picture. I might be in collusion with Sue; though I don't think anyone could suggest why I would go to such an incredible amount of trouble, or how I could convince Sue to join me in a plot. But I suppose it's easier for you to think that than to accept the only other conclusion."

"No," she said. "I know you don't like me, Jo, but give me credit for some intelligence. I'm—hit rather hard by this."

She was wearing another gorgeous outfit—a full hostess skirt, slit up the sides, over tight black slacks and jersey. But her face looked old—older and yet somehow softer. Old sucker Jo. I felt rather sorry for her.

"I don't dislike you," I protested. "I'm sorry if I gave you that impression."

"It's natural that you should feel hostility. You must think I've attempted to supplant you in Mary's affections. Of course I'm anxious to win her confidence, but her rejection of you is her own idea. You must have noticed that she's been avoiding you."

"Yes. I can't think why."

I could think of a reason, and it made me feel terrible. With my big mouth and my guilty conscience I might have spoken up if Anne hadn't spoken first.

"You can't? But it's obvious, surely. Mary is antagonistic towards all of you because you are thwarting her in the one thing she wants."

"What is it she wants?" I demanded, with sudden anger. "She can't really believe that—that thing that cries out there in the night is a human soul. If a child had been born, and died, I could see why she might cling to that idea, dreadful as it is. But even then—what does she want from it? She can't expect to—to call it back!"

"Now you're being illogical," Anne said. There were bright spots of colour on her cheeks. "You don't expect a woman in Mary's condition to be consistent, do you? Yet there is a consistency to her position, though she probably couldn't verbalize it. Whatever it is that cries in the night, it is unhappy. She wants it to stop crying; to be happy and at peace. It's as simple as that."

Her voice was unsteady. I looked at her in pleased surprise; it was reassuring to know that she could empathize so closely with a patient's feelings. Maybe she wasn't as hard as I had believed.

"But that's what we all want," I said. "That's what I'm trying to do."

Anne sat back. There was a pocket in the big skirt; she found her cigarettes and a slim silver lighter.

"So," she said, very much preoccupied with her cigarette, "you still won't consider the idea of a séance?"

"No, oh no. You wouldn't suggest it if you really believed in this."

"I don't dare believe, " she said, in an odd muted voice. "You don't know what it would mean to me to admit it . . ."

I remember that sentence, and the tone in which she said it, so clearly. If I had only had the compassion, or the intelligence, to inquire a little further. But I was too damned preoccupied with my own feelings.

"I know," I said. "It hasn't been easy for me either. I used to think of myself as rational. Are you staying over tonight? I certainly wouldn't want to drive in fog like this."

"The whole coast is fogbound, according to the radio," she said, in her normal voice. "I think I won't risk it tonight. I ought to be back by late tomorrow, I have a rather important appointment. But—well, we'll see what it's like in the morning."

"I'm afraid its going to be rather dull around here this afternoon."

"I've got letters to write. Might as well do it now, while my host and hostess are with one another. Jo . . . Thank you for showing me that."

"Sure," I said carelessly. I wasn't even thinking about her, I was so anxious to get back to my account books.

After a couple of hours my enthusiasm had waned. I started with the very first book, so as not to miss anything; and it was a terrible job, deciphering that finicky handwriting and stopping to wonder what some items might mean. If I had been looking for any one specific piece of information it might not have been so hard. I was looking for Miss Smith, but that wasn't all I wanted to find out about, and after what Will had said I was afraid to skip a single entry.

I got up to 1834 without finding a thing, and my eyeballs were beginning to roll around in my head; I knew I ought to stop for a while. The house had that Sunday afternoon hush which drives a lot of people into taking naps. Anne was presumably still writing letters; her door was closed and no sound came from behind it. I glanced into the library, and saw Ran and Mary both asleep in front of the television set. So I went to the kitchen. Mrs. Willard was cracking nuts for a cake and she pressed me into service. I had no sooner sat down than Jed came in. His hair was beaded with moisture.

"Good day for ducks," he said. "That fog is practically solid water. What's up, Jo?"

"I came to report," I said. "Look what we found."

I had already shown the box and the portrait to Mrs. Willard and she thought she had seen both before—that the portrait was probably the source of her memory of the face. Jed agreed.

"In fact, I'm sure this is what I saw. Haven't seen it for years, though. I remember the frame now, and the general look of the thing. But it must have been ten, fifteen years ago, wouldn't you say, Bertha? Haven't seen it since. And I don't remember ever seeing the child's face before. The picture must have been lying around the house, in a drawer, maybe, till the old ladies sold it."

"No," Mrs Willard said positively. "It was always in the box, just like it is. I remember the box well enough now that I see it again. Ugly thing, I always thought; it was on a shelf in one of the spare bedrooms for years."

"Well, that's nice to know, but it doesn't really get us any further," I said despondently. "We still don't know who these people were. All these separate facts, and no way to fit them together. Like that jigsaw puzzle of Mary's."

"But they do fit together," Jed said. "You just haven't found the key piece yet. What did Ran find out?"

I told him about Hezekiah's death. That piece of news and its concurrent facts startled him out of his usual composure.

"That is odd," he said. "I must have been in that room a half dozen times, and I never thought about those stairs, or wondered about 'em; and yet that is a very peculiar arrangement there. Those two upper rooms are self-contained, you realize that? You could shut 'em off from the rest of the house and nobody could get in or out. And the bars on the window—"

"If it was a child's room the bars make sense," I said. "It's the other angle I don't like. If Hezekiah died in that room, and Miss Smith called me to it—"

"Called you? It's interesting you should describe it that way. I've wondered about that before. You're the one that sees her, Jo. Why you? What does she want from you?"

"My God!" I dropped the walnut I was working on. "I'm sorry, Mrs. Willard, I didn't mean to swear; it just popped out . . . Jed, that's a horrible idea. Why should she want anything from me?"

"Well," Jed said apologetically, "she does keep getting closer, doesn't she?"

"Ugh," I said. "The last time was too close for comfort. What if she came into my room . . . or touched me . . . Jed, I think I'd lose my mind if she ever—"

"Calm down," Jed said sharply. "Don't you see, Jo, that is the only kind of damage a thing like that can do? It isn't solid; its only weapon is fear. If you're prepared for it you won't panic and you won't get hurt. You're young and healthy. But I'm worried about Mary. I wish I knew what she has been seeing and hearing."

"She's heard the crying. As we all have."

294

"Sure. But she must have heard more than that."

"Why?"

"How does she know its name is Kevin?"

It was one of those self-evident facts that none of us had put into words before. I was sorry Jed had done so now. I didn't like the picture those words brought to my mind.

"You mean," I said, "you mean it—it talks to her?"

"Seems as if it must."

"Oh, God." I put my head in my hands, and didn't apologize this time; nor did Mrs. Willard reproach me for taking the name of the Lord in vain.

"You see the problem," Jed went on. "With all these manifestations—sounds and sights and feelings, including that abnormal cold—we can't even define what we've got here. Is it one apparition or two? Is the hostile entity we call Miss Smith responsible for the pitiful weeping that fetches Mary out of her bed at night, into considerable danger? Or are there two ghosts?"

"There are two pictures," I said.

"Doesn't mean a thing . . . I think maybe I'll have another look at that room in the tower."

"Ran said he intended to do that too. I must admit I'm not anxious to see it again. I guess I'll go back to my dear account books."

On my way upstairs I went to the front door and looked out. San Franciscans boast of their fogs, but I had never seen one like this. Maybe it just seemed thicker because we were out in the country, where there were no lights or near-by objects. I couldn't see anything beyond the porch; the world might have ended ten feet away from the house. I was straining my eyes to see through the white opacity, and yet I was afraid of what I might see if I succeeded. In his own quiet way Jed was a master of the macabre. His suggestions were enough to make me abandon indefinitely the idea of sleeping. What if I woke up and found—her—standing by the bed—close enough to touch me?

That afternoon seemed to last for forty-eight hours. When Jed knocked at my door I was half asleep, nodding over the next account book. The look on his face woke me up fast enough, though.

"I've been up there," he said, without preamble. "That's a funny place, Jo, I never realized how funny. You know most of the furniture upstairs was sold or else stored away? There is still furniture in those rooms. The topmost one is a kind of bedroom. There's a brass bedstead up there, and some wardrobes and chests of drawer. How the Hades they got them up those stairs I hate to think, but there they are."

"You didn't know that?"

"Sure I did. I just never wondered about it. Why would I? None of these things we've found would mean anything unless we had a reason to notice them." He sounded exasperated. I knew he was annoyed with himself.

"That's a good point," I said soothingly. "What have you got there?"

One hand was behind his back. At my question his frown faded and a slight smile took its place.

"Something I think may surprise you. There were books in one of those cupboards. Look at this one."

It was an old-fashioned reader, or primer. I didn't pay much attention to the book itself, I was too fascinated by the inside front cover, which Jed displayed to me. There was a name on it, scrawled in big tipsy letters, like the printing of a small child who is just learning his alphabet. It said: "Kevin".

"Good gosh," I said. It was an inadequate expression of my feelings.

"Yep. We're getting there, Jo. I know it seems slow, but we are making progress."

"A child named Kevin did live in that room. Why not in the other nursery? And who was he? Not one of Hezekiah's children, we know their names . . . Wait a minute."

I picked up the genealogy from where I had tossed it on the floor, and we studied it together. Jed made mumbling sounds of satisfaction.

"Kevin was a family name before 1840. Must have come in with some Irish ancestress, before the Frasers ever emigrated. Yep; one, two, three—five times. The old man's own grandad was named Kevin. And he was the last. Never again."

"The one we want can't be any of the early ones," I said. "The house wasn't lived in by Frasers until Hezekiah's time. The book—yes, it was copyrighted in 1830."

"No, we haven't found the right Kevin yet," Jed said. "But we will. Back to your books, Jo. How far along are you?"

"Eighteen thirty-nine," I said, with a groan.

It was in the 1840 ledger that I found it.

The name seemed to jump out at me from the yellowing page.

"Wages, Miss Smith."

I sat back and rubbed my eyes. Yes, there it was; I had begun to think I would never find it.

I cheated then. Instead of continuing my entry-by-entry search, I jumped ahead. Miss Smith had first been paid in September of 1840. I checked that same month in succeeding years and it was there, regular as clockwork; "Miss Smith, wages". In 1842 she got a rise, from fifty dollars a year to fifty-five. In 1846 her name wasn't listed. I remembered the date on the tombstone, and I started looking back through that year. The search went much faster when I had a single specific question in mind; it took only minutes to find the entries.

"Coffin, for Miss Smith. To sexton, for digging grave. To Reverend Brown, for services."

So they had had the proper words said over her grave, improperly placed though it was. No black crepe. The family wouldn't go into mourning for a servant.

We'd been right about that. She was a dependant, who received wages; and since no housemaid or cook would be called "Miss", she had to be a governess or housekeeper.

And there was still no proven connection between Miss Smith and the woman in the miniature.

I sat back on my heels and rubbed my aching eyes. The problem was like a puzzle—not a jigsaw, but one of those involved exercises in symbolic logic. "Mr. Smith lives in the green house. The brown house is next to the blue house. The Frenchman drinks Scotch." Everyone has seen puzzles of that sort; they drive me wild, because I can never figure them out, and yet they have an unholy fascination for me. I can spend hours brooding over them. Usually I get about halfway through the necessary deductions, and then I get stuck. I never do find out who lives in the red house, or what the Canadian drinks.

I had the feeling that our puzzle was just as susceptible to reason, that it was only my lack of skill that kept me from reaching the answer. The woman in the miniature was the woman in the black dress. The woman in the black dress was Miss Smith. That would have made a neat equation, except that the second statement wasn't a fact, it was only a strong assumption. Miss Smith was a governess or housekeeper. The apparition in black had appeared, on one occasion, in a child's room. The woman in the miniature was connected with a child. Hezekiah had fallen to his death from the stairs in the tower room. The tower room was the room in which the apparition had appeared.

It was just like the puzzle about the houses. Only I couldn't be sure I had all the necessary statements.

I heard voices in the hall and glanced at my watch. It was much later than I had thought. The others must be getting ready to go downstairs. Wearily I got to my feet, kicking account books in all directions, and went to the bathroom to wash my dusty hands.

There was a knock at the door. I knew it must be Mary, from the sound of it, and I made a leap for the door. I didn't want her to see the books and the old trunk.

"What have you been doing all afternoon?" she asked. "You look like a grubby urchin."

"You look beautiful enough for both of us," I said, admiring her crimson hostess gown. "Do you want me to change? Who's going to be here?"

"Not Will," Mary said. "That old car of

301

his finally broke down. He just called to ask if Ran could meet him at the ferry. It doesn't get in till eight thirty."

"Oh. Well, I'll clean up, and then meet you downstairs. I could use a drink, on a dreary day like this."

"I want to show you something first."

"What?" I asked wearily.

"I've found Hezekiah."

If my teeth had been removable, they'd have fallen out. I got control of myself fairly well; but my voice sounded like a frog's when I responded.

"Where?"

"One of the guest rooms," Mary said. "It's an interesting picture, but Ran says his aunts couldn't stand it. That's why the guest room, instead of the parlour."

At the end of the corridor we turned into the cross-corridor and went down two steps into the east wing. When Mary opened the door of one of the guest rooms, I realized why I hadn't noticed Hezekiah's portrait on our house tour the first day. The old ladies really had disliked him; he was inconspicuously placed on a side wall, practically behind the door.

Artistically speaking, the painting wasn't

much. It was stiff and wooden, and it lacked the charm of a genuine primitive. It was simply poor work, done by a bad painter. It also needed cleaning. The varnish had darkened so badly that it was hard to make out the details of the figure, which was shown from the waist up against a background that seemed to be a *mélange* of seascapes, with a full-masted ship, a pagoda, and a palm tree as insignia.

As we stood there in front of the picture I heard someone calling Mary's name.

"That's Ran," she said. "He must have lost a button or a sock or something. If you're going to ponder over that handsome face, Jo, I'll leave you to it, before Ran bursts a blood vessel. He's like all men, no patience. Turn out the light and close the door, will you, when you're through?"

"Sure," I said vaguely.

At second and third glance the picture was more interesting than I had thought. The painter had caught the harshness of the features quite well. The face was almost square, the angles of the jaw and chin were so extreme. The nose wasn't good; it looked like a blob of modelling clay instead of the prow-like protuberance it must have been; but I imagined that the mouth, in real life, must have been almost as stiff and harsh as the artist had depicted it. The eyes, under heavy beetling brows, were failures; it's hard to capture expression in the eyes. All in all, it was close to my imaginary picture of the hard sea captain. Yet no one could call it lifelike or evocative; neither of those qualities existed to account for what happened to me then.

I was about to turn away when the air darkened around me. It was no ordinary power failure; the painted features were glowing, as if with a light of their own. There was a beating in the air, like the sound of great dark wings; and then, to my horror, the painted face moved. The features writhed soundlessly, as if in pain; the mouth opened in a silent scream of warning. I heard the words echoing inside my head:

"Get out . . . hurry, hurry . . . before it's too late . . ."

10

I DON'T remember how I got out of the room. I was halfway down the stairs before I came to my senses; I stopped there, hanging on to the banister and trying to catch my breath. I could hear voices from upstairs; Ran and Mary hadn't come down yet. So I decided it was safe to go on into the parlour, where I could collapse. I didn't want Mary to see me until I had myself under control.

The parlour wasn't deserted, however. Anne was standing by the window looking out. Against the darkness her profile was as sharply outlined as a face on a Roman coin. I was struck by an odd feeling of familiarity, and I wondered who or what it was she reminded me of as she stood there. But I didn't give the matter much thought. I was too far gone to worry about anything but my nerves.

She turned as I dropped heavily into a chair.

"Good heavens, Jo, what's the matter?"

I told her.

305

She didn't say anything. I assumed her lack of response indicated a perfectly natural scepticism, and I said wearily,

"You must think I'm as crazy as my sister. I'm beginning to wonder myself . . . Maybe I imagined this last thing. I'm in such a state. I don't really know what I'm seeing."

Her expression wasn't sceptical or hostile. It was abstracted, as if she were thinking about something else.

"I talked to Ran," she said.

"What about?"

"About your research investigations, what else? I think you've all been most ingenious."

"And naïve?"

"Not at all. In any case, you've got a pretty little family mystery on your hands. I'm particularly intrigued by the semi-anonymous grave."

"There's more," I said, and told her what Jed and I had ferreted out that afternoon. If she wasn't genuinely interested she was a good actress.

"It really is curious," she said. "Of course you realize that these things may have a perfectly innocent explanation? And that they may not be connected with your ghostly phenomena?"

"I do know that. That's our problem, that we can't get any definite facts."

She turned away, reaching for a cigarette. It seemed to me that she was smoking too much, but that was none of my business.

"There is one source of information you don't seem to have considered," she said.

"What's that?"

"The newspapers, of course. You aren't delving into ancient Babylonian history; there must have been a local paper in 1846."

"Of course!" I exclaimed. "I don't know why we didn't think of that. I'll bet they have copies at the local library. We can check tomorrow."

"It's a pity you can't check tonight."

"Why?"

She looked away.

"Now it's your turn to be sceptical," she said. "Maybe the atmosphere is affecting me . . . But I have a feeling that time is running out, and that the sooner you can arrive at some conclusion, the better."

"Why, Anne—"

"Don't be alarmed," she said quickly. "I'm not saying that because of any specific change I've observed in Mary's condition. All the same . . . This will be my last evening here; I called my secretary today and I find that I must be in Boston by tomorrow afternoon. Through fog and hail and dark of night, you know. At least I can be a good watchdog while the rest of you pursue your investigations. I can't seem to help in any other way."

I felt as if I ought to protest that last sentence, if only out of politeness; but she didn't sound bitter, only obscurely amused. And before I could think of anything to say, Ran and Mary came in.

Dinner was surprisingly pleasant. I say surprisingly because underneath the laughter and the casual talk I was very much concerned with Anne's remarks. She had said she wasn't worried about a worsening of Mary's condition, but I couldn't accept that statement at face value. If she didn't expect a crisis, why was she so concerned about the passage of time? I too had that sense of time running out, of the necessity for quick action. I knew the feeling was illogical. I had no reason to think that matters were any worse; if anything, Mary looked better that evening, bright-eyed and responsive and happy . . .

That in itself should have warned me. There had been other times when she seemed better; they had been followed by some of our

308

most disastrous nights. I didn't think of that at the time, however. The other problem that preoccupied me was how I was going to get out of the house after dinner. I had had time for a quick private exchange with Ran; Anne's suggestions about the newspapers had impressed him as much as it had me, and he was sure he could get the key of the library from the local woman who was in charge of it. He had to go into the village after dinner to pick up Will, so that would give him an excuse to leave the house. But I was determined to go with him and I didn't see how I was going to manage it.

It was easy. So easy that it should have made my suspicions flare up like a torch.

We had finished dessert and were having coffee at the table. Casually Ran glanced at his watch and then pushed his chair back.

"I'd better be leaving. Want to come along for a ride, Jo?"

"Well . . ." I glanced at Mary.

"Go ahead. The boat will probably be late, in this foul weather. You can both sit in the bar at the Inn and drink till it arrives. Then I'll know Ran isn't being seduced by any of the local sirens."

"If you're sure—"

"Of course I'm sure. I'm sorry things are so dull here, Jo; it isn't much fun for you sitting in the house all the time. Isn't there a movie in town, Ran? Why don't you treat your poor bored guest to a nice X film?"

"We can see what's on," Ran said. "I imagine Will will want to get home, but—well, don't worry if we don't come right back."

"No," Mary said. "I won't worry."

As we drove off down the road, I felt a qualm which had nothing to do with my concern about Mary. The fog was worse, or else it seemed thicker at night; I couldn't see anything. Ran didn't seem to be worried; he was whistling under his breath. After a while I relaxed too. I hadn't realized until we left it how tense the atmosphere in that house had become. A nice ordinary fog was a pleasure by contrast.

On the way to town we hashed over our deductions. I told Ran about my experience with the portrait, and my latest discoveries.

"It seems to me we have two major questions," he said thoughtfully. "First, who is the child, the boy named Kevin? Second—"

"What do you mean, who is he? We don't

even know he exists. If the boy who wrote his name in that book is—"

"Oh, hell, Jo, let's not be so dogmatic. I know we don't have concrete evidence for a lot of these points, but let's face it, we probably never will. I've reached the point where I'll accept a good strong presumption instead of proof. We have a name in a book and the picture of a fair-haired child and a child's voice that cries—and the name Mary has given to the voice. I'm going to assume that they all fit the same individual, and that his name was—is—Kevin. So we come back to the question—who was he? He wasn't one of Hezekiah's children and yet he seems to belong to Hezekiah's time. He is connected with the woman, not only because of the miniatures, but because of the concurrence of the weeping and the apparition of the woman in black. So let's do the same thing for Miss Smith that we did for Kevin; let's assume that all these identities are one and the same. The woman in the black cloak is Miss Smith, who is also the woman in the portrait.

"And that brings us to question number two. Who was Miss Smith, besides the governess? The miniature is not the portrait of a governess, it's the portrait of a woman who has the wealth and social position to commission such a work—or who is under the protection of a man who has those attributes. It is in that capacity that she is associated with the child. And yet Miss Smith is undoubtedly a member of Hezekiah's household staff. I ask again: what was she besides the governess?"

"All right, I know what you're thinking. The twin miniatures certainly suggest mother and child. If Miss Smith was the mother, who was the father? Kevin is a common Fraser family name—"

"And Hezekiah was a well-known lecher. Let me tell you a little thing, my innocent sister-in-law; if I had a girl like the one in that picture hanging around the house all day, I know what I'd be strongly tempted to do. From what we've heard, Hezekiah lacked my scruples."

"Hmmph," I said, impressed by his reasoning if not by his point of view. "Yes, but Ran—no wife, particularly a stiff-necked Bostonian like Mrs. Hezekiah, would keep her husband's mistress and their illegitimate child in her own house. The boy was there, in that tower room, if we can trust the evidence;

312

and Miss Smith was certainly in the house up till the year Hezekiah died."

"You underestimate the old boy, and the spirit of the times. Those were the good old days, when women knew their place."

We were on the outskirts of town now and I began to see lighted windows and an occasional electric sign through the mist. It made the fog seem less thick; but when Ran stopped the car and opened the door I heard a sound that is one of the most melancholy sounds in the world—the low, mournful wail of a foghorn, out at sea.

"Where are we?" I asked, looking out of the wet-streaked window. The street was a quiet residential street; a single streetlight tried valiantly to shine through the fog.

"I'm going to see if I can get the key to the library. You won't be afraid in the car alone, will you? This is the most law-abiding town I've ever been in, and if you come into the house it'll take time to make introductions and all that sort of thing. The ferry is due in five minutes."

"I'd rather wait here," I said, and watched him disappear along the sidewalk. It was like a disappearance, his tall body seemed to melt into the fog.

The time seemed longer than it was. As I sat in the misty darkness I could hear the foghorn still, even though doors and windows were closed. I began to feel like a character in one of those gloomy O'Neill plays; I remember one in which the foghorn hoots, with monotonous misery, through the entire second act. It's an extremely effective theatrical device for creating a mood of utter depression.

It couldn't have been more than ten minutes, though, before Ran came back, and I knew from his jaunty walk that he had succeeded. He put the car into gear and we started off. I wasn't really expecting to see Will that night, I couldn't imagine that anybody would be crazy enough to take a boat out in that fog. The ferry was not only functioning, it was early. When we reached the end of the main street where the dock began, we saw the boat's lights shining through the mist. Will was already waiting.

He blinked as the headlights struck him. The glare of the light robbed his face of identity, but it showed his general state of dishevelment quite clearly—his unkempt hair and the awkward way the old raincoat hung off his shoulders. He looked worse than I had ever seen him look; and I was so glad to see him I almost got out of the car and rushed to meet him. The sensation wasn't new. I had felt it coming on for a long time, but there didn't seem to be much point in encouraging it; between sexy Sue and brilliant Anne, my prospects didn't look too good.

Will got into the back seat of the car; and I thought, See? He doesn't even want to sit next to me.

"Everything okay?" he asked.

Ran started to talk, but I interrupted.

"The boy—your patient. How is he?"

"He'll be all right." Will chuckled; it was a funny chuckle, exasperated and yet triumphant. "Damn that woman, she was right. It wasn't a virus—it was appendicitis. We just got him there in time. The first time in ten years she's been right, and I don't imagine she'll ever let me hear the end of it."

"You must be exhausted," I said.

Will gave me a funny look.

"I'm a little tired," he said cautiously. "What's been going on this afternoon?"

"We've found out quite a bit," Ran said. "How about a drink and a steak at the Inn while we fill you in? If you can hold up for an hour or so, there's something I want to do

315

here in town before I drive you home. Of course if you're really too tired—"

"Hell, no," Will said indignantly. "But I won't turn down that steak."

He was definitely cool to me for the next five minutes; I was being punished for daring to intimate that four or five hours of work and worry could tire him. But he ate with the gusto, if not the table manners, of Henry VIII tearing into a haunch of beef.

Ran talked the whole time. When Will finally slowed down enough to comment, he remarked,

"Seems to me you do better when I'm not around . . . Jo, if I hadn't seen the lady in black myself, I'd begin to wonder about you. How come you're getting all the attention from the ghosts?"

"That's what Jed wondered. I don't like any of the possible answers. As for Hezekiah's portrait—"

"Yeah," Will said. "What about Hezekiah? I had him pegged as a villain, but it's beginning to look as if he might have been the victim."

"Will, I'm not sure," I said. "That business with the picture . . . It's a classic type of hallucination, isn't it?"

"Yes, it is," Will said.

"So maybe that's what it was. You know," I said, struck by the idea, "I wonder if that's why psychic phenomena are discredited. People see one genuine manifestation and it shakes them up so much they start imagining others. Naturally the false manifestations are easy to disprove, so the whole subject gets a bad name."

Will grinned.

"The SPR would love your descriptions. I commend your honesty, Jo, but this time I'll be the attorney for the defence. Your impression was not that you were being threatened; it was rather a feeling of warning, right? But that doesn't fit your conscious predispositions about Hezekiah. You thought of him as a villain too. If you had imagined that incident, you'd have seen him baring his teeth and reaching out to grab you."

Ran was beginning to fidget.

"I don't want to rush you, Will, but if we're going to spend any time in the library . . ."

I used to think of libraries as friendly, cosy places. But they can be eerie on a foggy night, when there are only three people in all the empty spaces. The fog seeped in through closed windows; long pale streaks of it drifted

317

down the shadowy aisles of the stacks. Footsteps echoed in those tunnel-like areas. The musty dusty smell of books, which is usually one of my favourite smells, took on a different significance in the gloom and seeping fog.

In the 1840s, the island had not boasted its own newspaper, but Richmond, the nearest mainland town, put out a weekly. Ran explained that it was our best bet. The Portland newspaper might have carried Hezekiah's obituary, since he was a fairly prominent citizen, but it was unlikely that they would print less important island news—certainly not the news of the death of a servant.

It was Miss Smith's obituary we were looking for. Ran had already seen the notice of Hezekiah's death; the clipping was among the family papers in the museum.

"I should have thought of a newspaper then," he admitted in disgust. "But the clipping was separate. Whoever cut it out didn't even include the name of the paper."

We were working with microfilm copies, not originals, but as soon as Ran saw the type and general setup of the pages, he was fairly sure that the notice of Hezekiah's death had been cut from this paper. We had to go through all the 1846 issues to reach the month in which Miss Smith had passed away, so when Will, who was operating the viewer, found Hezekiah's obituary, he stopped the machine, so that Ran could verify his assumption. Will and I hadn't seen the clipping, so we hastily scanned this copy of the obituary. Will is a faster reader than I am; I was still plodding through the names of local dignitaries who had attended the funeral when I heard him burst out with a single expressive expletive. It brought Ran back from his nervous pacing, and at the next moment my slower eyes found it too.

At the end of the column, the editor named the surviving relatives. There were a brother in Ohio and a sister in Rhode Island. The names of Hezekiah's wife and children followed. And last on the list was the name that had caused Will's outburst: "And his adopted son, Kevin."

II

"I swear it wasn't there," Ran said in utter bewilderment. "The clipping I saw ended . . . yes, right there. Third line from the bottom."

"Someone cut the last lines off," I said. "But why? Adopted son . . . Good Lord, we never thought of that."

"It makes sense," Will said. The microfilm reader was still switched on; the yellow light, shining upwards cast the weirdest shadows across his face. "When did you say Miss Smith first makes her appearance—1840? Suppose she had just had the baby. Hezekiah adopts it and brings it home, from Boston or wherever; and with it he thoughtfully brings a nursemaid-governess."

"Oh, I don't believe it," I said angrily. "Not even Hezekiah could do such a filthy thing. Why, it—it's horrible. And there isn't a scrap of proof."

"Proof, hell. I've known of people being hanged on less convincing circumstantial evidence. Go ahead, Will. We still haven't found Miss Smith."

Will touched the switch and the pages began to glide past. The next item appeared only a few weeks later, but it wasn't Miss Smith's obituary. Will almost missed it. The headline didn't include a name:

"Hope abandoned for missing heir."

"Wait," Ran said, and grabbed Will's arm.

We read the story together, in fascinated silence.

Kevin Fraser, missing since Friday night, is now believed to have been swept to sea after falling from the cliff near the Fraser mansion. Young Fraser was last seen on Friday morning heading towards the cliff. A search party, led by Joshua Beale, found the only trace of the boy—his cap, caught on a shrub just below the edge of the cliff. Kevin was the adopted son of Captain Hezekiah Fraser, whose accidental death occurred less than a month ago. The captain's will named the boy as one of his two principal heirs.

"Something a little pointed about the word 'accidental', don't you think?" Will suggested.

Ran was disturbed.

"My God, the poor little devil. How they must have hated him. They even tried to wipe out the memory of him."

"By 'they', I gather you mean your ancestors," I said. "Mercy and her son Jeremiah and all the rest. Ran, do you realize what you're suggesting?"

"It fits," Ran said. "It fits too damn well."

In the reflected light his face was ghastly. "He inherits a large chunk of the captain's estate and a month later he disappears. Talk about motives for murder . . ."

"Not to mention motives for haunting," I muttered. "Revenge? Oh no, surely not—not a child . . . Justice, then? Is that what he wants? No wonder he cries . . . How do you bring a murderer to justice when he's been dead for almost a century—even if you could identify him?"

Will started the machine again.

"Aren't you being a trifle melodramatic?" he said dryly, without looking up. "If you are willing to admit a disembodied intelligence that survives physical death, you ought to concede the likelihood of a Justice which can cope much more effectively with sin than any human court."

"And which is not deceived," Ran said.

"All right." I threw up my hands. "Maybe the child doesn't want anything except peace. Don't they say that violent death is a traumatic experience for the spirit? And time is meaningless in eternity. Maybe he's still in a state of shock—lost."

"That," said Will, continuing to scan pages, "is why I part company with spiritualism. If their benevolent creator can let a victim suffer that kind of torment all those years . . .''

"You want logic," I said angrily. "There isn't any. None of this makes any sense. But there has to be some point . . .''

"Exactly. And so far we haven't found it. We haven't even found . . . Ah, yes. Here she is.''

"One week after the boy disappeared," Ran said. "My God, it is like a curse. Isn't there an old superstition about death coming in threes?''

"Now you're being melodramatic," I said. "It sounds silly, but to me this is almost reassuring. She must have been very close to the boy, whether she was his mother or not. And she must have felt guilt as well as grief. She was responsible for him; a baby like that, she should have watched him more closely.''

"What makes you think it was suicide?" Will asked.

"Well, I certainly wouldn't buy three accidents within a month, all in the same house. What does the paper say? Ah—here you are. Empty glass and a bottle which had contained laudanum on the table beside her. The verdict . . . Hmmph. Accidental death?''

"Now wait a minute." Will was several lines ahead of me. "They didn't find a note, so they charitably assumed an accident. She mightn't have received Christian burial otherwise."

"You call that beyond-the-pale grave Christian burial? Oh, all right. You're arguing on my side."

"I don't know what I'm arguing for or against," Will muttered, scowling at the page. "Those three deaths are too coincidental. They ought to be connected, somehow."

"If it were a murder mystery, they would all be murders," I said, with a lightness I assuredly did not feel. "You know, the thing the police call the *mo* is the same in all three cases—making it look like an accident."

Will gave me a warning jab in the ribs and I stopped talking; Ran's grim face showed that he was taking all this seriously. I think the thing that bothered him most was the vindictiveness his family had displayed in wiping out all trace of the child. It had been deliberate; some record would surely have survived otherwise.

"Do you mind?" he said. "I can't take any more tonight. And we've been gone long enough; I don't like leaving Mary this late."

Will switched off the machine.

"We've got all we're going to find, unless we take a lot more time than we have at our disposal right now. Mary isn't alone, surely?"

"Of course not, Anne is with her. But it isn't fair to expect her to cope with Mary if she gets one of her spells."

"Funny thing," Will said casually, as Ran turned out the lights and locked the door. "I ran into a guy today, at the hospital, who used to know Anne in med school. He asked me about her husband. I said so far as I knew she wasn't married, and he seemed surprised. She was engaged when he knew her, to another student, and it was quite an affair."

"She was married," Ran said. We went down the steps and walked towards the car. "For less than a year. The guy who recommended her to me told me about it. Her husband was killed in Vietnam—or was it Korea, back then? She was badly shaken up. Had a breakdown. It was that that made her decide to go into psychiatry."

Right then I got the first faint prickle of alarm. I couldn't understand why I felt uneasy, but my subconscious must have been working on it. I remembered that it had been Anne's suggestion that had sent us to the

325

library that evening. I remembered Mary's acquiescence—eagerness, even. I remembered certain things that had been said—and the look on a woman's face as she stared out of a darkening window. And I knew, all at once, why Anne's face had reminded me of something. The resemblance had not been one of physical features. It had been an expression. The same expression, on Anne's face, that I had seen one other night on my sister's face as she stared out into the darkness where the crying child had its existence.

I caught at Ran's arm as he stopped the car in front of the librarian's house.

"Ran. Did Anne say anything more to you about holding a séance?"

"No . . . You mean lately? Not since that first time she mentioned it, and we all decided—"

"She's mentioned it to me several times," Will said. "Jo, what is it?"

"I'm overanxious. I must be. But tonight—she did seem glad to have us go, didn't she? She said it was her last night. She said—oh, God, what was it she said? 'I don't dare believe it; you don't know what it would mean to me—' Will. You don't think—"

"I think we'd better get back to the house

as fast as we can. Never mind the key, Ran; let's get moving."

Ran drove that road like a madman, and I kept urging him to go faster. In the faint glow from the dashboard his face looked like a death mask, and he never spoke a word. I kept babbling. I couldn't stand the silence.

"There's another theory, one we never considered. Suppose she's the murderess—Miss Smith? Hezekiah died in that room, falling down those stairs. A man like that, who had walked his quarterdeck in gales and storms, tripping on a stair? Suppose she pushed him. Suppose she hit him, with a poker or something, and made it look as if he'd fallen. The child might know. She would have to dispose of it to keep it from talking. Remorse, suicide—or maybe one of the family found out the truth and took the law into his own hands, to avoid scandal. I can see Mercy doing it, she must have hated the woman anyhow. Ran, can you go any faster?"

We met only one car on the road. It let out a long startled bleat of its horn, which faded as we swept past. Then we were among trees, swinging up the private road. The trunks loomed up and vanished like colossal columns in a pagan temple. And then, after far too long a time, we were in front of the house. Ran drove straight across the lawn. He was out of the car before the engine died, and we were right behind him.

Jed met us in the hall. His sombre face lit up at the sight of Ran.

"Glad you're back," he said, in what was clearly an understatement.

"Where are they?" Ran demanded. "Where's Mary?"

"They went upstairs an hour ago," Jed said. "I thought they went to bed. But Bertha went up a while back, just to check, and neither of them was in her room. I'm afraid—"

Ran made an inarticulate sound and started up the stairs. He, like the rest of us, had no doubt as to where to go.

The lights on the fourth-floor landing were on. That was the only sign that anyone had come this way. Everything was quiet; the tower door was closed. Then I heard a voice—it was Anne's, I learned later. I couldn't make out the words, but the tone was calm and regular, with a cadence almost like that of poetry.

The feeling hit me then—the same icy chill I had felt before, and with it came the sick malaise that was a sickness of the soul rather than the body.

I forgot that the others hadn't felt it, at least not so strongly. I saw Jed recoil, and saw the perspiration break out on Ran's face. He grabbed at the doorknob. It turned, but the door didn't open. They had barricaded it from within.

They heard us—or something heard us . . . Anne's voice rose, its tempo increasing; and from within the room there was a sickening grating groan and then a sob—a long, sobbing wail, the same sound we had heard before.

Will said something, through stretched lips; I didn't catch the words, but Jed did. He caught hold of Ran and pulled him back from his wild clawing at the door; and Will stepped back, raised his foot, and slammed it into the door.

I don't know whether it was karate, or what, but it was as effective as a battering ram. The door flew open.

The sound that burst out of that open door was hellish, and I use that word in its literal sense. It was the weeping we had heard before, but magnified beyond all endurance, like a powerful hi-fi set turned up as high at it will go. Even the sweetest sound is hideously distorted under those conditions. This sound had never been sweet. Now it sounded more like cackling laughter than grief.

The room was lit by candles—and by one other thing.

Not moonlight; the fog obscured the moonlight, and pushed at the barred window like a white monstrosity trying to break in. The other light came from an amorphous shape that hovered near the foot of the iron staircase.

It was like a cloud of luminous gas, or a patch of fog that has phosphorescent qualities. Its sickly grey light showed near-by objects clearly. The white bulk of the rocking horse looked obscenely out of place in that terrible atmosphere; the painted mouth seemed to grin, and I could have sworn that it was moving back and forth, as if something rode on its back.

The two women were sitting next to one another at a small round table in the centre of the room. After the first glance at Mary's frozen stare, I couldn't take my eyes off Anne's face. Mary had been through this, or something like it, before; but poor Anne . . . Half believing, half doubting, telling herself that this was only an experiment which couldn't harm Mary however it worked out. But the part of her mind that did believe believed in the pretty afterlife of the spiritualists, in flowers and singing and happy spirits who have passed over. Then the cold came to her, and the sickness, and the thing that was struggling to take shape against the darkness.

It was like a monstrous birth; the creature squirmed and writhed, fighting the bonds of the invisible. And all the while it kept up that mindless squealing. Sounds have direct emotional impact; animals make certain noises to attract sexual partners—or prey. I wondered how I could possibly have heard this call before and failed to realize that it fell into that same category—not a crying child but a counterfeit of one, deliberately created to attract a certain quarry, as a hunter reproduces the call of game birds to lure them within his weapon's range.

The whole thing couldn't have taken very long, but it seemed to go on for ever. Then, with a snap and a crackling flash, like an electrical short-circuit, the thing came into focus, complete and self-illuminated. It was distinct; and it was nothing like anything I had expected to see.

I had seen "Miss Smith" materialize before; it had been unpleasant, but it hadn't been nearly as bad as this. Yet I did expect to see her, because the only other face I might have anticipated was the cherub face with the golden curls, the face of the child in the miniature. That face would have suited the forlorn weeping, but it seemed blasphemous to associate it with this outrageous cacophony.

The thing we saw was a man; at least it was man-high and man-shaped, hulking and big. Shaggy dark hair fell over its forehead and ears. The mouth was open in a grimace of triumphant laughter. It was a brutish-looking shape, but its appearance was not the worst thing about it. The worst thing was the aura of abnormality that hung upon it.

Will claimed later that I was standing on his feet and trying to climb up on him. I may have been. I don't remember what I was doing, or what anyone else did or said. I wasn't even thinking about Mary. People talk about fear. They haven't the faintest idea what fear is. I could face a charging tiger or an earthquake or a maniac with a club now, and find all of them relatively unnerving.

Somebody started praying. It was me. The

prayer was a hodgepodge, bits of the "Our Father" and "Hail Mary" and miscellaneous lines from the ritual. I'm not claiming that the words themselves had any particular value. Maybe the multiplication table would have been just as effective—anything mechanical, learned by rote, to focus the mind and wrench it back to independent thought. The sound of my voice broke the rhythm of the wailing, and that may have helped; but it was no act of ours that saved us. The thickening shadows across the room didn't catch my attention at first, not until the shaping was almost complete; but there she was, the black-garbed woman, just as I had seen her once before. This time she moved. Her hands came up in an odd crossing movement; and simultaneously a light shone out—a powerful bright beam, cutting through the darkness like a sword. And they were gone, both of them; the room was empty.

The next thing I heard was a sodden thud, as Anne fell off her chair on to the floor in a dead faint. Jed kept the light focused. He was the only one who had had sense enough to remember to bring a flashlight.

Mary didn't stir. Her face was like wax, stiff and white and motionless. I had the feeling that I could have taken it between my hands and remoulded it into any shape I liked.

Tentatively Ran reached out and touched her arm. She didn't move. I could see her breathing, but that was all she did. Ran picked her up. She came up into his arms all in one piece, like a figure carved out of wood, and her face didn't change, not a muscle of it. Ran carried her out. Will scooped up Anne, with much speed and little ceremony, and followed them.

I turned to Jed.

"You're the lucky one," I said, in a croak. "I don't think you're going to have to carry anybody. Not if we get out of here . . . fast . . ."

He put his long arm around my shoulders and we went down the stairs together.

III

We spent the rest of the night in the kitchen, in what was more or less a state of siege. No one wanted to be alone.

Mary was still in shock; her eyes were open, but she didn't respond to anything.

334

Will seemed to find her condition relatively reassuring; at least he could give it a name.

"It looks like a form of catatonia. Ran, stop pacing; I called Vic and he thinks he can get the chopper down as soon as it gets light. Fog's supposed to lift. That's only a couple of hours from now; it's the fastest way, believe me."

Anne was made of stronger stuff than I had expected. Will shot her full of tranquillizers, but even so, she was doing pretty well. She didn't even indulge in guilt feelings.

"I couldn't possibly have known," she said steadily. She was thoroughly doped; her face had an almost oriental tranquillity, but she was thinking rationally. "What I did was stupid and unforgivable, but there's no point in berating myself now. Just tell me—what was that thing?"

"I don't know," Will said.

Ran wasn't taking any part in the conversation. He sat on a chair near the cot Jed had arranged for Mary. He just sat there holding her hand and watching her still face.

"We were calling the child," Anne said. "We were going to find out who it was. What it wanted. I thought if it didn't work, then she would accept the fact that there was nothing out there. And if it did . . ."

A spasm crossed the calm of her face, and Will said quickly,

"Never mind. I'm beginning to think it did work—better than you realize."

"Huh?" I stared at him. "That was no child, Will. It was a man. But not Hezekiah; I know his face."

"No, it wasn't the Captain," Jed said. He was sitting at the table with the Chinese box in front of him. He had been turning it idly in his hands. Now he tapped it with his finger. "Look at this, Will. I measured it this afternoon. There's a space of about an inch I can't account for. I hope Ran won't mind; but I took out the lining."

With the lining removed, the secret of the box wasn't hard to find. One of the nailheads on the bottom was false. When Jed pressed it, a drawer popped out. In the drawer was a single sheet of paper.

"It's a sort of birth certificate," Will said, studying it. "Not a formal one; but the colony had a doctor, and he wrote this out. A male child . . . mother's name, Georgianna Smith. Born in Macao. That was the summer colony of the Hong Kong merchants. Does it begin to make sense now?"

"She was one of the harem," I said sickly. "One of Hezekiah's Hong Kong harem. British, by her name—how on earth did he get a girl like that into—"

Will was staring at the paper.

"She was one of the lost people, I imagine," he said absently. "The orphans, the abandoned . . . The world is full of them. She might have been travelling to India or another British colony; maybe her parents died on shipboard, who's to know? If she was young and alone and met up with an experienced rake like Hezekiah . . . She must have loved him. She came back here and let herself be taken on as a hired servant."

"That I can't understand," I burst out. "That kind of crawling, obsequious—"

"It was another world," Will pointed out. "Not a very kind world for women. She came here in—1840, wasn't it? The first Opium War broke out about 1839; maybe it wasn't safe there, for her and the boy. Or maybe it was mother love that made her do it. If she let the old man adopt the kid, he'd be provided for. What other choice did she have? I'm surprised Hezekiah had the decency to do that much. Maybe he enjoyed aggravating his legitimate family."

"That I can believe. But Will, we still haven't solved the problem. What was the curious thing we saw up there? It couldn't have been—"

I broke off, seeing the expression that had come over Will's face.

"Not cretinous," he said in a hoarse voice. "Something else. Jo, we've been on the wrong track. All wrong. Listen: that room up there. The barred windows. The rocking horse. The book with the infantile scrawl. Is there any sign of an older child, an adolescent, in that room?"

"Of course not. He wasn't . . ."

"No crib," Will muttered. "Full-sized bed, furniture." His eyes were wild. "Think, Jo. The sensation of cold, the sick feeling. When you saw 'Miss Smith' in the graveyard you were frightened; but did you feel the coldness then?"

"No," I said, without hesitation. "But it was outside, Will."

"It was during the daytime," Will said. "Daylight, Jo. The crying only came at night, and the cold came at night. She came at night too, sometimes, but does that mean the cold, the unique sensation of terror, is her attribute? What if it is a quality associated with the weeping instead? Because of our various prejudices we've tended towards a certain theory—that the woman and the child haunt the Frasers because one generation of Frasers was responsible for their deaths—morally if not literally. But that doesn't explain what we saw tonight. There's another explanation, Jo. It doesn't absolve the Captain. In a way, he was responsible for the whole tragedy. But he couldn't anticipate what happened. He was away, at sea, so much of the time . . . And the symptoms may not have developed until long after he brought them home . . ."

"There's something caught up under the top of the drawer," Jed interrupted. He scooped the paper out with his fingertip. After he had scanned it, he looked at Will.

"She did leave a note," he said quietly. Then he read it aloud.

"They said he had sold his soul to Satan. He was Satan's child, the fruit of sin. The sins of the fathers are visited upon the children; but on whom are the sins of the children visited? The crime of Absalom was his, but the Lord sent Joab to spare Maacah. She did not sin as I have sinned. The punish-

339

ment was fair, but I am weak. And so I sin again, for the last time, because I cannot live with what I had to do. Absalom sinned, but David wept for him."

There was a moment of silence.

"I don't get it," I said.

"It's the pronouns that confuse you," Will said. He was looking rather pale. "There are two of 'him'—her son and her lover. How well do you know your Bible?"

"I know Absalom. He rebelled against his father—was that his sin? He got killed, but David wept for him anyhow. 'O Absalom, my son, my son.' But I don't know Joab."

"'And he took three darts in his hand and thrust them through the heart of Absalom.'"

The voice was the voice of Mrs. Willard. She looked up, from where she shared Ran's vigil by Mary's cot.

"Maacah," she added, in her flat voice, "was the mother of Absalom."

Gradually the meaning dawned on me, and I felt a little pale myself.

"It's not possible, Will. She killed the boy? Because he killed his father?"

"He was Satan's child," Jed quoted. "That's the boy she's talking about. The sins of the children . . . Yes, I'd say it was pretty clear."

"That little boy?"

"How old do you think he was?"

"Five . . . six . . ."

"That's one of those prejudices I was talking about. Stop and think, Jo; have we found anything that gave us the slightest indication of the boy's age?" Will held up the worn paper on which the child's birth had been recorded. "He was born in 1832."

I stared, horrified, as the truth dawned.

"He was fourteen years old," Jed said. "And he took after his father. A husky hulking body and a violent temper. Couldn't you see—tonight—that he had the look of the old man?"

IV

Will stood up.

"I'm going upstairs."

"I'll go with you," Jed said.

"Take the Book with you," Mrs. Willard said calmly.

I had an insane desire to laugh.

"What good is that going to do?" I demanded. "Anne! You aren't going back up there?"

She was on her feet, pale and unsteady but very calm.

"Yes, I am. I don't know what I'll feel like when this injection wears off, but I'd like to show a little dignity while I can."

"Oh, hell," I said. "All right. But you're all crazy."

At the door Will turned and glared at me.

"Where are you going?"

"With you. I'm just as"—I gulped—"as nosy as the rest of you."

"No, you're not. Not going, I mean. God knows you're nosy enough. That's probably why poor old Miss Smith picked you to come to."

"You think she was trying to warn me?"

"Yes, I do. She couldn't help scaring you to death; that's an inevitable result of materialization."

"Then I'd better go along as interpreter."

"Jo." He took me by the shoulders, and at the look in his eyes a selfish pang of pure joy went through me. "Stay in one piece, will you? I worry about you. You haven't got any sense of self-preservation."

"I'm going."

"I thought you would," Will said coolly. "Well, just in case we don't come back—"

He kissed me. When my head stopped spinning I followed them.

Jed had flashlights for everybody this time. We stood in the doorway and shone our lights around the room; and I said irritably,

"Why can't we wait till daylight? It's the darkness that makes this place so awful."

"We'll never be sure," Will said. "Not unless we can come here at night."

"Wait a minute," I said. I handed Anne my flashlight. "I want to try something."

Will made a grab for me, but it was too late; I walked out into the middle of the room and stood there. It was the bravest thing I've ever done, and I'm very proud of myself for doing it. I was quaking like a jelly, especially when I passed that hideous iron staircase.

I didn't say anything. I couldn't think of any words that weren't theatrical or corny. I just stood there and thought of that poor woman; only a girl, really, when she got involved with Hezekiah. Yet she wasn't so much his victim as she was a victim of the times, times which condemned women to a single role in society and damned them for eternity if they accepted the role without the magic scrap of paper which legitimized it. If there could be such a thing as a psychotic

343

ghost, she was it—caught in the vicious trap of the guilt her culture had brainwashed her into accepting.

I stood there for perhaps a minute and a half; it's a long time when you are quaking with fear and pity. I never saw a thing, not certainly. I might have imagined a slight thickening of the shadows in the far corner. There was no cold, no fear; only a long, shaken sigh and then silence. The room was empty; and I had a feeling that it would always be empty now.

When I went back to the door Will grabbed me and held me so tightly I couldn't breathe for a minute.

"We'd better get moving," he said. "It will be light soon. Jed, you and Bertha won't be afraid here alone?"

"We've been alone all this time," Jed said calmly. "And you'll all be back."

"You think it's gone?"

"I think so. But I'll tell you what I'm going to do anyhow. I'm going to haul out every book and every removable item in these two rooms and burn them. Starting now."

Will didn't say anything; he just reached out and took hold of a chair. When we went back down the stairs we each carried a load.

Jed and Will went back again and again as the windows slowly lightened, and Anne sat staring at her hands in a silence I didn't care to break. When the helicopter lifted, with a full complement of passengers, I looked down; and I saw a great tongue of flame rise up from the stableyard, like a beacon, or a banner.

EPILOGUE

MARY'S fine. She and Ran are in Switzerland now. Will and I will join them next week for our honeymoon. We'll be married in Zurich. I'm sorry the Willards can't be there, but we'll be seeing a lot of them after we get back.

Mary has no memory of what happened at the house. She thinks she had a conventional nervous breakdown, and she's rather ashamed of herself. One day we'll tell her. We don't believe in lying; there's always a danger that you'll get caught.

I have found a new kitchen table. The first thing I'm going to do when we get back is relegate that green plastic horror to the barn. The second thing I'm going to do is buy a few new records for Will's collection. The Beatles, of course, and Cream, and a few more. He'll get used to them.

There have been no manifestations since that night. Opinions differ as to what did the trick. Will thinks the bonfire was the decisive factor; he's really a materialist at heart. I am convinced that my courage and sensitivity in communicating with "Miss Smith" gave her the strength to detach herself and her wretched offspring from the pattern in which they had been trapped. Mrs. Willard says nonsense, it was prayers, and the Good Book.

"It was simple," Jed says, in his calm voice. "All we had to do was find out the truth."

When he is questioned, he will sometimes elaborate.

I remember one time, when we were sitting in the kitchen eating doughnuts as fast as Mrs. Willard could turn them out. Will had just finished reading through the last of the account books. He hadn't been putting me on about his fondness for the dry bones of history; he actually enjoyed reading them. He was telling us, that day, about certain entries which in his opinion confirmed his diagnosis of Kevin Fraser's illness.

"It hit me when Jo mentioned cretinism," he explained. "That wasn't it, of course, but the word made me think of a physical ailment, and then I realized that the stigmata were all there—the high brow, saddle nose radiating scars around the mouth, bowed tibia. Even the teeth had the characteristic shape. You don't see it often nowadays; treatment is so effective. It can be prevented, if the mother is treated during pregnancy. But it wasn't till after 1910 that Ehrlich made the first significant breakthrough. In the mid-nineteenth century it might not even be recognized for what it was. Yet when you talk about the sins of the fathers being visited upon the children . . ."

"And eventually it causes insanity?" I asked.

"Paresis is only one of the possible results," Will said. "In such cases there is a general deterioration of mental function; that was one of the things that finally struck me about that room, that it was designed for an individual who was physically mature and mentally retarded. In the final stages the brain is actually destroyed, and violent rages are one of the symptoms. Of course all this is theory; I've never tried to diagnose a ghost before. But all the evidence indicates mental illness of some kind. What I found in that 1845 account book confirms it; in that year, when Kevin was thirteen, the tower rooms were fitted up and the bars were put on the windows. Evidently his condition wasn't considered dangerous until then."

"Poor child," I said, shivering.

"It's curious," Will said. "You know Mercy never mentions his name? There are certain items purchased 'for the child', but not once did she write the name."

"Not surprising that she should feel that way," Jed uttered. "You suppose she was the one who put the papers and the miniature in the box?"

"I think so. She would be the first one called when Georgianna's body was found; she wouldn't let that note become public property. But she didn't destroy it. She put the relevant documents into the box, and there they remained. A beautiful example of the New England conscience at work: avoid scandal, but never destroy the truth."

"Sounds like Jed," I said, smiling at him.

He nodded soberly.

"You remember, Jo, I said to you once that these creatures couldn't do any physical harm; all they could do was scare people. And a lot of the fear comes from ignorance. There's a lot of nonsense talked about the reasons for this kind of disturbance—hauntings, if you want to use that word. But they all hinge on the same thing. When the lost treasure is discovered, or the murderer is brought to justice, or the truth is known—

then the trouble stops. So that's why I say our trouble is over and done with. It's more like one of those old Greek tragedies than a mystery story, with a villain that's got to be discovered and punished. There aren't any villains in our story—not even Hezekiah, though he was as near to one as we can get. But even he was driven by the patterns of his time, and his station in life; he didn't act that much worse than a lot of men, and in the end he got his punishment, no question of that. The boy? You can't blame a poor creature like that for what his father unwittingly made of him. And the woman is the most tragic figure of them all."

"Not so much a Greek tragedy," Will said, "as one of those grim biblical stories of nemesis and doom. The sins of the fathers . . . I can't get that verse out of my mind."

"It's not such a terrible verse," Jed said. "If you think of it as a warning instead of a threat. It's true, in more ways than we like to admit. But there are a lot of verses in that Book, Will, and there's another one that sticks in my mind."

"I know," I said. "I know the one you mean. 'You shall know the truth . . .'"

"'And the truth shall make you free.'"

ROMANCE TITLES
in the
Ulverscroft Large Print Series

MYSTERY TITLES
in the
Ulverscroft Large Print Series

Henrietta Who?	*Catherine Aird*
Slight Mourning	*Catherine Aird*
The China Governess	*Margery Allingham*
Coroner's Pidgin	*Margery Allingham*
Crime at Black Dudley	*Margery Allingham*
Look to the Lady	*Margery Allingham*
More Work for the Undertaker	
	Margery Allingham
Death in the Channel	*J. R. L. Anderson*
Death in the City	*J. R. L. Anderson*
Death on the Rocks	*J. R. L. Anderson*
A Sprig of Sea Lavender	*J. R. L. Anderson*
Death of a Poison-Tongue	*Josephine Bell*
Murder Adrift	*George Bellairs*
Strangers Among the Dead	*George Bellairs*
The Case of the Abominable Snowman	
	Nicholas Blake
The Widow's Cruise	*Nicholas Blake*
The Brides of Friedberg	*Gwendoline Butler*
Murder By Proxy	*Harry Carmichael*
Post Mortem	*Harry Carmichael*
Suicide Clause	*Harry Carmichael*
After the Funeral	*Agatha Christie*
The Body in the Library	*Agatha Christie*

THE SHADOWS
OF THE CROWN TITLES
in the
Ulverscroft Large Print Series

The Tudor Rose   *Margaret Campbell Barnes*
Brief Gaudy Hour *Margaret Campbell Barnes*
Mistress Jane Seymour   *Frances B. Clark*
My Lady of Cleves
                    Margaret Campbell Barnes
Katheryn The Wanton Queen
                             Maureen Peters
The Sixth Wife   *Jean Plaidy*
The Last Tudor King   *Hester Chapman*
Young Bess   *Margaret Irwin*
Lady Jane Grey   *Hester Chapman*
Elizabeth, Captive Princess   *Margaret Irwin*
Elizabeth and The Prince of Spain
                              Margaret Irwin
Gay Lord Robert   *Jean Plaidy*
Here Was A Man   *Norah Lofts*
Mary Queen of Scotland:
The Triumphant Year   *Jean Plaidy*
The Captive Queen of Scots   *Jean Plaidy*
The Murder in the Tower   *Jean Plaidy*
The Young and Lonely King   *Jane Lane*
King's Adversary   *Monica Beardsworth*
A Call of Trumpets   *Jane Lane*